Talking Dirty

Also by Jennifer Seasons

The Fortune, Colorado Series
Getting Lucky

Coming Soon
Playing Rough

The Diamonds and Dugouts Series
Stealing Home
Playing the Field
Throwing Heat
"Major League Crush" in *Confessions of a Secret Admirer*

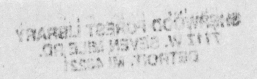

Talking Dirty

A Fortune, Colorado Novel

JENNIFER SEASONS

AVONIMPULSE
An Imprint of HarperCollinsPublishers

HarperCollins
P U B L I S H E R S
— Since 1817 —

Excerpt from *Getting Lucky* copyright © 2015 by Candice Wakoff.

Digital Edition JANUARY 2017 ISBN: 978-0-06-236504-0
Print Edition ISBN: 978-0-06-236505-7

Avon Impulse and the Avon Impulse logo are registered trademarks of HarperCollins Publishers in the United States of America.

Avon and HarperCollins are registered trademarks of HarperCollins Publishers in the United States of America and other countries

AM 10 9 8 7 6 5 4 3 2 1

For all those who believe in love—who spread it. You know that love is the answer to everything. This one's for you.

Chapter One

"You know what your problem is?"

Apple Woodman smiled victoriously, glad she'd finally gotten close enough to Jake Stone for him to hear her from across the short stretch of sidewalk separating them in downtown Fortune, Colorado. Shuffling the bag of produce she'd just purchased from the local co-op, she settled the fabric straps on her shoulder and frowned at his broad, muscular back. Not that she was noticing that it was muscular or anything. "You're not a nice person."

There, she'd finally said it. That had been floating around inside her for weeks.

Wow, she felt *so much* better.

"That hurts my feelings," the man turned around and had the gall to say, with a blatantly fake hurt-puppy expression on his handsome face.

"You know, if it weren't against everything I've been taught about how a person treated others, I'd kick you in the shins so hard right now." Annoyance flooded Apple. Most of it was directed at the most aggravating male in the entire known universe. The man had mad skills when it came to driving women crazy.

She should know. Jake Stone had been under her skin and scrambling her brains since before the last ice age. Once, just once, she'd like to have all her mental faculties fully functioning in his presence long enough to tell him exactly what she'd thought of him since kindergarten.

Or, well, *mostly* everything.

No way would she ever admit that another tiny little part of her was also currently annoyed at herself for considering him "handsome." She should be so over that about him by now.

Turning her attention back to his tall, broad-shouldered form, Apple scrunched her nose against the sun and shaded her eyes with a hand just in time to see the unrighteous gleam in his eye as he taunted her. "I dare you to even *try* that, woman. Here, I'll hold a shin up for you to kick." He raised a jean-clad leg and waggled it slowly at her. She could only scowl at him, because she was stuck somewhere between flabbergasted and infuriated instead of making some fabulously pithy comeback as she'd prefer. Jake must have taken that as a sign of defeat because a low rumble of humor came from him, and he smirked, dropping his leg back down. "You couldn't hurt a hornet if it stung you on your ass, sweetheart."

"You don't know that," Apple instantly defended, frowning at him. She conveniently ignored the fact that he'd called her "sweetheart" and the responding quiver that had darted through her lower abdomen.

Sigh.

Back to the point: simply because they'd known each other since forever didn't mean he actually *knew* her. Not one single bit. If there'd been a time that she might have wished differently, that time was *long* past. Like, ancient as the Indus Valley past.

There was only one thing she wanted from him now— and it was purely business. One hundred percent. So on the up-and-up platonic end of things that it was *beyond* vanilla.

And the damned man wasn't cooperating. Hadn't even *budged.*

Which was ridiculous. It was *vanilla*, for chrissake. Totally harmless. Who would be afraid of harmless?

Jake raked a hand through his recently cut hair and sighed, his brown eyes oddly restless on her before they slid away. "You're wrong there, Apple." His gruff voice held an edge she didn't understand any more than that look he'd just given her.

"Nice haircut, by the way," she retorted because it was the only thing she could come up with. Lame, but what else could she expect? He had a way of reducing her to juvenile, brainless behavior.

"You like it?" He shot her a grin and winked, his eyes dancing with sudden humor. Angsty one minute, amused the next. She swore the man's moods shifted faster than the Colorado weather. "Thought it was time for a change."

Apple couldn't help it. She snorted. Right out loud on Main Street with pedestrians strolling by. "Ha! Since when do *you* do change?" He might not know her as well as she once might have wished he did, but she for sure knew *him*. He hated change. It was like a dirty word to him. Simply look at the women he dated. They were all *exactly* the same—and had been since his first girlfriend, Scarlet Floozy, from way back in junior high school (not her actual name, sadly).

That thought had her frown deepening. Why couldn't he just do what she wanted so she could stop harassing him? Stalking wasn't her most flattering behavior. But darn it, the blasted man had reduced her to it.

Jake braced his long, heavily muscled legs apart and crossed his arms, his biceps flexing in a rather flattering, masculine way—she supposed. She'd barely noticed. Her eyes were firmly glued to where the ponytail he'd worn for the past twenty years had been. Now his sun-bleached light brown hair was a lush, tousled mass that stopped just short of his collar. She had to admit that it was a little shocking to see him with the short hair. If she'd thought his features rugged before, the new haircut made them even more so.

His brown eyes were locked on her, his expression unreadable. "You'd be surprised by what I can do, Apple. You've always underestimated me."

"That's because I *know* you."

"Now, that's not nice. My feelings are back to being hurt."

Which was a total lie. She could see his lips twitching at the corners. "I've been *nice* to you my whole life, Jake.

It's only the past four months that I've turned into some crazy lady. But you've forced me to it. You know this book is incredibly important to me. I can't finish writing the history of Fortune without your input—what you know about your family. And you promised to tell me." Now she was getting all riled up a third time. Grabbing the fabric straps of her reusable grocery bag, she hitched it back onto her shoulder in a jerky motion. "And you absolutely know that being published is my dream, so it's killing me that you won't just sit down and talk to me. What's so damn secretive about people from a hundred and fifty years ago that you can't share it?"

He opened his mouth to reply, face stubble glinting bronze in the sunlight, and then snapped it shut again.

"Tell me, please." Her voice sounded pleading even to her own ears. Ouch, this was demeaning. Begging Jake to *talk* to her. Jesus. Most women begged him for sex. He'd always been popular with the ladies. God, how many times had she seen him get hit on while trying to wear him down at his brewpub over the past few months? Apparently, she was the only single woman in Fortune under the age of sixty-five who wanted what was in his brain instead of his pants.

"Why can't you finish your book for your fancy publishing house without me? It seems to me that the town librarian ought to be able to research enough to figure it out on her own." He honestly looked perplexed, she'd give him that.

Like she was explaining this to an elementary school student, Apple took a breath and said in her patient-librarian voice, "*Because*, dear Jake, I've looked through every public record at City Hall already, as well as searched through every old periodical still at the library. I've scoured the Internet. I've interviewed every other person whose family traced back to the second wave of Fortune's settlers. I've played amateur sleuth on my own and tried to dig up any crumb of useful information about the first wave of settlers. Who just so happen to be *your* family. And you and your dad are the only ones left I have to talk to." Belatedly she realized how insensitive that might have come across with that last sentence and quickly added, "I'm still sorry about your loss."

Jake braced his legs farther apart and shot her a look full of consternation. "You don't have to keep apologizing, Apple. My grandfather has been dead for a while now."

Her shoulders slumped a little. "I know, but I still miss him. He had the best stories."

Jake's firm, full lips tipped into a slight grin and she smiled back, the two of them sharing a moment of remembrance for Harvey Stone, prospector and storyteller extraordinaire. "Remember that one he loved to tell about the gold rush of seventy-two and the bear who stole his stash of gold?" he asked softly.

Her eyes lit up, and she chuckled. "You mean the bear that had escaped from the circus and had been caught and trained by thieving prospectors to raid other camps for nuggets?"

"That's the one," he replied, his slight grin blooming into a full-on smile.

She laughed outright and then had a thought. Tipping her head to the side, she pondered out loud, "Do you ever wonder how many of those stories were actually true?"

"Nah. Probably less than half though, if I did have to gauge." He shrugged when she gave him a quizzical look. "Harvey liked to tell stories. I learned when I was a kid to take them with a grain of salt. Who knows, maybe some were true. It would be a kick if they were. But we'll never really know."

Apple pressed, "Wouldn't Verle know?"

A veil seemed to drop over Jake, and he closed up tighter than a clamshell, his eyes back to being unreadable when a moment before they had been warm with memories. "My dad wouldn't know anything, you know that. He regularly forgets what day it is."

Now she felt bad. She hadn't meant to upset him. Apple pressed her lips in a firm line and then tried to apologize and turn the topic back to what she'd hunted him down for: her book. "I'm sorry to bring him up. But back to why I stopped you. I'm up against deadline, Jake. I've already spent my advance and would really love to not have to pay it back—"

He raised a hand and frowned, stopping her midsentence. "Wait. Explain to me how your spending habits are my problem."

Okay, now she was insulted. "My *spending habits* are just fine." She had the IRA and retirement plan to prove it. "And I would have turned my book in months ago if you'd have sat down and answered my questions about what you know about that first founding party—and you can't pretend you don't know, because I know you do—like you'd said you would. So come on, Jake, for once in your freaking life follow through on something you said you'd do." She clenched her hands into fists and added on a rush of emotion—no thought—"Damn it, just for *once* commit to something. Commit to *me*."

In an instant his face went pale and his eyes went dark. "Excuse me?" Then his whole body seemed to snap like a stretched wire, and he jerked, nearly stammering, "W-what did you just say?"

What had she just said? She had this unladylike quirk of blurting things out without thinking about them, especially when overwhelmed. So what were her last few words again...?

Oh, shit.

She started waving her hands in front of her like an umpire calling safe, her head shaking in vehement denial. "No, no, no. I didn't mean it like that! I just meant...oh, you know...maybe...spend some time with me." God, now she was just making it worse. *Mouth, shut up now.*

Apple clamped it shut and promptly bit her tongue. Served her right, she thought as she winced from pain. A swollen tongue ought to keep her quiet for a while and out of trouble.

But Jake didn't answer. He just gave her the oddest look before he moved his legs and began walking, pulling away from her. His long stride ate up the concrete. Being on the short side of five foot three, her legs weren't equipped to keep up, and he had her breaking into a run to catch up to him again. Not even once had he turned around and looked at her.

But then she caught his profile just right and saw that quick grin. And she knew he'd heard her verbal slip—even if he was trying hard to pretend like she didn't exist. For whatever reason, he simply loved to antagonize her.

Which had her irrationally irritated and circling right back to the beginning of their conversation. Had her back to thinking just one thing about him.

"Did you hear me earlier, Jake Stone? Because I'm saying it again." Apple planted her feet, rooting herself to the sidewalk under a shady honey locust tree as the past four months of stress and frustration came out at his back in one big rush. *"You're not a nice person!"* she ended on a shout, her hands fisted at her sides.

"I beg your pardon!" A balding, elderly man who had been walking by just then spun his head toward her, looking mortified as he leaned on his cane and blinked at her from behind his slipping bifocals.

"Oh, not you, Mr. Parsons!" Reaching out a hand, Apple placed it on his frail shoulder and gave it a quick, reassuring squeeze. "You're a doll," she insisted with a smile. God, her stupid mouth sometimes.

"I was talking about that big oaf over there," she said and tipped her head toward Jake as he opened up the door to his establishment and tossed her a wink, his brown eyes sparkling with mischief.

She forgot all about offending Mr. Parsons as she spun on her flats toward Jake. "I'll just follow you inside, you know. You can't get away from me."

Jake's collar-length hair shimmered in the September sunlight as he tossed back his head and laughed, the deep sound rumbling in his chest. Then he pulled out a set of keys and jangled them together. "Wanna bet?" he threatened, one brow raised.

Apple narrowed her eyes, her blood beginning to boil. "You wouldn't dare."

He smiled then, a slow turn of his lips that transformed his rugged face into something so primal and so sexually charged that she instantly forgot her own name, her mother's—and her current address too.

Good Lord, Jake Stone had a *smile*.

Suddenly feeling a little warm—though she decided to blame it on the temperature that was still hanging around the mideighties—Apple cleared her throat and tried not to think too much about how dry her mouth had just become. And then she thought about all the time she'd spent agonizing over his lack of cooperation, and she realized it was a good thing that he didn't often bring out his smile in full force. It was raw sex on a platter—and it was potent enough to make her want to forgive him every transgression.

Which, of course, she couldn't.

And now she was back to frowning. "I don't understand you."

Placing his hand on the edge of the saloon-style front door of Two Moons as she approached, making it clear she was serious about following him inside, he replied, "I'm a simple guy, Apple. There's not much to understand."

Bullshit.

If he was simple, then she was a runway model. And they both knew that being petite and curvy, she wasn't exactly the stick-figure model type. She was more like the exaggerated cartoon pinup type. And she was fine with her body type. The point was that she was at least honest with herself.

Jake clearly lacked objectivity.

Knowing that he was waiting for her to decide if she was coming inside Two Moons or not, she moved toward him, readjusting her reading glasses as they slid down her nose. "I just wish you would talk to me. Seriously. An hour of your time and then it's over."

The moment she brushed past him, her shoulder gently bumped his chest, and electricity darted through her body. Stopping cold, Apple looked up at him, her eyes wide. *Whoa, what was that?*

Jake must have felt something too because his brown eyes narrowed, searching her face and coming to rest on her lips—which suddenly felt very, very dry. She swallowed hard as her heartbeat sped up and her breathing went shallow. The way he held his focus on her made her squirmy.

There was no way that a man who housed that kind of intensity could be simple.

No way, no how.

"Interesting," he said with a heavy breath, his gaze intense. "What have we here?"

"I don't know," she whispered back, confused and transfixed at the same time. " 'What have we here,' what?" There was no breaking from his gaze. Just. None.

"I've wondered about this." He shifted closer, just a fraction, but it sent fireworks skittering along her skin. She'd never been more aware of another person in her life. His nostrils flared as he inhaled deeply, almost like he was taking in her scent, absorbing it. *Feeding* off it. "There it is, right there." His face seemed to grow more tense, his body too. "I can smell it on you."

"What are you doing?" she squeaked softly. Smell *what* on her? She'd showered that morning. At least she was pretty sure she had. Right now she couldn't remember with his big body so close to her, frying all her signals. Still, she was almost positive she didn't stink. "What can you smell on me?"

Something seemed to have shifted inside him. He suddenly seemed resolved. About what, she had no idea. But he gave a quick smile of satisfaction and nodded once, decisively. "Chemistry."

And, of course, he didn't fill her in on what that was about. Nope, he just said in that low, gruff voice of his, "I won't do your thing for free, Apple. If I give you an hour of my time, it'd better be worth it. Mutually satisfying for us both." He had a way of speaking that made him sound like he'd just rolled out of bed after a good romp, all relaxed and gravelly—even late in the afternoon. Knowing his reputation and the fact that he'd been walking to work just now, it was an actual distinct possibility that his voice was indeed postcoitus gravelly.

Somehow, right now that didn't seem to irk her like it usually did. Not when that voice of his was doing funny things to her insides and her brain was scrambled sunny-side up.

Because his gaze was still locked on her mouth, she inhaled a shallow breath and licked her lips self-consciously. "What do I have that you want?" She honestly had no idea.

His eyes flashed, molten chocolate. "Whatever makes it worth my time," he retorted, answering her question.

"Oh, I've got something. Trust me." The words popped right out of her mouth before she had a chance to stop them. Just. Great.

"Oh yeah?" he murmured, his expression just this side of mocking. "Okay, I'll bite. What's in it for me?" He cocked a brow, clearly waiting to be blown away.

See? This was why having no verbal filter was a problem. Oh, the pickles it got her into.

"Something irresistible?" she finally ventured, her brain as empty as a Buddhist temple.

His lips curled up into a quick, crooked grin so full of naughtiness that heat pooled unexpectedly in her belly, and she gasped softly. It just wasn't fair that such a pain-in-the-butt man could possess so much sex appeal. Not fair at all.

Just then, Jake's gaze dropped, and he glanced at her chest—her rather *sizeable* double-D chest. "I'm beginning to think it might be," he murmured quietly, almost contemplatively, his tone ripe with appreciation, before he looked away.

The expression on his face made her brain instantly transplant her into the middle of a vivid memory. It was Jake's senior year, and she'd just driven him in his souped-up old car back to his dad's wreck of a single-wide trailer after he'd had too many beers at Aidan's one and only house party. He'd been way too wasted to drive. She'd just parked in the dirt driveway of his place and had killed the engine. Jake had been passed out in the passenger seat. She had leaned toward him to shake him gently awake, and he'd shifted, mumbling under his breath.

"What did you say?" she whispered, confused and excited at their nearness in the dark interior of the car.

Jake slowly opened his eyes and focused on her, his gaze heavy-lidded yet surprisingly steady. "I said, I dream of you." He reached toward her and slid a large, confident hand up her rib cage until he reached the underside of her breast. Her breath froze in her throat as his hand traced gently over it, and he brushed his palm over her sensitive nipple that craved more of his touch. "Every night about sweet, sexy you. And these." He cupped her suddenly heavy and aching breast and held, his big teenaged hand already hard and calloused from work. "They're magnificent. Fuck, Apple, I'd give anything to see them." Before she could respond, his hand slipped down her body and he passed out again, his snoring and her short, rapid breathing deafening sounds in the suddenly quiet interior of the car.

Before she'd even been able to calm her racing heart, Aidan had pulled into the driveway behind her, arriving to give her a ride home. She'd scrambled out of that Camaro like her pants were on fire, confused and excited and a little scared at the new feelings Jake had awakened in her. Aidan poked his head through the open car window, took in the situation, and decided to just let Jake sleep it off right where he was. Apple had agreed, so she'd stuck his keys in the mailbox for him to find in the morning. Then they'd left, her young reality shaken from what had just happened between her and Jake.

Snapping back to the present, Apple blinked. Holy crap, what a memory! She'd never forgotten the details of that night, not even for a nanosecond. *Phew.*

That had been a seriously hot little exchange between the two of them. No wonder she'd been so into him back then. Who wouldn't be after hearing a confession like that? Even now her heart was beating furiously over the words.

Fuck, Apple, I'd give anything to see them.

He'd said anything. *Anything.* Had he really meant it? Apple's eyes began to light up like lights on a Christmas tree as the realization that maybe he *had* actually meant it began to sink in.

It gave her an idea.

An absolutely *irresistible* idea.

Excitement flooded her and broke the spell Jake had on her. Suddenly confident that she'd finally discovered a way to make him talk, Apple shifted and walked into the pub, her vintage sundress swishing around her knees flirtatiously. Barely noticing the brewpub's patrons; the huge sign advertising its upcoming Theme Night and charity of choice, computer literacy; or the live band that was playing Taylor Swift covers on the patio, she went straight to the bar without waiting for Jake. She wanted a few seconds to plot and get it straight in her head before offering her new proposition. She was pretty darn sure she was on to something. It really just might work.

Alone for a few blessed heartbeats, Apple closed her eyes and briefly grappled with the reality of what she was about to do. In all honestly it caused a wide range of emotions to shuffle through her. From excitement and eagerness all the way to a little frustration. She was a woman who derived so much of her self-esteem from her personhood—her intelligence, heart, kindness, and compassion. It didn't settle easily inside her to use her body for personal gain. And yet, at the end of the day, there she was about to do just that.

Why? Maybe it was because she had always wondered a tiny bit about how honest Jake had been that night in the car when he'd been drunk, and this was a chance to find out. But mostly because she'd run out of time and choices. And because nobody—not even her parents—thought she was going to finish this book and turn it in on time.

Okay, so it wasn't on time—she was on her second deadline extension already—but she was going to finish it. Damn it, Apple was going to assert herself enough in the world to achieve her goal. She was going to show that she had the gumption to fight, really fight, for what she wanted. Persistence had always been one of her best qualities. It was finally time for her to put it to good use—toward something that really mattered.

Everyone thought of her as just Apple Woodman, the sweet, plump little town librarian with big boobs, big glasses, and a big heart.

But she was *so much* more than that. Only nobody knew. Not even her parents.

And that right there was the heart of it. Even her parents, as loving and wonderful and supportive as they were, didn't really believe she could follow through and commit to a writing career—not when it required a boatload of self-discipline and self-motivation every single day—and she had always had a tendency to lose interest in projects before they were complete. Or she'd found a reason why they weren't the right thing for her anymore, even *if* they were what her heart wanted most, deep down.

But, it galled the hell out of her that she *had* committed to this—to her book and to her publisher. It wasn't her fault that someone else was standing in her way to the finish line. Still, her mom would just give her that warm, affectionate smile and say, "Well, honey, you've given it your best, and that's what really counts."

This, coming from a free-spirited bohemian clay artist who spent her days singing Joni Mitchell songs and playing with mud.

It was aggravating, and if she was honest with herself, also belittling. Beyond that, it cut into her self-confidence and brought doubt. But she had staying power and follow-through. Oh, yes she did.

And she was going to prove it right now.

Jake joined her at the bar, turning her attention, and she took a deep, steadying breath. It was now or never. She placed her elbows on the bar and leaned toward him.

He scowled.

Of course he did. He was always scowling around her. Earlier had merely been his five-minute reprieve. "Put those away before you hurt someone."

Now he was sounding downright grumpy too. *Huh, funny thing.* "Why would I do that?" she asked and gave her girls a little squeeze with her elbows and inwardly sighed at the lengths she was willing to go to for the things that mattered most to her. He muttered under his breath and scowled some more. *Good.* "I don't see anyone here complaining," she added just to taunt him.

Not that anyone could, really. Her back was to the tables. Jake was the only one who was getting the full display, exactly as she'd intended.

"I'm complaining." He practically growled. He yanked a white bar towel from its holder and began polishing the bar top.

He sounded surly, but Apple knew that secret about Jake, and she was not at all ashamed to take advantage of it now. He'd forced her to it. "Why? Because you've been trying to scam a peek at my boobs since I started growing them in sixth grade?" She tipped her head to the side and blinked all big and innocent behind her oversize reading glasses. "Are you feeling sad about that?"

He scoffed at that—*after* he glanced at her chest again. She totally had him. "Of what? All the cases of blue balls your rack gave me when I was fifteen?"

"What if I offered to make up for all those missed opportunities? All those spin the bottles and sixty seconds in heaven that didn't pan out?"

Jake stopped wiping the bar and pegged her with a look, his dark eyes filled with barely controlled skepticism. "And how would you do that, juicy fruit?" he asked, referencing her childhood nickname—the one *he'd* given her the year she'd come into her body.

If letting Jake finally see her topless was going to get him to actually open up and tell her what she needed to know about that first settlement in Fortune, then by all means she'd take her shirt off. It was worth it to her. Plus, it would quell that one nagging question she'd *never* had about them, which was awesome. Because she'd *never* wondered, "What if?" Not once. Why would she?

More to the point, she was willing to do it because she was desperate. Enough so that she'd bare what she had for Jake. Because the truth was, beyond needing to prove to herself that she could achieve her dreams, he wasn't all that wrong about her "spending habits." Not that she was a mess with finances or anything. But she didn't make that much as the librarian, and it had been a hefty advance (with which she'd paid off the last big hunk of her school loans. Responsible. Appropriate). And now she was out of cash, out of savings—debt-free, but still broke.

This was her opportunity. Her shot. Right here and now. No matter how devalued she felt over how it was playing out.

Being a published author had always been her dream. And she was *this close*. She'd be an idiot not to flash him her goods if it meant finally wrapping things up. Only this time he wasn't drunk—and she was no longer such an innocent little good girl. It was just Jake. They'd known each other since she was three. Besides, if there was a question mark dangling over them—which there *wasn't*, not in her head anyway—then this was a quick and painless way to turn that question mark into a period.

No question mark, no doubts—no dissatisfaction over what might have or might not have been.

Apple took a deep breath. "I'm offering a trade. If you finally tell me what happened to the original founders of Fortune, I'll show you my breasts. You've always wanted to see them." Or so his drunken teenaged self had said, if that source could be trusted.

Jake laughed at that. "What makes you think I'm still interested?"

"Because you're a guy." Apple gave him a level look, unfazed.

He merely shrugged, his broad, defined shoulders moving under his faded green T-shirt. Then he slid her a quick glance. "Maybe I am. But you're going to have to do better than that if you want me talking."

Apple leveled him with an incredulous look. "This is a big deal. Big offer from me here, Jake. What else could you possibly want?" And then she thought of everything she'd tried already and felt exasperated all over again, so she added on a frustrated rush, "What's it going to take to get you to finally spill your family's story?"

The look he shot her had Apple slowly straightening from the bar, her pulse skittering. She'd never seen that particular gleam in his eye before. It was dark and intense and unreadable. Dangerous even.

She swallowed hard.

Then he placed his elbows on the bar and leaned toward her. He didn't stop until they were almost nose to nose and she could see amber flecks in his chocolate eyes.

"Here's the deal, all right? If you really want me to talk about myself, my family—hell, about *all* my frigging secrets, because I know you, and you're too damned nosy and won't stop with just my ancestors…" He stopped suddenly and took a deep breath, his last words hanging suspended between them. But his gaze held hers steadily as one uncomfortable heartbeat, then two, passed before he continued speaking. This time he was more animated, seemingly building up steam about something.

"Shit, you won't stop until you've taken up permanent residence inside my head and know things about me that I don't even care to understand. Why? Because you're Apple Woodman and you can't help yourself. It's what you've always done. And you think caving and fulfilling some outdated PG-13-rated teenage fantasy is going to be all it'll take to get me singing about stuff I've never told *anybody*?"

He straightened and crossed his arms, his face set in stern lines as he shook his head once—just once—with impact. "Nope. No good. There's only one thing you can do." He raised a hand, his long, thick index finger pointed straight in the air.

Apple eyed him warily now as she slowly inched back from the bar, feminine fear racing across her skin. Maybe this wasn't her brightest idea, after all.

"Oh yeah, what could that be?"

Jake leaned over the bar toward her again and crooked his finger at her, urging her closer. His gaze held hers as he smiled, slow and devastating, and said the words that sent her reeling. "If you want me to talk, juicy fruit, I get to see *all* of you naked."

Chapter Two

"YOU GET NAKED!"

Jake bit his lip to keep from grinning at Apple's outraged response. "I am serious. I want to see bare skin."

"Oh, you are *such* a dog!"

Jake laughed out loud then. He couldn't help it. The way she was eyeing him in openmouthed shock, like he had said something crude enough to upset her delicate sensibilities, had him feeling a perverse sense of satisfaction. God, the woman was fun to rile.

For the better part of his life, Apple had caused him problems of one form or another. Always in his business, always offering unsolicited opinions or advice, her big blue eyes and even bigger boobs clouding his otherwise clear vision. Couldn't blame a guy for taking the opportunity to cause her some strife in return when the chance arose. Heckling Apple was his way of evening the scales some.

He cut to the chase, knowing Apple wouldn't bite and not really meaning it anyway, but loving that expression on her face all the same. "Look, that's the deal. Take it or leave it." To prove his (not really) point, he threw the bar towel over his shoulder and turned his back on her to start pulling a pint of his signature ale from the tap. Why? Because he could—and because he knew it would drive her bat-shit crazy. He had to fight the urge to laugh when he heard her grumble, but he couldn't keep his lips from twitching.

She sputtered and moved down the bar toward him, absently saying hello to the few people seated nearby as she passed, because that was Apple. Polite to the core—to everyone except him. Once she was in front of him again, she leaned in close and whispered fiercely, her eyes still round behind her ridiculously huge glasses, "You can't be serious!"

Jake closed the tap and set the pint glass on the counter, facing her again. "Why not?" He really wanted to know. Apple was far too much a good girl to agree, but man was it fun egging her on.

She glanced up and down the bar and then leaned even closer, both hands planted on the edge of the counter, her cheeks flushed. "Because, well, because that's just absurd! You can't jump from a boob-flash to full-on nudity in one fell swoop. There's economy of scale to consider, Jake. Jesus. Besides, since when have you ever wanted to see me naked, aside from that one night your senior year in your car when you said you did?"

Jake stopped dead. "Really?" He couldn't even compute how naïve that question was, even coming from

Apple. The woman could say some random shit some-times, but this? "Come on, girl. You really think that I've never had thoughts about you naked? Especially after you got tossed into the lake the summer I graduated high school and came out looking like a soaked *Sports Illustrated* model? Please."

She tipped her head to the side slightly, her high bun slouching a little, and narrowed her eyes on him. Then she straightened and held up a finger just like he'd done earlier.

"For one," she started, in that sassy tone of hers that drove him crazy, "you've never said anything about it to me other than that one drunken confession, and every-body knows better than to believe that stuff. Chances were, I probably wouldn't have done anything back then—"

"Don't I know it," he interjected with a mutter. Apple had been pure as fresh snow back then. And his hands had always been dirty. One touch from him and she'd have lost that innocent perfection. Which was just one of the thousand or so reasons he'd kept his distance.

She continued, obviously ignoring his comment. "And two, we both know that in no way do I resemble a *Sports Illustrated* model. Never have, never will. That magazine couldn't handle all this jelly. So how much of your granddaddy's hooch had you been drinking at the lake when you saw me all wet?"

He smirked. He couldn't help it. One of the irritating truths about Apple was that she understood people. She paid attention. "I don't remember how much, honestly.

But that was also the day Aidan rode old man Taber's prize Brahma bull, remember? So it must have been a respectable amount."

Her eyes went big. "Oh God, I remember that. He'd never even ridden a horse bareback before, much less a rodeo bucking bull."

Jake shook his head, a small smile playing across his lips at the memory. Dumb like only a teenage boy could be and drunk off backyard moonshine. To get Becky Hartman's attention, a besotted Aidan had crossed the fence separating the lake from Taber's field and jumped on the grazing bull's back just like it was the PBR finals. It was amazing he hadn't killed himself.

What was even more amazing was that they'd timed him and he'd lasted the full eight seconds—just like he was Ty Murray.

Apple dropped her chin into her palm, reminiscing now. "Wasn't that also the night of your last performance with Redneck Rockstars?"

He shook his head. "Different one," he said and watched a patron slide onto an empty stool two seats down from Apple and signal him for a drink. Scooting down the bar, Jake eyed the guy in the expensive outdoor clothing that still looked new and said, "Visiting?"

The man nodded and asked for a pint of signature ale, his perfectly trimmed salt-and-pepper hair and pale skin pegging him for a desk jockey. Jake noticed the Rolex and guessed stock market. Day trader. And the way the man was absently rubbing his left ring finger, Jake would bet recently divorced too.

Apple rotated her chin on her palm and inquired of Day Trader, "What brings you to Fortune?"

Jake was about to hand over the pint when the guy openly checked out her cleavage, and he had to fight a sudden urge to dump the glass on the asshole's perfectly coifed head. "Yeah, what brings you here?" he said instead, more abruptly than intended.

Day Trader was clearly reluctant to pull his gaze away from Apple because he said with his eyes still locked on her, "Hiking trip with some buddies. We're here for the weekend." Then he reached out a hand to her, smiling now. "Hi, Steve Baker. Bond trader. Manhattan. And you are?"

Really close to throwing your sorry ass out of my pub.

Jake was about to open his mouth to say something to protect Apple's virtue, when she straightened and placed a hand on her hip. She turned toward the rich douche, smiled widely, and slid the other hand across the glossy mahogany bar until it reached Jake's. He jerked at the contact, at the surge of energy where their fingertips touched. Then she slipped her tiny hand inside his, so warm and soft, and he squeezed it tight for a heartbeat before releasing. Out of reflex, of course.

Why else would he do that?

With the nerves in his hand still jumping, he glanced questioningly at Apple, but she wasn't looking at him. Her gaze was on the wannabe as she said sweetly, "Why, I'm Apple, and this big handsome guy is my fella, Jake Stone. He owns this place." Then she pushed onto her toes, leaned over the bar, and planted a kiss on his cheek.

Feelings tumbled inside him, one after the other. So many he couldn't name them. Didn't want to, honestly.

Picking up on Apple's cue, and trying to ignore the fact that his cheek was tingling, Jake played along. "Welcome to my place, man. This lady's taken." As soon as he said the words, something stirred deep in his subconscious—something base and male and primal. Something that seemed to very much agree with that statement.

Jesus, just what he needed.

The pasty number pusher in spanking-new North Face rose hastily to his feet, his gaze sliding quickly away from Apple now. "Great place you got," he mumbled and walked quickly toward the open French doors that led out onto the patio, melting into the growing dusk.

Which left Jake alone again with Apple. She on one side of the bar, he on the other, leaning close and still holding hands. Surprise sparked in him as he noticed that. Why hadn't she let go?

Why hadn't *he*?

He cleared his throat and released her hand, his palm oddly bereft now without her warmth. "Where were we?"

She rolled her eyes, but he couldn't help noticing that she was rubbing her own palm slowly. "You want me naked."

The plainspoken statement had lust pouring through his veins like liquid gold, heating his body and making him tingle. Seeing Apple naked had been one of his life-long secret dreams. But he still couldn't resist teasing her. "It's not about what I want, Apple. It's about what's fair and equitable, given the value of the content of this exchange."

That was his story, and he was sticking to it.

She grimaced, shifting gently—and damned if her breasts didn't jiggle enticingly enough from that small movement to make his dick grow hard. Christ. The woman should be required to carry a permit for those things.

"Look," she started to say, both hands planted above her full hips now. It only served to showcase her exaggerated hourglass shape and cause him further torment. "We both know that that's not a reasonable request."

"How are you to judge what's reasonable for me to request or not? I'm the one spilling the beans."

"*Fine,*" she said with a sigh. Apple must have seen that he was about to retort, because she held up a hand and closed her eyes briefly, cutting him off before he began. "I'm willing to find a fair compromise."

"How charitable of you," he couldn't help poking.

Her blue eyes flashed. "You bet it is. You've caused me a lot of grief."

Jake leaned forward until they were only inches apart again, desire and irritation mixing inside him. "Oh, honey, you don't want to get me started on who's caused who the most grief over the years."

She didn't even flinch. She just stood there, nose to nose with him as she raised a finger and slowly pushed her big-ass glasses back into place. "Maybe I do."

They stood rooted there, the two of them staring each other down. Apple's eyes were full of challenge, but he couldn't tell whether it was just bluster or not. There was one way to find out.

"Okay, fine. You think I've caused the most grief?"

"I do." She nodded.

"You want me to answer your questions?"

Again she nodded, her blue eyes bright with determination. "Yes, yes I do."

He winked and tapped the tip of her pert little nose with a finger. "Then here's how this is going to go down. For every question you ask, you have to take off an article of clothing."

Her eyes narrowed, but she didn't budge. "Not happening."

That was the response he was expecting. "Well, now that's just too bad. I was really looking forward to reading your book." He winked to let her know he was joking, laughter humming in his chest when she glared at him. He had her bluff now. Any moment she was going to cave and declare the whole thing off.

She blew out a breath and said unexpectedly instead, "You're talking a game of strip poker, only with interview questions, right?"

It was his turn to nod as surprise darted through him. "Yeah."

"Do shoes count as a pair or individually?"

He thought about it for a moment, amused now that she seemed to be standing her ground. God, she was fun to banter with. "They would count as a pair."

Apple began chewing her bottom lip like she always did when she was thinking, and he realized she was actually considering it. His gut instantly tightened with arousal, damn her.

"And is this a graduated, cumulative sort of thing? Or do I get to start over with a full set of clothes for each group of questions?"

Damn, Jake hadn't realized there were going to be multiple events. This could wind up being a whole lot of fun. "I'll take it easy on you. New clothes, new questions. *But*"— he added hastily when he saw her expression change and her eyes go shrewd—"you have to wear weather-appropriate outfits. No layering, no hats, and jewelry doesn't count. Just a good old-fashioned traditional game of striptease. The braver you are about what you're willing to take off, the more questions you'll get answered."

Apple went quiet, and he could see that she was mulling it over. Suddenly jittery, with unexpected excitement tugging at his belly, Jake pushed back from the bar and clapped his hands together, smiling because he just couldn't help himself. "That's the deal, woman. Take it or leave it."

"Hmm, I think I'll leave it. That's a crap-ass deal, and you know it," Apple said, looking him dead in the eye.

It was, and he did know it. He also knew Apple. She'd never make such a lopsided pact where she was giving too much and not getting enough in return.

Jake took a breath and waited for it, knowing there was a big pushback coming from her. It didn't take more than three seconds for it to arrive.

"If this is what you want in exchange for talking to me, then I want something too." The way she said it left zero room for argument.

"Oh yeah? What's that?" This was going to be good.

"You have to get naked too."

"Excuse me?" His eyebrows shot up to his hairline.

She crossed her arms and nodded. "You heard me right. I want to see you in your birthday suit too. It makes this whole thing equal."

Taken off guard, Jake shot her a look and teased in an attempt to regain his bearings, "Honey, if you've been angling to get me naked this whole time, there were easier ways to go about it than hounding me about your book. You could have just asked."

"Ha-ha," she deadpanned, her eyes completely serious on him. "I don't have a burning desire to see you in the buff. However, I *do* have a very keen interest in fulfilling my publishing contract, and I'm willing to consider all options. But I won't do it willy-nilly, Jake. Equal exchange only. If I'm taking it off, so are you. Whatever piece of clothing I lose, it comes off for you too."

He honestly had no idea if she was serious or not. But he was so intrigued by her "compromise" that he said through a slight smirk, "I'm game. If you think you can handle it, that is."

"*Really?*" Her voice was ripe with exasperation. "Getting naked is just that easy for you?"

"I'm comfortable in my own skin," he said casually and shrugged, coughing to cover his laughter when she looked like she wanted to clock him. "Hey, don't get mad," he added. "It was your idea. I'm just saying that I'm in, if you think you can handle it."

For a full minute she stood there quietly, her lips pursed and eyes averted somewhere over his shoulder. Then she inhaled deeply like she was about to speak. But she didn't, and he stood there with growing impatience, waiting for her to open her mouth and tell him *something*.

Jake shifted on his feet, bracing them farther apart like he was preparing for impact. His heart rate had gone from slow and steady to just this side of racing. If she didn't use that pretty little mouth of hers soon, he was in real danger of doing something asinine—like try to kiss a response out of her.

At that moment her shoulders slumped, her mouth snapped shut as her nose scrunched up like a rabbit's, and she placed a single finger over her mouth. "Hmm…" Apple's eyes rolled toward the ceiling like she was in deep contemplation.

"Oh for fuck's sake!" he snapped as impatience won the battle and burst into a million prickly pieces inside him. Pushing away from the bar, Jake snatched up the nearest towel and began furiously polishing the mahogany surface. Christ, she could try the patience of a saint. And he—well, everybody in this whole damned town knew he wasn't one.

"*What?*" Apple rebuffed with a look, her hands palm up as she shrugged, trying to act innocent. "I was thinking! It's not as easy a decision as you'd probably like to believe it is, Mr. Sleeps-With-Everybody. Just because you get around faster than a case of mange in a pack of junkyard dogs doesn't mean I do too. I run the risk of full bodily exposure, which for *me* isn't a casual consideration, and I hadn't anticipated that. So you'll have to forgive me if I need a few minutes to process," she finished with a healthy dose of sarcasm.

The woman couldn't do a damn thing simple even if she tried.

She drove him crazy. Really she did—about half the time. And the other half…well, the other part of the time he wanted to do things to Apple he couldn't talk about in polite company. Or any company, honestly, because the other things he wanted to do to her were *dirty*.

And it would no doubt terrify her sweet, good little soul clear down to her toes if she were to ever discover it.

"Time's up. I've changed my mind. Offer withdrawn," he said, having decided he'd waited long enough for her to make a choice. The fact that a part of him was feeling downright prickly that she hadn't jumped up and down, shouting, "Yes!" the moment he'd made the offer had him scowling and crossing his arms defensively. Why should he care when he'd known the minute he'd made the suggestion that the answer would be no? This vague sense of disappointment had to be for some other reason.

Apple's eyes went wide, and she blinked behind her glasses. "Wait, what?" She began waving her hands back and forth and shaking her head. "No, no, no, you can't take it back! I need this!"

He shrugged and drawled, "Who says I can't take it back?" And oh, it was killing her. She *glared* at him. After all the sleepless nights she'd given him over the years, it felt good to see her all stirred up for once.

Obviously having made a decision, Apple stood up straight and slapped her hands on the bar. "Fine. Let's do it! We have a deal."

He smiled, slowly and with great satisfaction.

Hot damn, yes they did.

Chapter Three

THE NEXT MORNING, Apple was up bright and early. Her brain was way too busy scheming and planning to let her sleep. Which was unfortunate since being short on rest meant she was going to look like crap all day. But whatever. She had bigger concerns. Like how she was going to remain dressed during her talks with Jake. If she didn't *have* to show him any skin, she certainly wasn't going to. Even if it meant not getting to see any of his gorgeous bronzed flesh in return.

That thought was maybe a little more disappointing to her than she'd like to admit.

Still, the more she thought about it (which was *a lot*), the more she was sure she could come up with a plan to keep her clothed—and get all the information she needed. Just because she'd agreed to a bet like this didn't mean she couldn't still rely on her brain to get what she wanted without dropping her pants. She could figure it out. Right? And the *teeny tiny* little part inside her that got all fluttery at the idea of them seeing each other naked after all these years?

Nothing but aftershock.

Stumbling through her living room in the predawn light, she stepped on something pointy with her bare foot and yelped when it let out a squeak. "What the—?"

She reached down and retrieved the offender—a dog toy. "Where are you, Waffles?" Her recently adopted family member was almost always underfoot.

Not hearing a sound in reply, Apple shrugged and tossed the spiny rubber ball onto the couch. Yawning loudly, she stretched and made her way toward the kitchen. Just then a scuffling sound came from under the couch, and out popped Waffles, who ran over to her, her little scraggily tail wagging.

Apple had taken one look at the tiny mixed-breed dog and fallen hopelessly in love. The veterinarian at Fortune's pet adoption event had said the six-pound dog was a Chorkie—a Yorkshire terrier and Chihuahua mix—but she wasn't so sure about that. Waffles looked like her mom had gotten *around*.

Her funny look was precisely why Apple adored her. Waffles was so ugly, she was cute. Scooping her up, Apple snuggled the tiny brown dog with her crazy white Einstein eyebrows and gave her a good pat.

Jake had been at the event too, as part of the "Bachelors of Fortune" celebrity trio, which included her cousin Aidan Booker and Sean Muldoon. It still made her chuckle and shake her head that the local media had dubbed them that a few years back after they'd literally struck gold in the river behind Jake's house. Once word had gotten out about their incredible discovery, between the media outlets and women fawning over them, they'd become the three most popular men on the Western Slope of Colorado. And years later their popularity was still going strong. They even made public appearances like the pet adoption fair.

They'd signed autographs and had their picture taken, and Jake had practically laughed in her face when he'd seen her new pet.

Which just showed how little he knew.

Waffles was the quintessence of awesome.

Apple clicked on the overhead light in the kitchen and flinched at the sudden brightness. "Ouch, shit." Quickly flipping it back off, she breathed a sigh of relief and placed Waffles on her small purple dog bed. "You hang out here, love. I'm going to scrounge some coffee."

Apple placed her hand on her hips as the large dry-erase calendar on the wall by the refrigerator caught her attention in the budding light. The whiteness of it was particularly jarring this morning against the poppy-pink wall color.

Yes, she'd painted her kitchen pink. She wasn't ashamed.

Padding across the scarred wood floors of her small 1920s bungalow, Apple grabbed a dry-erase marker, found the day's date—Sunday—and drew a big red X through it. Then, taking up Monday, Tuesday, and, oh, pretty much every other day of the week, she wrote the words that filled her with dread: *FIVE WEEKS TO DEADLINE*. Just below it, she wrote a short motivational sentence in small letters: *Get your ass moving!!* With two exclamation marks. That's right. She wanted that motivation screaming at her.

Straightening again, Apple took a steadying breath. She had five weeks to get the information she needed from Jake and to finish her book. If she was clever and played her cards right, one strategic interview session with him would be all she needed.

Her stomach went shaky at the thought.

If she wasn't clever, she might wind up doing the full Monty with Jake.

Apple yanked open the white cupboard door in front of her, rose onto her toes, and searched for her coffee. Only it wasn't there. Not this time.

Frowning until she remembered that she'd meant to grab more at the co-op, but had chased after Jake instead, Apple let the cupboard slap shut. "Looks like we're going out for coffee."

Giving herself a quick once-over and deciding that her ancient *Reading Is for Awesome People* T-shirt and pink sweatpants were good enough for a coffee shop run at seven thirty in the morning, Apple moved back through her house to retrieve her reading glasses.

She put them on and grabbed a hairband from her dresser. Finding a pair of flip-flops hiding under the corner of her white vintage wrought iron bed, she snagged them and slid them on. When she turned around, Waffles was in the doorway wagging her tail and looking irresistible.

"I just need to grab your leash." Which shouldn't have been too hard to find. She'd left it on the coat hooks by the front door yesterday, right? That's where she always kept it.

Wrong.

Ten minutes later, decidedly irritated with her space-brained self for having left the leash in her sock drawer, Apple stepped onto her front porch and closed the door behind her. Waffles pranced excitedly next to her in her slender rainbow-colored leash and matching collar.

The sun had dawned, and soft white light filtered through the canopy of huge old trees that lined her quiet side street, their brilliant green leaves still in the calm, cool air. September had just come to Fortune, pronouncing that autumn was just around the corner.

Taking a moment to appreciate the gorgeous morning, Apple inhaled the sweet, earthy scent of pine and grinned. It was her favorite smell in the whole world. Well, that and the smell of flowers and dirt and wet grass. Or pretty much anything from nature. The simple scents of Mother Nature delighted her senses clear down to her toes.

She was a Taurus. What could she say? Earth was kind of her thing.

And it's also why she had a vegetable garden and flower beds in a riot of blooms all around her yard that rivaled any master gardener's. And until she had a whole gaggle of children to tend to like her heart longed for, her flowers and vegetables—and now Waffles—filled that need.

Apple sighed. She was thirty-two. If she wanted that gaggle of babies then she kind of needed to get moving pretty soon. Having a man would help too.

She sighed again. Not at the thought of finding someone, although that did cause her some consternation on its own, but because she didn't want just any man. She wanted *the* man.

The man of her dreams.

An image of Jake came to mind and was gone, leaving her briefly shocked and short on air. She shook her head and blinked hard. Had her brain just short-circuited? Because no way did she have any romantic designs on Jake. Not anymore.

Besides, he wasn't dream-man material.

But *someone* was.

"Where are you?" she said under her breath, wistfully, like maybe her knight in shining armor—*not* Jake—would magically appear if she asked just right. But just like pretty much every other time she'd asked the question—besides that one glorious day when a crow had taken a dump on her head to shake things up—the only response she got was silence.

Wasn't the universe supposed to be chock-full of signs? Over every hill and dale, in every nook and cranny, or plastered to the side of a bus that just so happened to pass directly in front of her? Unfortunately for her, the only thing the Great Beyond was choosing to reveal at that particular moment was the neighbor's dog sneaking a squat behind Apple's lilac bush, leaving her a big, fat pile of stink to deal with later.

Fan-tastic.

Muttering, Apple bounded down the steps after the mutt before he decided to pee on her zinnias, and in her haste she almost forgot poor Waffles was still attached to the leash in her hand. At the last minute she let it go, thank goodness, and dashed across the dew-dampened grass, belatedly noticing her neighbor perched on her front porch in a large wicker chair while she sipped something from a blue mug.

"Lovely morning, isn't it?"

"Awesome," Apple replied, not really meaning it. She already had a list of things she was annoyed about. Pulling up short and nearly losing a flip-flop in the process, she pasted on a smile. There was always the chance for improvement, right? Maybe an actual dream man—*not* Jake—would show up and make up for her brain betraying her with that flash image. "Morning, Mrs. Walton. I was, uh, just helping Buddy find his way home. He seems to be lost in my yard again."

Bless her heart, but at nearly eighty years of age, her neighbor had a hard time keeping track of her yellow Lab mix. And because Mrs. Walton could barely hear, that dog got away with everything and had horrible manners.

"Thank you, dear. He can be such a wanderer. Now, when are you going out with my Drew again? The way he talked, you two seemed to hit it off."

Apple groaned softly. Never let it be said that she wasn't a good sport, because that blind date with Mrs. Walton's grandson had been a mess. She was all for love, really she was—but she wanted passion too. Not some guy who spent the better part of an evening going on and on about his sci-fi addiction and the genius of the remade *Battlestar Galactica* series. She was more excited about the idea of deep cleaning her refrigerator than spending another three hours in his company.

But she couldn't tell Mrs. Walton that. "The library has me so busy lately. We got a huge donation and all the sorting and filing and logging—oh, you know how it is. I've just started teaching a new computer literacy class too. Maybe soon though, okay?"

Her neighbor nodded and gave a small wave. "I'll tell him you said so."

Fabulous. "You're too sweet, Mrs. Walton. Have a good day now."

Before she could be waylaid from coffee any longer, Apple grabbed up the leash from the grass and started walking with Waffles, noting the late-summer flowers blooming in front yards up and down the street. An occasional hammock or tire swing hung from the mature trees, adding texture to her already charming neighborhood. She loved all the unique old houses painted unexpected color combinations and tiny bungalows with their creative additions.

But the best part about her neighborhood was that it was tucked just off Main Street, a leisurely ten-minute walk away from the library and her all-time favorite coffee shop, the Mother Lode. The café paid homage to Fortune's humble beginnings as a gold mining town with a rustic interior reminiscent of an Old West apothecary, with gorgeous glass jars showcasing select whole beans and black-and-white photos of early prospectors hung on the walls.

Apple had just turned onto Main, Waffles keeping up beside her like a champ, when she spotted a bright orange, perfectly restored '72 GMC pickup parked in front of Two Moons. The song that had been playing in her head abruptly went off track with a *screech* like a needle on a record player. And there she'd been working so hard to improve her mood. The best day of her life, her ass. Those American Authors didn't know what they were talking about.

How could any day be great when it had started off with no coffee and a reminder from her neighbor of how low she was willing to go in her quest for true love—and went directly into seeing Jake's truck parked in front of his pub? And *right* after she'd had that disturbing thought about him being her dream man? Plus, it bugged the hell out of her that his truck hadn't moved since yesterday. Had he left the pub with some random woman last night, instead of going home? Ugh, just the thought made her stomach uneasy. Which it shouldn't.

What he did on his time was his business. What did it matter to her?

Just to prove to herself how little it mattered, she didn't look over even *once* to see if he was inside already. Let him have his casual encounters. All she needed from him was some key information.

So then why did the thought of him doing the mattress mambo with some random woman make her so irritated? It was an irrational response to say the least.

Hmm. Maybe she was shorter on sleep than she'd realized. Would explain the burgeoning irrationality.

It seemed a plausible explanation and eased the tightness building between her shoulder blades. The idea that she cared what Jake did with his personal time was laughable. Seriously. She might be a little too open-minded in her search for love, and the bar may not be set very high, but she wasn't that desperate or crazy.

Jake Stone was most women's dream man for the night, but he wasn't marriage material. He was too busy chasing skirts. And that was fine with Apple because she didn't have any interest in him that way anyway. Not since she was fifteen and had learned the hard way that he wasn't to be counted on. He'd promised her a ride in his souped-up old Chevy to Jenny Ballard's homecoming party where the *real* man of her young dreams had been waiting to give her her very first kiss. Only Jake had failed to arrive, and Ryan had danced with Shelley Peters instead that night. The two of them had become an official item by the following day. *Apple*, on the other hand, had been stuck home alone waiting for a ride that had never showed. To this day Jake still refused to explain his actions from that night.

Once she was past Two Moons, she admired the enormous planters full of flowers on Main Street and the colorful banner that spanned it, advertising Fortune's famous upcoming annual Blues and Brews Festival. In just a few short weeks the frost would come and take the flowers, but for now they were still going strong. And they were gorgeous. Focusing on them and thoughts of the upcoming brew fest helped her get all the way down to the Mother Lode, where two couples in casual outdoor gear were already sitting at the tables outside, and the rich, pungent scent of roasted coffee poured out through the open door of the cedar clapboard building. Some acoustic folk singer was quietly playing through the speakers, and the bike rack was already a third full.

Apple stopped and assessed where would be the best spot to leave her dog for the moment, feeling conflicted about abandoning Waffles even though she was simply going inside for a quick coffee and would be out in two minutes. Still, she felt like a bad parent who'd leave her kids in the car while running into the department store.

"Having problems, juicy fruit?"

Apple let out a tiny squeal and jumped. *Jake.* Rounding on him, she frowned instantly at the happy, relaxed look on his face. *Wonder what put that there?* "Don't you dare sneak up on me like that again! You scared the daylights out of me. Where'd you come from?"

"There." His thumb hitched over his shoulder in the direction of Two Moons. "Just got to work."

She just bet he had.

And now she was seeing him in the soft early light, looking all rugged and outdoorsy and sexy with his stubble, worn cargo pants, and ancient hiking boots. Then she noticed the slight dark circles under his eyes, and all she wanted to do was stomp on his foot for causing her so much trouble. And maybe a little bit for leaving his truck at work and going home with some stupid chick for the night.

A smile played on his lips as he crossed his arms over his chest, causing his pecs to bulge all masculine-like and yummy and further annoying her. "Looks like somebody woke up on the wrong side of the bed."

Something hot flared to life in the pit of her stomach, and she snapped, "At least I woke up in my own damn bed."

Jake rocked back on his heels, eyebrows raised in surprise and his dark eyes going bright. "What's that supposed to mean?" He looked over at his truck then and started laughing. "Did you think I went home with someone from the pub last night? Because I didn't. Wait, are you *jealous*?"

"Of course not," she instantly sniffed, offended. Jealousy was for insecure people. "I don't care what you do in your free time." She notched up her chin for emphasis just to prove she really meant it and ignored the tiny spark in her that was relieved he'd slept alone last night.

His eyes narrowed suspiciously, damn him. "Then why the attitude?"

"Why the interest?"

"Because you're acting weird." He leaned down until his broad shoulders filled her entire field of vision and she was staring into his unfairly gorgeous eyes. "Also because I think you're intimidated about our new arrangement and that's why you're being prickly."

"As if," Apple replied on a huff, agitated. God, the man was full of himself. Like a little game of striptease was going to faze her. *Please*. "You don't scare me."

He smiled then, slow and lazy, and to her extreme annoyance, her core began to heat. "Then why don't you ask your questions now? Why wait? We can do it in my office at Two Moons."

Apple took a deep breath as something like panic slammed into her chest. *Not now!* God, she wasn't even close to ready. "I don't have them with me," she scrambled to say. "Sorry." Then before he could open his big mouth and say anything else frazzling to further throw her off, she shoved Waffle's leash at him and ordered, "Here, take her. I'm going inside for coffee."

Jake's mouth dropped open a little as he fumbled with the leash. Waffles sat on her butt whimpering up at him, her enormous brown eyes begging for love.

"Enjoy!" Apple chirped with an overblown smile and strode toward the open coffee shop door.

But before she got all the way there, Jake recovered and said in that deep, rough voice of his that made her lady parts quiver, "Tomorrow night at my place. You bring those questions you've been hounding me about."

Apple gaped at him, her glasses slipping down her nose. It was just too damn early for this. "Fine," she finally grumbled. "Your place, tomorrow night."

The man whipped out that smile of his again. Her knees went weak as her brain blanked like a clean slate. And she could *swear* she suddenly heard the sound of someone laughing evilly off in the distance like some B-grade horror movie, warning her she'd just fallen into a trap. A very big, potentially naked trap.

"Here." He held out the leash toward her, Waffles sitting like such a good girl next to him. "Come take your mutt back."

The hormone haze caused by his smile disappeared in a *poof*! Jerk. How dare he? Waffles was a unique beauty.

Apple *hmphed* and gave him a good glare. "You wouldn't know quality if it bit you on the butt. Now stay there and apologize to Waffles while I finally get my darn coffee." With that she left him on the sidewalk, glancing over her shoulder to see his expression shifting between bafflement and a frown as he stared after her.

Jake might not be her knight in shining armor—and certainly *not* her dream man—but he could at least hold a damn leash.

As soon as she'd pushed through the front door, Apple spotted her best friend, Nell, without her son, waiting in line at the counter. Relief poured through her, and she quietly burst out, "You wouldn't believe the morning I'm having!"

Nell gave her a thorough once-over, tipping her head to the side and causing her long honey-colored braid to slide over her shoulder. "By the looks of you, I can believe it. What's up?"

An espresso machine began to whir and buzz, causing Apple to raise her voice some to be heard. "For starters, Buddy dumped in my yard again. The leaves are beginning to die on that lilac because of him utilizing it as his toilet, and you know how sad that makes me."

Her best friend's soft green eyes were full of sympathy. "I'm sorry, sweetie. I know that dog drives you crazy. Maybe you should think about building a fence to keep him off your property?"

Apple sighed greatly and pushed her glasses back into place. "Can't afford it. Plus, it would break Mrs. Walton's heart if I suddenly threw up a hard boundary between us. *Who also*, by the way, is insisting on setting me up on a second date with her grandson."

"Oh God, no, really?" Nell's look of horror was a comforting balm to her ego. "Didn't he list off his favorite baby names and ask you to pick one each for a boy and girl?"

"That and *so* much more. There was also a brief, one-sided discussion of whether or not I had sufficiently wide birthing hips. Seriously. It was appalling."

"Wow, and I thought my last date was bad."

Apple glanced at her best friend and smiled wide. "Nope. I win!" And then she added on a more somber note, "I always do."

Nell gave her a reassuring squeeze, her tall, fit body almost towering over Apple's petite and curvy frame. "Maybe someday we'll win the man lottery. Keep your chin up, hon."

They reached the counter, and before Apple could speak, Nell winked at her and said, "It's on me. You deserve it after the yard bomb and bad-date reminder."

"Thanks, love. Appreciate it. But that's not even the worst of it."

"No?" Nell gave their order to the cashier—two grande vanilla lattes with extra shots. "What else is going on?"

Apple just pointed over her shoulder toward the man standing out on the sidewalk holding her dog. "That."

This time Nell chuckled while she paid for their drinks. "Oh, I think Jake looks cute holding Waffles. What'd he do to get under your skin?"

"Exist?"

Nell gave her a look—that look that only a mother can give. "Is he still refusing to talk to you for your book?"

They stepped off to the side to wait for their drinks as a road cyclist dressed all in shiny spandex took their place in line to order, and Nell snapped a picture of Jake on her cell phone. "For posterity." She grinned. "Proof he can be sweet."

Apple just rolled her eyes and answered Nell's question. "It's worse than just him still refusing to talk. I got so desperate and frazzled yesterday when I saw Jake after work that I ended up agreeing to something really dumb but potentially fun to get him to talk about his family."

"Uh-oh." And then, "You didn't agree to sleep with him, did you?"

Pretty close. "Oh God, no. Well, not technically. There's no touching involved."

Nell's mouth dropped open, and her usually calm, controlled demeanor faltered as she sputtered softly, "Wh-what the shit, Apple?" Her round eyes searched the sidewalk until they landed on Jake. "What did you agree to do with him?"

"A game of strip poker with questions." Turned out that it was embarrassing to admit it out loud. At least she was going to get to see him strip too.

"But don't worry," she assured Nell. "He has to get naked too." Her stomach went jittery with nerves as soon as the words popped out. Seeing Jake in the buff was the stuff dreams were made of. Or at least old dreams anyway. She hadn't actively wanted that since high school. But now that the opportunity had presented itself…yeah, she was maybe still a little interested.

Her best friend finally regained her composure and quipped, nudging Apple with a shoulder good-naturedly, "Well, that's a relief. At least now's your chance to find out what all the fuss is about. See why all the ladies *crave* Jake."

Crave.

The word shot straight to the pit of her stomach and curled into an unexpectedly hot, sizzling ball of primal agreement. Before she could even react to it, she saw a couple with a stroller outside walk up to Jake and start talking. The smile he gave them was warm and friendly, kicking that sudden craving up a notch. And when he bent over the stroller, reaching out a hand only to have his index finger gripped by a tiny little infant hand in return?

Kaboom!

She just flat exploded with hormones and need and yearning that she didn't even know were there inside her.

"Would you look at that?" came Nell quietly from next to her as they both stared out the window, amazed.

Apple couldn't stop looking, and it was churning up her insides in ways she didn't like or understand. Babies. Jake. Him holding Waffles. Naked question games. It had her all kinds of twisted up and discombobulated.

Just then the barista announced their order was ready, and Apple snatched up her coffee cup, taking a long scalding drink. "Ouch! Shit that's hot." Her tongue began to sting fiercely.

"Things are crazy busy right now at work, what with the blues fest later this month. I had to hire extra help to get through the crush." Thank goodness Nell had changed the topic. Bless her best friend and her ability to read her like an open book. She must have known that she needed a break.

"It still amazes me that your rock-climbing club gets so packed. I mean, it's great for you. Yay, money! But, it's just weird that they come so early to Fortune to spend time playing on rocks before the concerts. I don't understand rock climbers."

A shadow played over Nell's pretty eyes. "Honey, I was married to one. Trust me, I know the sentiment."

More than most anybody else, Apple thought. Nell had married a world-famous climber, and it hadn't ended well. He'd died taking on a treacherous climb in the Swiss Alps and had left her pregnant and widowed less than a year after she'd said, "I do." All that she had left of that short relationship was an indoor climbing club that she'd inherited from him and hated owning—and her son, Sam.

Speaking of… "Where's your boy this morning?"

Just mentioning her son brought light and humor back into Nell's eyes. "Actually, he's with your mom making me a birthday present."

The cyclist stepped closer to them, crowding them, so Apple began slowly meandering her way back through the tables to the front of the store. For some reason she wasn't in much of a rush to get back to Jake and Waffles. Especially not when he was now actually *holding* the baby and her heart was beating heavy in her chest from the sight.

Big masculine man, soft sweet little baby snuggling together. All of Apple's deepest dreams right there rolled into one.

Sigh.

She was toast. Toast with a side of massive yearning. *Mmm-mmm*, yum.

Forcing herself to tune back in to what Nell was saying, Apple replied distractedly, "That's great. I'm sure Mom has some amazing clay project planned." Which was true, actually. Sedona Woodman was a world-renowned ceramicist, her work displayed in galleries from San Francisco to Paris. Nell was in for one heck of a birthday gift.

Still, Apple couldn't take her mind off the fact that Jake was out there cuddling a baby while holding a dog on a leash and looking all domesticated. Her brain was all like: *me Apple, you hot man with baby. Mate me now.*

As if pulled by some invisible cord, she was outside on the sidewalk and had said good-bye to Nell like she'd been on autopilot, barely registering their exchange and parting hug. After a promise to call her later, she turned her gaze on Jake. He'd shifted positions, and now the baby was resting on his chest, its little downy-covered head on his shoulder with its eyes closed tight, sleeping soundly. And Jake was very subtly rocking his big, fit body from side to side in that way that parents do—that natural, instinctive soothing motion that had been putting babies out like lights for eons.

She tuned in just in time to hear him say to the couple, "He's happy, and I'm already babysitting anyway. It's fine, really. Go on inside and grab some coffee. Branson and I will hang out here until you get back."

Her heart stopped dead. Flat, *dead*.

What alternate universe had she slipped into that Jake Stone had suddenly turned into an affable guy who willingly offered to cuddle babies? Was the coffee shop the portal? And what did it mean that she didn't want to step back through and spoil it?

Man, maybe she needed to see a therapist because this morning her thoughts were uninhibited *crazy*.

"Thanks, Jake. We'll be back in a flash. We'll be keeping an eye out, so if he wakes and starts to fuss just flag us down through the window," the baby's father said as he slid his arm around his uncertain-looking wife and gave her a reassuring squeeze.

Jake shifted in his ancient hiking boots and gave the new mom an easy smile. "It'll be fine." He tipped his head toward the shop. "Now go on and enjoy five minutes of adult time before this little fella wakes up and demands you back."

Before she could protest, the man bustled his wife off, leaving Apple alone with Jake and an irresistibly adorable baby. "Who are they?" she blurted out, her fingertips itching to touch all that soft, newborn hair.

"Friend of mine from college. Chris and his wife, Julia, just recently moved here after he took a job teaching chemistry at the high school." Jake rotated his shoulder slightly so that she could get a better look at the infant's sleeping face. "And this guy is Branson. He's six weeks today."

Unable to stop it, Apple leaned in and traced a fingertip over the puff of silky blond hair. Her insides went to mush. She inhaled that sweet baby scent and felt her sigh come straight from the heart. "I want," was all she said, but there was a lifetime of hope and longing in those two simple words.

"I know." Jake's voice came soft, gentle from just above her head—and heavy with some emotion that she didn't understand, but it laced his tone like rum in a drink. Resignation? Annoyance? What was it?

"Babies fill my cup," was all she said, completely lost in the sight, scent, and feel of the infant. If she could have three or four of these, she'd be set and happy for life. Heck, right now she'd settle for just *one*.

"Why don't you start then?" Jake asked, his voice quiet yet questioning. "Have a baby?"

Apple leaned in farther, tracing her finger across Branson's tender cheek. She was *such* a goner. Jake's words were barely registering. "Need the right man," she mumbled in reply, smiling when the infant let out a tiny sigh and pursed his lips.

Jake was still gently rocking, slowly, barely moving. "There're sperm banks, you know."

She scrunched her nose. "Uh-uh, not for me." As if Branson heard her, his angelic newborn face molded into a deep frown and he let out a tiny cry, pulling his knees farther under himself against Jake's chest before settling comfortably again. "Call me a traditionalist. I want my babies to come from a union of love."

Jake rocked closer, and his head was mere inches above hers now. "Not very feminist of you, Apple."

She just shrugged. "Want a man, want marriage, want babies. Nothing antifeminist about that. It's what I want and choose. That's the heart of feminism anyway: a woman's choice." Apple caved and leaned in to kiss that downy baby head. "And I choose the traditional route."

She looked up then, and her eyes went round. Jake was staring at her with the darkest, most intense and unreadable expression in his eyes. A jolt of awareness barreled through her, slicing straight through her heart and down through her stomach to her very toes. Her pulse leapt into action like it was a racehorse from the starting gate.

Their gazes locked.

One heartbeat.

Two.

Tension mounted between them as Jake just kept giving her that unfathomable look. Unthinking, Apple licked her suddenly parched lips and blurted, "You're good with him." Referring to the baby he was holding.

Not even a flinch. Not a blink. Why was he staring at her like he could bore right into her soul?

"Maybe you should have kids." It was all she could muster and come up with.

And just like that, the spell was broken. *Poof!*

Jake blinked, and his expression went blank, as unreadable as any professional poker player. "Never going to happen," he growled, the instant edge in his voice confusing to her.

Apple frowned, wondering why he was getting so agitated. "Why are you getting so upset? I just said that you should think about having kids. You're a natural with them," she added, nodding toward the way he was cradling Branson. "And if I'm not wrong, you actually seem to like them too."

Jake began to scowl, rocking the baby a little more animatedly now. "You're wrong. I'm never having kids."

"But—"

He pegged her with a glare that nearly melted her from the heat. "*No*, Apple."

"But—" she tried again.

"Never. Going. To happen," Jake ground out between clenched teeth.

"*Fine,*" she said on a huge sigh. Let him have whatever this was. "I was wrong. You don't like kids, and you're never going to have any. End of story."

Jake nodded, his jaw set in tense lines. "Damn straight." He held out his hand with the leash. "Now take your mutt so I can get on with my day."

"You don't have to get so pissy, you know."

Just then Branson's parents stepped out onto the sidewalk, steaming-hot cups of java in their hands. Apple took that as her sign to leave. Twisted up and confused inside, she couldn't resist poking Jake one more time as she turned toward home, her own forgotten coffee cup still in hand.

She opened her mouth, and he cut her off.

"No." A single word, but the man said it with *emphasis*.

Apple started to walk away, Waffles obedient beside her. She got a dozen steps and stopped. Turned around only to catch Jake nuzzling the baby's head. He straightened the minute he spotted her and tossed her a defiant look.

But she knew the truth now, and it warmed her from the inside out.

"You don't like kids? Never having any?" she said again as she strolled away, suddenly feeling lighter.

"That's right," he nearly shouted back.

Apple turned to face him and kept walking backward down the sidewalk. He scowled after her, and she just smiled. "You sure about that?" she asked, almost bursting with happiness inside and not wanting to care why.

"Yeah." He braced his legs apart and stared her down, challenged her to call his bluff.

The grin that came to her lips was full throttle. "You're *such* a liar."

She spun and left him there, adding a little swish to her stride for dramatic effect as she sauntered away. It was going to annoy him so much—that extra bit of unnecessary sass.

Huh, imagine that.

It was turning out to be a great day after all.

Chapter Four

THE NEXT MORNING Jake was up and in town early again. He parked on Main in front of Two Moons and enjoyed the underlying crispness to the morning air as he left his truck behind, walking down the street toward the coffee shop. Fall was coming in hard and fast, and he was glad. It meant firing up his woodstove at the cabin soon—and *that* meant warm, relaxing evenings at home with nothing but the sound of snapping logs to keep him company. He liked the sense of solitude that fall and winter brought to his neck of Glacier Valley.

Hunkering into his coat some as a gust of cold wind kicked up, Jake sighed to himself. This was the fourth or fifth morning in a row that he'd been into town before the roosters crowed. But this time, instead of heading to his brewpub to experiment with a new ale recipe in a last-ditch attempt to turn his recent insomnia into something productive, he was headed for the Mother Lode.

He smirked wryly after he stopped in front of the already bustling shop and realized it was the exact same spot he'd stood in with Apple yesterday. At least this time he wasn't holding the leash to a tiny mutt-dog like an idiot while its owner took her slow, sweet time inside purchasing some frou-frou overcomplicated drink.

Because it was the only time that would work with everyone's current schedules, this morning he was here to meet Aidan and Sean to discuss his upcoming nineties-themed night at the pub. Once a year, Two Moons put on a Decade of Music Theme Night with all proceeds going to a chosen charity. Last year they'd raised over ten thousand large for the elementary school.

To pick the year's theme, Jake wrote every decade from the last sixty years on scraps of paper and then had a pub patron choose one from an old miner's hat—a tradition. Everyone was welcome to dress in historically accurate clothing when they attended the party, and they did. Oh, the good people of Fortune most certainly did. They got into the spirit in a big way.

This year, Tommy Wilcox had yanked out the nineties, Jake's favorite decade.

He stepped inside the coffee shop, his mind instantly flashing back to the summer of '99. He, Aidan, and his old band buddy Elijah Goldman had pulled into the local gas station one blazing-hot afternoon, having just returned to town from a three-week-long backpacking trip in the San Juan Mountains to celebrate their graduation. They'd taken his old car, a '78 red Camaro with black rally stripes that had gotten him laid by pretty much the entire cheerleading squad junior and senior year. As they'd pulled up to the gas station, the windows were down and the stereo was cranked to his favorite Fly song, "Got You Where I Want You." Jake remembered being obsessed with listening to it daily. And the funny thing was, he'd always ended up thinking of Apple when it played.

And then, lo and behold like he'd conjured her out of thin air, Apple came sashaying over to his car in some sweet little sundress that tortured his imagination. Jake had suddenly been acutely aware that he hadn't had a proper shower or shaved in three weeks. He felt unclean. It was a feeling he'd already had too many times around her, and it always left him feeling substandard and inadequate.

So he'd greeted her with a scowl from behind his sunglasses.

It hadn't fazed her. She'd just leaned down through his open window, completely oblivious to the fact that she'd shoved her juicy tits right in his hormone-crazed face, and smiled at her cousin all warm and sweet and nice. "Hi, Aidan. How was the camping?"

He noticed The Fly's lyrics coming through the speakers just then and couldn't have agreed with them more. She was killing him. Apple's nipple had puckered tightly beneath her dress, and it had taken all his willpower not to open his mouth and nibble that perfect little bud. God, he'd wanted to tongue it until she moaned. It had given him such a monster hard-on.

And apparently that unexpectedly hot little memory was enough to give him a hard-on all over again, even now. At thirty-five years of age. Waiting in line in a damn coffee shop just like he was eighteen and horny as hell all over again.

Jake grumbled under his breath and shifted to alleviate some of the pressure in his jeans. Sometimes he really frigging wondered who had whom. Because if the way he was standing right now was any indication—uncomfortable and a little awkward with a semi in his pants—then it was pretty clear who was coming out on top.

He got a mental picture of her in that position and couldn't stop the quick grin that followed.

"Hey, Stone. Over here."

Turning his head in the direction of Aidan's voice, Jake found the guys already set up at a scarred wood table. "Let me grab a coffee and I'll be right there."

Stepping up to the long L-shaped counter, Jake took stock of the menu written in colored chalk on the blackboards hung on the wall and made it simple. He really liked simple. "Large coffee, black."

The young barista smiled at him through her lashes and flipped her dark braid over her shoulder. "Is there anything else I can get you, Jake?"

Having never seen her before, he had no idea what her name was, but Jake had given up wondering how people knew his. It was always one of two things: his old, wild reputation (which was always blown *way* out of proportion), or because he was a Bachelor of Fortune. In the barista's case, since she was probably just about nineteen, he figured it was the latter.

Which made him inwardly sigh and say with a polite smile, "I'm good, thanks"—he scanned her nametag—"Bethany."

When he, Aidan, and Sean had struck it rich panning for gold behind his cabin five years ago, they'd never anticipated the amount of media and public interest that had resulted. But practically overnight they'd gone from simply being three normal guys to local celebrities with regional newspapers and TV outlets going crazy over their story. All the press had gained them a following—a mostly *female* following, but still. Some days it was weird being asked for an autograph or photo, because in his mind he'd forever just be Jake Stone, misfit son of the town drunk...no matter how many millions might be sitting in his bank account.

Still, he and the guys recognized how fortunate they were, and whenever they were asked to make public appearances or do events, they did. And this time it was Jake who was going to be doing the asking.

The Bachelors of Fortune were going to become bartenders for a night.

Coffee in hand, he pulled out a chair at Aidan and Sean's table.

"Morning, mate," Sean said in his lyrical Irish accent, before narrowing his eyes and stating flatly, "You look like shite."

"Gee, thanks," Jake retorted and popped the lid off his coffee to help it cool. "I haven't been sleeping the best lately."

Aidan raked his gaze over him and took a pull from his drink. "You okay?"

Having known each other since kindergarten, there wasn't much that his oldest friend didn't know about him. In fact, there was only one thing he could think of that he'd ever kept from Aidan. But it was for a lot of good reasons.

So it really wasn't an option right then to tell the guys that he hadn't been able to sleep since Apple had decided to strip for him. Every time he closed his eyes, he began to fantasize about her—which made him hard and frustrated, and robbed him of any hope of sleeping.

Yeah, he didn't think that confession would go over too well. Particularly since Apple and Aidan were more like sister and brother than cousins.

So instead of answering right away, he kicked his legs out in front of him and crossed his ancient Merrell hiking boots, taking a long, leisurely pull of straight dark roast Columbian. At last he replied casually, "I'm good, man. Just have a lot on my mind these days."

Aidan smirked and slid him a glance. "I bet."

"Hey, I have shit to worry about." Jake took mock offense. "Just because I don't own southwest Colorado's largest construction company and I don't have a thousand employees to run herd on doesn't mean my life is always a breeze, man." Then he broke into a grin. "It just means I have more fun."

Aidan laughed and said, "You always seemed to, man. Which is bullshit, by the way." He shook his auburn head. "How was it that you and I did everything together from the time we were five, but you always had more fun? Even when it was mundane crap like shoveling the driveway?"

Sean chuckled and merely shook his head, looking at them. "You two. You're like ornery siblings."

Jake just grinned at Sean before raising a brow and replying over the rim of his cup to Aidan, "I have the joie de vivre, brother. You were always so serious."

"And you never were," Aidan retorted. "You were always breaking the rules."

"That's why you got beat up on the bus every day after school until I started riding with you, man. You needed to loosen up." Jake leaned forward and clapped him on the back, laughing.

"I'm plenty loose," Aidan muttered and tugged at the brim of his worn blue BOOKER CONSTRUCTION ball cap, resetting it on his head and flashing a grin. "See?"

"Of course you are, mate," Sean said with a laugh.

Aidan was about as relaxed as a cheetah on the prowl. The last time Jake had seen him completely at ease was before his dad had died and left him his company, back when he'd been twenty-three and head over heels in love with that environmental science major. Whatever magic she'd worked, she'd brought out a different side of him and made him happy. Right up until the day she'd crushed his heart. But with her, Aidan had been easygoing, laid-back, and carefree. So different from the earnest kid Aidan had usually been.

Scratching his chin, Jake said, "We're just saying that you could stand to cut loose sometimes. Which brings me to why I called you guys to meet me here this morning." It had absolutely nothing to do with the fact that the Mother Lode was Apple's favorite morning haunt and there was a chance he'd run in to her. None at all. "It's that time of year again at Two Moons: Theme Night for charity."

"I've told Shannon about your parties. Since experiencing the general enthusiasm Fortune displays for karaoke, she's excited to see the fun to be had at Theme Night." Sean grinned, his green eyes dancing.

Jake smirked. "Then your woman is going to really love this: you get to play bartender for the night." He glanced at Aidan and winked. "You too, pretty boy."

Aidan frowned and uncrossed his heavy work boots. "What do you mean? Did somebody quit on you?"

The doorbell jangled, and Jake's gaze shot to the door. But it was only Jerry Gibbons, not the person he wanted to see. Which was no one. He wasn't looking for a single person.

Jake took another sip and ignored his heavy heartbeat. "Nah, man. Everyone is good. I've just got a specific fundraising goal this year and want to outdo last year's earnings. Having the Bachelors in attendance and bartending will boost attendance, which in turn will net more money."

"Of course. What's this year's charity?" Sean asked.

Jake grimaced slightly, instantly self-conscious, and hedged, "Yeah, so, the thing is, well…it's, um, for Apple."

Aidan raised a brow. "Excuse me?"

Jake took a hot sip, frowning slightly into his cup. For some reason he felt a little embarrassed to admit the reason he'd chosen this year's charity. "Not Apple,

specifically—but the library. Since she's taken up residence at the pub to hound me about her book, I've been
listening to her talk for months about the condition and
age of the library's computers. Especially the ones in the
computer lab. They're ancient, and she's starting a basic
literacy class for senior citizens next month. I thought
it'd be nice if they had new computers to learn on. And
having the Bachelors there will make sure we can raise
enough to meet the library's needs." He ended abruptly
and took another long drink, swallowing hard. "I thought
it could be kind of, you know, like, a gift for Apple. You
know, keep the announced charity general, like 'computer literacy,' so that she doesn't know it's specifically
for the library, and then surprise her with the check after.
I thought she might like that…" He trailed off. Christ,
why did he feel so awkward? Like a goddamn schoolboy
giving a pretty girl a fresh-picked dandelion. He really
hoped new computers would make Apple happy—and
he didn't want anyone to know that he wanted that so
much—her happiness. *Especially* her.

Shit, now he was even acting childish. What the hell?
"What do you say, are you guys up for it?"

"Goes without saying," Aidan said, nodding.

"Of course, mate. After the way you helped save my
ass against O'Banion, you don't even have to ask," said
Sean.

"That wasn't a favor." Jake shook his head. "That was
taking care of family."

Before coming to Fortune five years ago, Sean had been
a bare-knuckle boxer in Dublin where an unfortunate

entanglement had left him on the run from the Irish mob. The boss, O'Banion, had found him a few months back, and he and Aidan had helped Sean secure his freedom, along with the help of Shannon Charlemagne—Sean's stable manager and the love of his life.

Aidan nodded and pulled his smartphone out of his pants when it went off. He scanned the message and broke out laughing. Then he handed it to Jake and said around a grin, "Sissy dogs are a good look for you."

What the hell?

Jake snatched the phone from Aidan and looked at the screen to see a text that Apple had sent. There he was crouched next to her puny dog while he scratched its ears with a dumb smile on his face. Below the picture read: *There's not a single lady this guy can resist. Besides me, that is. Thank God. :-)*

Irritation washed over him and settled between his shoulder blades at the same time a slow burn of desire started low in his belly. Which was pretty much what happened every time Apple was involved. Arousal and irritation all at once. It was like his body went bipolar at the mention of her name.

He was so used to it by now that he just rode it out and forced a chuckle. "I like females, what can I say?"

That used to very much be true. One hundred percent. Jake and the ladies had enjoyed each other on the physical level. Who could blame him? It's all they'd ever wanted from him anyway.

So yeah, he'd liked a variety of women. Right up until about four or five months ago when Apple had started invading his life on a regular basis again, just like back in high school when she'd always tagged along with Aidan, making a nuisance of herself. His feelings for her then had been nothing more than the intense cravings of a hormone-raged teenager, and he'd believed he'd simply outgrown them.

But then she had to go and text a photo of him to Aidan with a comment implying she was glad he wasn't interested in her in *that way*, and his stomach went hollow and achy. Like he was that easy and beneath her standards.

Jake glared into his coffee cup until he realized something else: that was the second time Apple had made a pissy comment about his sex life in just as many days. He wanted to know why.

Sean cut into his thoughts. "So what's the decade for Theme Night?"

"The nineties, man," he drawled with a grin.

"Sweet." Aidan laughed. "We get to pull out the flannel."

"So we're good then? You guys will help out at Two Moons in a few weeks?"

The guys nodded and agreed. Jake pushed away from the table just as two young women sidled up to the table in T-shirts that tagged them as sorority sisters from the state college in Archer, the town one valley over. The short blonde twisted her braid between her fingers and smiled, showcasing perfectly bleached teeth and deep dimples. "Hi, guys. I'm Britney, and this is my Gamma Phi Gamma sorority sister Heather." She gestured to the tall redhead standing next to her. "We're seniors at Archer State."

"You're the Bachelors of Fortune, aren't you?" the redhead demanded to know, all business.

Aidan nodded and gave them a friendly smile. "Good eye. Yes, we are."

Britney squealed a little. "We love you guys! We went to the Blues and Brews Festival here last year and saw all of you perform with the Redneck Rockstars. *Total* shocker that you all play instruments! It was *so* awesome. Are you really going to do that again this year?"

Jake crossed his arms, nodding. "We're planning to, yeah. We're trying to make it an annual thing."

The girls giggled and glanced at each other. Then they looked back to the three of them with expectant expressions. Sean was shifting in his seat, looking a little uncomfortable with all the young, enthusiastic female attention. Apparently being in love made one less inclined to enjoy such interest from the opposite sex. *Eesh*. Someone would have to kill Jake before he stopped enjoying looking at attractive women.

So why wasn't he feeling the least bit interested in looking now at the two who were standing just a few feet away?

An image of Apple's voluptuous, womanly body popped into his head. Naked. And he was suddenly very, *very* interested.

He hadn't once stopped being aware—not for one nanosecond—that tonight was the night he was finally going to see all that warm, gorgeous skin of hers in person. It didn't matter one shit to him that he had to bare it too, not when the reward was Apple unclothed. No wonder the co-eds didn't interest him. He had the image of Apple undressing with every question she asked taking up all his brain space.

Cursing under his breath, Jake stood up. "It was nice to meet you," he said with his head inclined toward the sorority sisters before turning to Aidan and Sean. "I've got to jet."

Aidan's eyebrow's shot up in surprise, and his gaze slid to the co-eds and back. "So soon?"

"Yeah." It was weird to him too. But the only thing he knew was that something inside him didn't feel right. And for some reason, that was enough.

"Wait, you can't go yet!" Redhead held her hands out. "Can we get a selfie with you guys first?"

She and the blonde put their heads together and smiled wide. Then they chimed in unison, *"Please?"*

Aidan looked back and forth between Jake and Sean when neither of them spoke, clearly puzzled. Or maybe he was just confused about Jake's general lack of enthusiasm and was looking to Sean for clues. Who knew? "Sure, we'll hop in a picture," he finally answered for them.

Jake had just squeezed in behind the redhead and next to Aidan when he caught a blur of movement out of the corner of his eye. He turned his head just as the camera on the phone snapped, just in time to watch Apple swish by out on the sidewalk in one of her girlie dresses with her best friend, Nell Taylor.

They were laughing, and Apple had an unhindered, carefree smile on her face. On her fresh-skinned, sweet round face—and it transformed her from pretty into something far more beautiful. Something luminescent.

This time when the lust slammed into him at the sight of Apple, he was prepared for it. What he *wasn't* prepared for was the not-so-vague feeling of yearning and the pang in his heart that accompanied it.

Fuck.

Just…well…

Fuck.

Chapter Five

LATER THAT AFTERNOON, Apple looked up from behind the desk in the children's department at Fortune Public Library. She'd been searching the computer database to see if the latest Geronimo Stilton had been checked back in, while Pam Butler and her daughter Sarah stood waiting patiently. Luckily the search indicated that it was returned—it just hadn't been shelved yet.

"Let me check the cart in the back room real quick," she said with a smile and rose from her chair. Then she looked at Sarah and added, "Have you read any of the newer Thea Stilton novels? They're just as adventurous and fun-filled."

The Butlers were regulars at the library, what with having six kids to entertain. It seemed like Apple had been helping at least one of them with books ever since she'd started working there eight years ago.

The youngest Butler shook her head and said quietly, "I haven't read them. Is she Geronimo's sister?"

Apple rounded the desk and came out on the other side, her comfy blue flats moving silently over the beige carpet. "I believe she's his cousin, but I could be wrong about that. Would you like me to double-check?"

Sarah just shook her head and shuffled restlessly in her scuffed sneakers. Being patient was hard at seven.

Clasping her hands together, Apple said, "Okay, I'll be right back."

Making her way through the maze of short, child-sized bookcases painted in shades of green, yellow, and orange, she crossed over the huge play rug, beneath the giant reading tree, and headed toward the back. She noted that the play train set had been in a colossal wreck and poor Thomas and his friends needed some assistance to get set back to rights. As soon as she finished helping Sarah, she'd go tidy up.

Housed in the old water mill that abutted Glacier River at the end of Main Street closest to Jasper's Peak, Fortune's library was a testament to the creativity and ingenuity of its citizens. Once abandoned and derelict, the old mill with the working paddle wheel and quirky design had been renovated by a group of volunteers led by Aidan's construction company after asbestos had been discovered in the old library and they'd had to find a new space to house the books until repairs were finished.

But then Aidan had gotten it in his head to completely renovate the mill with LEED-certified green materials and make it a permanent space for the books. So now the library was a quirky red-brick haven of literacy. And she loved it more than anything else.

Reaching the back room, Apple stepped inside and was, as always, immediately taken with the view from the huge window directly opposite her. On the backside of the mill, they were three floors directly up from the wide, fast-moving river, with a thick bank of aspens and pines standing on the far side. The sound of water rushing through the wheel created a constant low-level white noise that was super relaxing.

Apple should know; she'd fallen asleep in that room cataloging books after hours more than once, but especially in the summer when the windows were open. For her, the library became a tranquil paradise retreat.

Quickly finding the newly returned book, Apple crossed back through the cheerfully decorated room and returned to the front desk. "Here you are, sweetie. I think you'll really like this one. Geronimo goes on safari."

"Thanks!" The girl took the book and made a beeline for the reading tree, plopping down on the thick rug and starting to read the moment she got over there.

Mrs. Butler had been staring hard through the wide archway that led from the children's section to the front room and circulation desk. At the sound of Apple's voice she swiveled her head and asked, "Is it true that you're trying to get the Bachelors of Fortune to do some sort of event here at the library?"

She fumbled the book and nearly dropped it. "Not, not that I know of, no. Why do you ask?" She was the second woman already that day to mention that same thing. It was becoming unnerving.

The exhausted-looking mom replied with a nod toward the entrance where Apple noticed with surprise that Jake was standing just inside the entrance frowning at the circulation desk. "Because Jake Stone just walked in, and I don't think I've ever seen him come here. Plus, I heard it from Carol King at the donut shop just this morning." She leaned in close and added with a whisper, "Not that I'm complaining that he's here. I'm married, not dead. He's gorgeous."

Apple could only sigh. "Yes, he is."

"So you are having them do something?"

How had admitting that Jake was good-looking automatically mean she had the Bachelors doing an event? She didn't have anything planned. Besides, since helping with the remodel, this had to be the first time in four years that Jake had stepped foot inside the library.

What was he doing there?

Mrs. Butler adjusted her shoulder bag and pressed, "Are you sure? Carol King said Sharon Riley told her over coffee that Barbara Keeley saw you make an agreement to do something with Jake at the pub last week. And then Carol overheard him with the other Bachelors this morning at the Mother Lode, and your name came up."

Crap.

Humiliation and embarrassment flooded her. The town's biggest gossip had overheard her make the deal with Jake! Oh, good God. She could die. Just curl up on the floor and die right then and there. No way in hell did she want everyone to know about her Q&A striptease agreement with Jake.

God, her big stupid mouth. See? Tourette's.

Wait, why did her name come up at the coffee shop? Was he *telling* everyone?

Patting the brunette on the arm briefly in a display of reassurance, Apple faked a calm she didn't feel and smiled. "Oh, you mean *that* thing." She tried for flippant and added a little laugh for effect. "I'd forgotten. But yes, now that you mention it, there is something I've arranged."

Mrs. Butler's eyes lit up. "What is it?"

Shit if she knew. Stuff was just flying right out of her mouth now. She was making it all up. A desperate need to keep her business private could make a gal do that.

"I'm not at liberty to say quite yet," Apple hedged as she prayed for inspiration to strike and give her a decent excuse. "But I'll be sure to let you know as soon as I am."

However, inspiration was less than forthcoming with gifts at the moment. Even more so than the universe had been that morning when she'd asked for a sign. Which meant that it wasn't forthcoming at all. In any way, shape, or form. But at least this time she didn't have a pile of dog crap to clean up.

"Oh, I'll be sure to let Kay Greer know," Mrs. Butler said as Jake walked up behind her without her notice. He stood with his feet braced apart and arms crossed, listening. "Between Two Moons' big party and this thing you're cooking up, she's sure to have a chance at snagging one of those guys. It would be such a lift in her spirit, being as her divorce just finalized and all. A sweaty night with a young, hot Bachelor would be just the thing to cheer her up."

Heat flooded Apple's cheeks. No doubt she looked as red as her name implied.

"Now, that sounds like quite the invitation," Jake said. Then he grinned full out with wicked humor. Apple was still blushing when he raised one thick, well-shaped brow and winked right at her.

The audacity.

"Oh my God, you heard that?" Mrs. Butler looked mortified. Just mortified.

"Mmm-hmm," he drawled, clearly enjoying himself.

Apple clasped her hands together and cleared her throat, flustered but trying to get beyond the embarrassing moment and keep the conversation moving. "Well, I can only *imagine* what that would be like," she began absently until what she was actually saying registered and her gaze flew to Jake, her eyes huge. *Hello, awkward.*

He was giving her that same dark, intense look—the one that made her squirm. Her stomach dropped, and her heart made a distinctive *thud* inside her chest.

It had changed some over the years though and grown hotter, darker—edgier. But she knew that expression. It was the same look he used to give her when they were teenagers and in the same space together for more than a few minutes. Apparently her response to it hadn't changed either. She was instantly sixteen and keyed up all over again.

She suddenly had the strongest urge to strip and cool the steam rising from her like a hot spring. Right there in the Fortune Public Library. With a mother and her daughter in attendance, waiting patiently to check out a book.

Good Lord, what was wrong with her?

"What I meant to say was that I can imagine *Kay* could use a morale booster after that messy divorce." Big, wide-eyed smile. "Now, why don't we get that book checked out for you?"

Phew. Disaster avoided. Dumb mouth.

Apple swooped past Mrs. Butler and Jake. She had just made it to the archway when she heard the woman say from the other room in a voice that had a decidedly flirtatious vibe, "Can't wait to hear more about this little adventure of yours, Jake. Apple told me all about it. *So* looking forward to it." Clearly her mortification could be soothed away much more quickly than Apple's.

Had she actually thought she'd escaped the calamity caused by her mouth?

Yeah, well, she'd been wrong. "Just this way!" she called behind her. Though what she really wanted to do was wave her hands and make everybody freeze until she could figure out a way to keep her secret agreement with Jake, well, *secret*. Not that she was a prude or anything. She just didn't think it would do well for everyone to believe that the town librarian took it all off for cheap.

Just when she'd been beginning to hope that he might not respond to Mrs. Butler, Jake inquired, "What adventure?"

Apple squeezed her eyes tight and grimaced. Here it came.

"Oh, the one you and Apple are cooking up."

"She told you about that?" Surprise colored his deep, rough voice.

Where was a hole to crawl into when she needed it?

"That's right. She said you were just getting started."

Because she was almost sure that Jake was staring after her through the archway, she swallowed hard and tried to respond lightly, "That's right!"

Sounding clearly puzzled, Jake added, "Tonight, as a matter of fact."

"Oh, that's wonderful to hear!" Mrs. Butler clapped. "I'm sure you'll do good work together and we'll all have something to look forward to soon."

And the day had started off so well. "We will, Mrs. Butler. It will be great, I promise." Apple lightly rapped her knuckles on the circulation desk, making a faint sound. "Now, if you and your daughter just want to come in here, we'll get that book checked right out."

Jake walked into the front room, his expression one of both confusion and curiosity as he looked over his shoulder back toward the children's section. "You told Greg's wife about our arrangement?"

Mortified at the idea of telling *anyone* about her agreement with Jake, Apple glanced around him to make sure the coast was clear before hissing back, "God, not *that*! I said something else." She spotted the mother/daughter duo coming and finished whispering quickly, "Just play along, okay?"

"Why?"

"Because we were overheard at the bar last week, and I don't want everyone knowing what we're up to. Now just hush and play along."

His rich brown gaze dropped to her chest briefly, and he smirked. "What's it worth to you, juicy fruit?"

Apple fought the urge to roll her eyes. She had a reputation to consider, even if he didn't. "I'm already coming over tonight. What more do you want?" she demanded in the fiercest whisper she could use without drawing attention.

He seemed to think about it. "Tonight, I get to pick which items of clothing you have to remove."

What?

Apple forgot about the Butlers and exclaimed, "You've got to be kidding!"

"What's he joking about?" Sarah asked from behind Jake, her little round face full of innocent curiosity.

Jake just cocked a brow at Apple and grinned as she stammered, "Oh, oh, he's just being silly. You know how boys are." She pulled a face, making the girl laugh, and it helped calm her nerves a little.

Until Jake said, "You know, I saw the funniest text message today on your cousin's cell…" And she realized what he was talking about. "You seem awfully interested in my personal life. Why's that?"

Warning bells went off in her head, and she knew he was up to no good, especially since he was bringing up her message to Aidan in front of other people. Glancing around the circulation desk, Apple took a deep breath and considered her options while she checked out the girl's book, making small talk about the weather. Bringing up her text now was just a tactic meant to press her. "You weren't supposed to see that. It was a joke for Aidan."

"But I did, and I'm awfully curious why you care so much about my sex life."

"*Shhh*! They'll overhear." Apple could feel her face flaming again, tossing a worried glance at the duo who were thankfully preoccupied putting books in a cloth carry bag and didn't seem to be listening.

He laughed. "That's the point."

"So it's my agreement or my embarrassment?"

"Yep." The jerk just grinned like the dickens, obviously having the best time. Neither choice was great, but the bottom line was that she'd really prefer to not have the entire town know the lengths (or rather how low) she was willing to go for her story.

"Whatever I take off, you have to as well. Equal treatment," she quietly reminded.

"That might be hard. I don't typically wear a bra."

"Typically?" She eyed him with question.

"*Ever.*" His gaze waffled and then slid away. "Okay, there was that one time in college when I dressed up as Marilyn Monroe for a Halloween party, but that's it. I swear."

"How'd it feel?" Apple couldn't help asking through a sudden grin.

"Uncomfortable as hell, actually. I feel for all you ladies who have to endure that bra shit every day."

She laughed. "Well, that's gallant of you."

"That's the kind of guy I am, sweetheart. Gallant to the core."

"If that were true, then we wouldn't be here right now having this dumb conversation."

"But what fun would that be?"

"I'm not having fun." She glared at him to prove her point.

He grinned. "How about I agree that we take off the same clothes? More fun now?"

Actually, yes, that did sound kind of fun.

"Yep." *Shit.*

Jake laughed out loud at that, earning them a curious glance from Mrs. Butler.

She slid Jake a resigned glance, her decision made, and said under her breath, "*Fine*, it's agreed. Tonight, you get to pick what *we* take off."

And now she was going to go find that hole.

"*Oh my God*, there's a naked man in the river!" Mrs. Butler suddenly exclaimed from in front of the large picture window overlooking the water.

"What?" Apple looked at Jake before they both dashed over to see. "Who is it?"

Jake got there first, and his quiet swearing and sudden scowl answered her question. There was only one person Apple had ever known who had the ability to kill Jake's mood instantly.

His dad.

She glanced down the rocky bank just as Verle Stone stuck his head under the mill's still-working water wheel and let it splash over him, a bar of soap in his hands. The man was naked as the day he was born, his clothes laid out nice and tidy on a wide, flat rock farther up the bank. A filthy, ratty camping backpack was tossed haphazardly next to them. And there, sitting on top of the heap, was an empty liquor bottle.

Mrs. Butler coughed and darted a look at Jake. "We'll just be going now. Thanks again for the books, Apple."

Sympathy for Jake flooded Apple. She couldn't imagine what it was like to have that kind of prejudice to deal with on a regular basis. God, she couldn't stand small-mindedness. It was bad enough he had an alcoholic father to deal with. He didn't need people judging him for it.

"Would you like me to call someone?" She touched his arm for comfort.

His large, hard hand covered hers briefly in return, squeezing tight before letting go. "Nah, I've got it. Just give me a few minutes to get him bundled up and out of here, okay? Don't call anyone."

She looked up into his dark eyes and smiled easily, hoping to lessen some of his tension. "You got it. Is there anything I can do to help?"

He scrubbed his hands over his face wearily and blew out a long, slow breath. "No, but thanks." Then he smiled at her, only it looked a lot more like a snarl than a grin, especially with that one slightly crooked incisor of his. Still, she had to give him points for trying. "I'll have him gone in ten minutes."

Maybe more like fifteen, Apple thought, after glancing down again against her better judgment and discovering

Verle soaping his armpits and singing a unique version of "She'll Be Coming 'Round the Mountain" at the top of his lungs like he was the happiest, freest man on earth. Which in a way he kind of was, if free-balling counted for anything.

Promptly reeling back, Apple closed her eyes tight. "Jesus, I didn't need to see that."

Jake looked out the window, mumbled something under his breath, and made a beeline for the door, stopping long enough at the entrance to say, "My place tonight. Seven o'clock. You know the way." Two footsteps more and he cleared his throat. "Also, thanks for being cool about my old man."

Then he was gone. Apple blew out a breath. Looked like she had four hours to get her questions in order. Just a mere 240 short minutes to become more clever and succinct with words than she'd ever been in her life.

Otherwise she was going to be sporting the same damn outfit as Verle.

Chapter Six

JAKE POPPED THE top off a beer and tossed the cap into the trash before stepping out onto his back porch to watch the sun dip low behind Jasper's Peak. It was almost time for Apple to arrive, and his stomach was a tangle of knots. He told himself it was because of the subject they were going to discuss, that it was sensitive material for him.

Which it was, that was true enough. He never talked about his family. There wasn't anything good to share anyway.

Just a pot full of losers sprinkled with crazy sauce.

His dad's behavior that morning was simply one good example why he kept his personal business personal. That hadn't even been the first time in the past week he'd had to rescue his dad from doing something illegal or stupid. It was also not the drunkest he'd seen him.

Jake shook his head and took a drink of the cold, crisp brew, glad as shit that he didn't have the alcoholic gene that ran in his family. As if skinny-dipping at the public library wasn't bad enough. One of these times his old man was going to land himself in jail, get hurt—or worse.

And, well, there wasn't a damn thing Jake could do about it.

Because alcoholism was only a symptom of the real problem Verle faced: the Stone family genetic defect, otherwise known in medical terms as familial glioma. An inheritable disease that caused one or more tumors to grow in mostly untreatable areas of the brain, it affected different nervous systems based on the individual. In his pop's case, MRIs showed that his tumor grew on his amygdala—the emotion center of the brain. Untreatable and inoperable, as it grew larger, Verle's behavior became more and more erratic. All Jake could do was sit back with a heavy heart and watch his dad slowly unravel.

It was hard.

Knowing that it was a sex-linked trait that appeared only in the males in his family didn't make it any easier. Nor did knowing that it could randomly appear not to affect a generation like it had with Harvey, and like it had since his ancestors—the first founders of Fortune—had arrived. Most especially, it didn't help knowing that the disease often lay latent in an affected male until his early to midthirties. *Then* the tumor started to grow, and life as that guy knew it was over.

There was no way to tell if it was going to happen. Genetic testing wasn't available to the public yet that could code for the mutated gene that caused the glioma. He'd been keeping tabs, hoping. But no such luck.

There weren't even any early warning signs he could rely on to help him know. The men in his family carried the gene and it either crippled them or didn't. Jake had no idea where he stood. He could be one of the few whom the mutated gene affected only mildly like Harvey. Or the glioma could affect his nervous system and he could wake up one day with his left arm feeling numb—and end up paralyzed from the neck down for the rest of his life. It could also grow near his amygdala and he could become emotionally unstable like his pop.

He just didn't know.

It killed him.

And it made a future for him to plan—a *real* future— all but impossible. How could he ask a woman to accept that kind of instability, sharing a future with him? He couldn't. There was no way he could leave a woman or a family devastated while he lost the fight to glioma. What if *he* went insane? He just couldn't do that to someone.

Not only that, he couldn't risk the disease passing on. Not through him. That's why he'd taken action to prevent it from happening the day he'd turned twenty-one. After he'd explained his medical condition to a urologist over in Archer, the doctor had agreed to give him a vasectomy, even though it wasn't typically done at such a young age. With his genes, they'd both felt the responsible choice was to make certain there was no risk of impregnation.

The one consideration he'd overlooked in his eagerness to stop the spread of the disease was someone else's feelings. Say like a potential partner's. He'd never stopped to consider that someday a woman might want to have kids with him. Or vice versa.

Apple leapt into his mind, and he sighed. Yeah, that right there. She was human perfection personified in one soft, gentle, beautiful package. Everything he'd wanted his whole life and could never have because of his god-damn family disease.

Sometimes biology could be a real bitch.

That thought made him wonder if his dad had gotten the brochures for the retirement community that he'd left for him last week. If he was going to develop a glioma that debilitated him, he needed to make sure Verle was going to be taken care of. Before it was too late. With so much of his future uncertain, Jake needed to cover all the bases. That thought hovered over him like a black cloud, and he wanted it gone. He could carry only around so much.

A snorting sound turned his attention, and Jake reached down to scratch the ears of Dregs, his late grand-pop's bulldog. "Hey, buddy. Are you missing him?" It had been only a few months since Harvey Stone had dropped dead of a heart attack while working outside at his home-made distillery, and sometimes Jake could swear the dog still got sad about it. He knew he did. Spending time up the side of Jasper's Peak with his grandpop in that old miner's shack he'd called home had been some of the best times of his life. Having Harvey had helped make up for having a drunk dad and no real mom—only an occa-sional birthday card that showed up postmarked from various places throughout the Midwest.

The old dog snuffled and groaned as he leaned heavily into Jake, making him grin. For a few minutes, they enjoyed each other's company, until the sound of tires crunching gravel turned his attention. *Apple.*

His gut tightened almost painfully at the thought of her. Taking another drink as his pulse began to race, Jake surveyed his backyard and listened for the sound of footsteps. It was amazing how acutely he was tuned into Apple's movements, how very aware he was of her presence even though she was clear on the other side of the cabin. He frowned. How was that even possible?

But he knew the moment she rounded the corner of his cabin. He *felt* it.

"All right, Jake. I'm here. Let's do this," Apple said as she started up the stairs, looking tense and determined with her notebook clamped in her fists.

And so it began.

Excitement and nerves jolted him and had him pushing away from the railing. "What? No warm-up, no verbal foreplay? What's the rush, Apple?"

Color flooded her sweet cheeks, turning her face red. "Considering our relationship, I don't think foreplay is necessary. I don't need it. Really, I'm good. You've got me ready and raring to go. So let's just get right to it, okay?"

Jake laughed. He couldn't help it. God, he loved the way stuff came out of her mouth. Her *phraseology.* Guaranteed she had no idea what she'd just said. "Oh, honey, it's necessary all right. And if you don't think so, then you've had some shit partners."

The look she slid him had heat pooling straight to his groin. It was a mixture of embarrassment, annoyance, and—if he wasn't mistaken—curiosity. "My sex life isn't up for discussion."

Jake absently licked a drop of ale off his bottom lip and grinned. "Maybe if it was better, you'd be up for talking about it."

She rolled her eyes as she reached the porch landing, a canvas bag hung over her shoulders. "Maybe you should just mind your own business."

He held up his hands. "Hey, I'm only offering advice." Though he realized he wasn't. Not in the least. He didn't actually like the idea of Apple having sex with anyone. But damned if he knew why he felt that way.

Dregs waddled over to her then, snorting and sniffing up her skirt. She gave him a good, sound pat. "I know he's old and a little smelly, but I'm glad you took him in after your grandfather passed," she said. Her hand was already busy scratching the dog under his chins. "So, where do you want to do this?" she added, sounding nervous as she brought their conversation back around to business.

Jake looked her over, really taking in her attire for the first time. Normally she liked dresses, but tonight Apple was wearing a long green skirt with some Indian-style print on it and a plain white V-neck T-shirt. *And* she was wearing pink flip-flops with chunky argyle-print socks.

He raised a brow. "Interesting choice of footwear."

"I get cold feet," she retorted defensively.

"Clearly."

She glanced at the river just through the stand of trees and said, "Is that the actual spot where you, Aidan, and Sean struck gold?"

He nodded and leaned back against the log cabin, crossing his arms. "It is, yeah." He indicated the spot with a tip of his chin. "A sandbar goes out almost to the middle, and we were set up just past it. Well, Aidan and I were. Sean was actually *on* the sandbar when he found his obscenely large nugget."

Her eyes were focused on the rushing water and went wide behind her glasses. "Is that the very same spot your ancestors panned when they first arrived?"

Jake flicked her a glance, his lips twitching. "Why yes, yes it is."

Apple was so entranced with whatever she was imagining that she obviously didn't realize what she'd done. Jake couldn't keep from laughing. This was going to be so easy.

First question down.

"Socks off, woman. I don't normally give a shit about that stuff, but you look like a fashion nightmare. So be gone with them."

"What, why?" Sputtering, her mouth dropped open and floundered for a bit until, looking thoroughly discomfited, she finally managed to say, "Seriously, you're calling that a question? That didn't count! I wasn't ready."

Jake enjoyed the look of indignation on her face and gave a short laugh. "Sorry, but them's the breaks, kid. Rules are rules. You ask a personal question, we strip. That's the deal we made."

Grumbling, Apple heaved a sigh and started toeing off her flip-flops while he got rid of his socks and put his boots back on. "Why are you so amused by all of this, Jake Stone?"

"Because it's funny."

She glared at him as she wiggled her sock-covered toes, trying to extricate the V-shaped cotton from between them. "To you, maybe. I'm actually trying to accomplish something important."

So was he. Seeing Apple naked had been important to him ever since she'd begun haunting his dreams nightly. But he also knew if that were all he really wanted from her, he'd have gotten her in the buff years ago.

Begrudgingly he had to confess that there was more to his feelings toward Apple than he understood. They weren't straightforward and simple, as much as he'd like them to be. Instead, just like the woman who spawned them, his feelings were confusing and complex. And that grated like hell on his nerves, because it was the exact opposite of the simplicity that he craved. If there was any justice in the world, seeing her naked would fix that. Or even better, make the feelings go away completely.

There was only one way to find out. "Let's move on to the next question, shall we?" Pushing away from the cabin logs, Jake snagged a blue camp chair and took a seat.

Dregs was already sacked out and snoring like a champ in the waning afternoon sunshine. Warm day, soft breeze, quiet surroundings. For an old dog like him, that was about as good as it got. Shit, Jake thought that sounded pretty damned great too. Nothing complicated, nothing jarring him out of his serenity. Just him, nature, and good ol' peace and quiet.

"You're expecting us to do this interview here, *outside*?"

And Apple.

Damned if there wasn't almost always Apple too.

At least tonight he got to call the shots. "Bet your der-riere I do." He caught her uneasy glance toward the forest that surrounded his place and laughed, shaking his head. "You really think someone's going to see?"

The woman sniffed and began unfolding a green camp chair directly across from him, her back to the river. "Maybe I'm modest."

That had been the right of it back in high school, for sure. But something about Apple made him wonder if that still held as true today as it had then. It was the way she moved sometimes, with such natural sensuality, that made him wonder what she was like behind closed doors.

"Do you ever wear your hair down?" he suddenly asked, more gruffly than he'd intended. Apple was across from him now, sitting with her notebook in her lap. Her hair was pulled up like always in a thick twisty bun thing, and she had on those enormous schoolmarm glasses. The graceful curve of her neck was displayed temptingly, backlit now as it was by the sunset. In fact, her whole head was in that light, the rays turning her hair into a golden halo.

A feeling began to stir in the pit of his stomach. That wasn't as far off the truth as he'd like to admit. Apple had always embodied this light, gentle energy—like an angel's. It had called to him in ways he'd never understood and had resented for being unable to resist the lure.

She'd captivated him.

Glancing up from whatever she was scribbling in her yellow notebook, she raised a brow, her blue eyes sharp. "If I answer your question do I get a freebie?"

Like he was giving up any chance of seeing Apple's naked skin. Never. "Sure."

She smiled. "Then *maybe* I do."

Saucy wench.

"Boots off, Stone," she added, sounding damned pleased with herself.

Amusement warmed his chest as he kicked his boots off and set them aside. "Tell me about this book thing of yours, then. Why write about Fortune?"

Dregs let out a huge snort, rolling onto his stomach with all four legs pointed out on each side. Then he resettled with his chin on the ground and closed his eyes, all of his loose fur wrinkling around his ugly mug. The comical underbite just made him that much more awesome.

Apple crossed her shapely legs, her argyle sock-covered foot tapping with nervous energy before she remembered and quickly pulled the garments off both feet, setting them aside. She slipped back into her flip-flops and chewed on the end of her pen before answering. "The reason is simple, really. I love where we live, Jake. I'm proud of it. And I've always wondered why no one has taken the time to compile our town's history." She smiled tightly. "Now, with your assistance, I get to be the first."

"Great." Jake held his bottle of ale out to Apple, offering her a drink. "I can get you one of your own if you want," he added with a nod toward the kitchen.

She took his and drank deeply, handing it back when she was done. "No thanks, I'm good with this."

He took it and immediately brought it to his own lips, a funny feeling in the pit of his stomach over the knowledge that her mouth had just been there. "Why do you love it here so much? I know why I do; I'm just curious what your reasons are. What's so great about this place that it's worth writing about and telling the whole world?"

Apple gave him a look like he was dumb. Just plain dumb. "You really need me to explain it?"

No, he didn't. Not really. He knew what made Fortune so special. It was just for some reason, now that the moment of truth had come, Jake found himself stalling like he was nervous or something. But that was ridiculous. Why would finally seeing Apple naked make him nervous?

"Fine, let's get on with it then, shall we?"

Jake kicked his legs out in front of him and placed his bottle on his thigh. As he watched, Apple pulled a minirecorder from her backpack and fidgeted with her notebook, pushing her big-ass glasses back up her nose.

She clicked the tape recorder on and exhaled quickly. "September ninth, interview with Jake Stone regarding Fortune's first settlers." Her eyes fluttered closed for a heartbeat before snapping open and zeroing in on him. "All right, let's do this."

His entire body went tense as something deep down inside him awakened, rearing its head with one simple message—one coherent thought—but it was enough to start him slow burning.

Finally.

Chapter Seven

IT WAS GO time.

Apple opened her mouth to ask the first question on the list she'd compiled earlier that afternoon, but the words refused to come out. Stumped, she swallowed and cleared her throat, then tried again. Still nothing.

Crap in a hand basket.

Jake cocked a brow and grinned wolfishly, making heat pool in her belly. "Problems, honey? A little frog in your throat perhaps?"

Torn between wanting to kick him really, really hard in the shins for teasing her and a sudden urge to give the man a dose of his own medicine by tormenting him, Apple decided to take charge. She was going to give him that dose. No way was she letting her embarrassment over what they were doing win and make her too timid to play the game. Jake didn't intimidate her.

"Nope, I'm good. Just needed a few more minutes to organize my thoughts." She acted like she was writing something in her notebook and glanced at him through her lashes. For a guy who claimed to be easygoing, he sure looked on edge. If he gripped his beer bottle any harder there was real risk of it shattering.

Why was he so tense?

"You look really uncomfortable." The words just popped right out of her mouth before she could stop them. She inwardly groaned and cringed. Where was her freeze button? Or better yet, rewind?

Jake slowly rubbed the palm of his hand against the thigh of his jeans, his movements almost mechanical and stilted. "I'm not uncomfortable, Apple," he said finally, quietly after a few awkward moments.

He couldn't even look her in the eye when he said that. Not very convincing. But she was just going to keep her thoughts to herself and move on.

She opened her mouth to speak, intent on asking one of her interview questions. "You're sure acting like it," is what came out instead. Lovely.

His gaze whipped to her, dark and unreadable, and she began to squirm. "I'm comfortable okay. Just trust me."

Something hot and dangerous flickered in his eyes at the words, and her core trembled in response. But she decided to seize the moment and gain the upper hand...

It was worth a shot at least, right?

Apple leaned forward, placing her elbows on her knees, and bit the inside of her lip to keep from laughing when his gaze instantly dropped to the deep-V neckline and her girls.

"How about we start again?" she asked, leaning forward a little more to scratch a pretend itch on her ankle, knowing the movements made her breasts push up against her knees and nearly pop out of her shirt.

His eyes flashed before lifting back up to meet hers. Now she had his attention.

"Let's do," he said.

"Awesome. Okay, I'll start with my first question." She sat back up and smiled pretty, preparing to take off her flip-flops. "What happened to Fortune's first group of settlers back in 1869?"

His gaze held on her steady as he took a drink from his bottle, saying around the rim, "They died."

"Are you going to be difficult every time I ask you a question?"

"It was an answer."

Apple leveled a look at him. "It was a bullshit one, and you know it."

He smirked, his dark gaze holding hers steady. "It's still an answer."

Slowly starting to fume as it became clear that Jake was going to be obstinate as usual, Apple bit her tongue to keep from making a snarky comment and closed her eyes for a second. A few long breaths and a count to ten had her refocused and goal oriented, so as she opened her eyes she pretended to bobble her pen and let it drop from her fingers, rolling to the wood plank porch.

Two could play his game. "Whoops!"

He cocked a brow. "Really?"

Yep. She smiled. "Silly me!"

With wide, innocent eyes, Apple leisurely bent forward to retrieve the Bic, stopping halfway down when he said, "Are you sure you want to do that, juicy fruit?"

She looked right at him and slowly bent the rest of the way down, biting back a laugh when her boobs pushed against her knees, plumping considerably. "Do what, exactly? I'm just retrieving my pen." To prove her point, she held her hand up and waggled it at him, smiling brightly. "See?"

Jake laughed low in his chest and shook his head, his sun-streaked hair shimmering in the light coming in low from the horizon. "You seem to have forgotten something about tonight. Might not be a big deal." He shrugged and took a pull from the bottle. Long and slow, just to drive her crazy. When he was done he set it on the porch and laced his fingers behind his head, his brown eyes lit with mischief. "Then again, it might be worth a reminder."

"What should I be reminded about, exactly?"

He grinned, sly and with a whole lot of naughty, successfully emptying her mind of any coherent thought. She really despised how that look of his had the ability to make her insides quiver. Tipping her head to the side, Apple took him in—every last masculine, rugged inch. *Why* did he have to have such a sexy, muscular frame? It made staying focused way more difficult than she needed it to be.

"That *I* choose which clothes we take off, and you just asked another question. It's not your flip-flops I'm after, juicy fruit."

"What—" she started to say, but her voice broke. Clearing it, Apple tried again. "What answer? You didn't *answer* anything."

"Okay, that's fair. Ask me another one."

She straightened up, glancing quickly at the list of questions in her notebook. "Hmm, let's try this: Where did your family originally come from?"

"You mean, where'd they emigrate from?"

"Yeah."

Jake scratched the stubble on his chin, looking thoughtful. "If my memory's right, they came over from northern England, up near the Scottish border. He was a bookbinder with a penchant for adventure, and she was the youngest daughter of a Scottish laird who decided a life in America with a bookmaker was better than a boring, normal aristocratic life." He took a drink, and added, "They eloped to Gretna Green and spent their honeymoon on a ship."

Her eyes went round. "Seriously?"

Jake nodded. "Mmm-hmm."

"God, that's such a cool story!" Excitement burst inside her. Oh, what a scintillating tidbit to add to her book! As fast as her pen would go, Apple retold the story to her notebook. "Thanks for telling me."

She looked up from her notebook then to see Jake staring intently at her, and it stopped her cold. "What? Did I do something?"

"No." He shook his head, his eyes dark and intense. "But you're going to. So am I."

Her heart began to pound, but she couldn't break his gaze. "What do you mean?"

"That this is a game of strip questions."

"And you just answered one," she concluded a little breathlessly as the implication sunk in.

He nodded again. "Mmm-hmm."

Damn it, and it'd been a good and honest answer too. There was no balking this time. The two of them were about to be short an item of clothing. And he got to choose.

It was unnerving. A little daring. *Exciting.*

Apple took a deep breath. "What would you like us to remove?" Unease skittered down her spine, and she straightened, moistening her suddenly dry lips with the tip of her tongue. Oh man. The sudden glint in his eyes told her this wasn't good.

His brow shot up at that, and he chuckled softly, shifting a little in his seat. "I would *like* you to take off your bra."

Her mouth dropped open. "Why?"

"Why not?"

"Because you don't have one on!"

His lips twitched. "That's because I'm a guy, honey. Don't wear one."

"Well, you're taking off something, Jake Stone." A quick assessment of his wardrobe showed her there weren't many options for him. He was going to be naked as a jaybird in no time.

Too bad for him. "Lose the shirt, I'll lose my bra."

Jake grinned then. "With pleasure."

Heat flared in the pit of her stomach as he reached behind his head and pulled his shirt off, revealing a body that was as hard and masculine as the rest of him.

Muscles flexed with every little move he made, and the small patch of chest hair grabbed her attention like a homing beacon. So did the happy trail that ran down his flat, defined abdomen before it disappeared into the waistband of his jeans. Goodness, the man was sculpted bronze everywhere.

For a moment their gazes met, and Apple felt something inside her go soft and supple with need. With *desire*.

Her notebook slipped from her limp fingers and landed on the deck with a thump, startling her. "Shit!" Reacting quickly, Apple scooped it up and pressed it against her racing heart. "Sorry about that."

Jake just took another long, slow pull of his beer. "Your turn, juicy fruit."

She pulled a face—a very *flushed* face—and stalled because she realized the tactical error she'd made. Her shirt was old and thin. The minute she took off her bra, her nipples would be highly visible. Apple sighed, knowing that feeling shy was pointless.

The things people did for their art, right?

"Fine," she muttered and reached behind her for the clasp to her bra. Grappling with it since that one stupid hook was caught again, Apple huffed and looked at Jake, who was smirking. The jerk was clearly amused. She stilled and demanded, "Remember this moment."

He laughed. "Oh, I will, trust me."

That's not what she meant. Not even close. "I *meant*, remember this moment, you jerk, because you finally got me out of my bra." The clasp finally gave, and Apple quickly pulled the straps down one arm, then the other.

She was just starting to pull it out the sleeve of her shirt when she caught his expression and faltered, snagging the hook on the V-neck of her shirt and pulling it far to the side. A large portion of bare skin was exposed with the movement, and his gaze zeroed right in on it.

Swallowing hard, Apple unhooked it and pulled the bra the rest of the way loose, dropping it gently on the porch. Her full breasts swung free, her nipples puckering instantly. She was unprepared for how vulnerable and exposed she suddenly felt.

Jake made a strangled sort of sound and coughed, and she darted him a quick glance just in time to see him shift in his seat. Dropping her gaze farther, she gasped at the sight of his jeans stretched tight across his lap and rapidly looked away.

But Jake wasn't shy. "You're surprised by that?"

"Surprised by what?" she pretended not to know even as she'd gone slick and achy at the sight of him.

Suddenly the air changed around them, charging with rising energy, and she inhaled, holding her breath.

Jake looked her in the eye. "Are you surprised that your breasts made me hard?"

Good heavens.

Apple couldn't help it; she glanced at his lap again, becoming transfixed. At his *impressively* bulging lap. "A little," she admitted honestly. She absently licked her lips with the tip of her tongue.

"Ask me another question." His voice came to her then—quietly, coaxing.

For the life of her she couldn't look away. She knew she should, but she couldn't. Jake's thick erection in his jeans was just so *erotic*. And it made it nearly impossible to think. "D-do you know their names, that couple?"

"I do..." he said casually, his eyes beginning to smolder as they raked over her from hair to toes. "They were Charles Stone and Margaret Ferguson."

"Thank you." She jotted their names down while nerves exploded under her skin and raced along her veins as she waited for him to tell her what they were going to take off next. She reminded herself as her breath drew shallow that this was all for a purpose—it mattered. This wasn't gratuitous nudity.

"Is one of the rumors true about what happened to the Fortune settlement?" she asked, unthinking. "You know—cannibalism, avalanche, rival prospecting party?"

He shook his head. "Uh-uh. That's two questions. Take off your top first."

Apple's heart stopped. Just plain stopped for an entire beat. "If I'm taking off my shirt, Jake, you're taking off your pants." It was about all he had left.

He seemed to consider it. "Deal." Standing up, he reached for the button on his jeans and stopped. "I should probably mention something before I do though."

Her stomach flopped, but damned if she was backing down now. She needed to know what happened, and this was her chance. "Yeah, what's that?"

Jake's fingers began working the button loose, and then he tugged the zipper down slowly, exposing golden skin and a small thatch of curly brown hair. "I'm not wearing any underwear."

Apple went hot and throbbing and wet all at once.

Before she could chicken out, she said, "Prove it," and reached for the hem of her shirt. Yanking it over her head, she dislodged her glasses. Crying out as they fell to the floor, she temporarily forgot her topless state. "My glasses!" she exclaimed, bending forward.

"I've got them," Jake said at the same time and bent down too.

And they nearly collided, his face stopping mere inches from her bare breasts. The heat of his breath fanned over her already puckered nipples. But he didn't back away.

He was naked.

Full-on *naked*.

Apple sucked in a breath and held it. She'd never seen anything like him before in her life. Built and sculpted and strong. Bronzed, muscled thighs with their dusting of brown hair filled her vision. Swallowing hard, her heart thundering, she stole a quick glance at the heavy, thick erection between his legs.

Oh. My. God.

Another wave of desire captured her. She wanted to touch, to feel, to taste. *Bad.*

Apple's gaze flew to Jake's, and she waited for him to say something. Anything. But he didn't. He merely devoured the sight of her breasts, his gaze intense and hungry as it raked over her bare skin.

"Do you like them?" she whispered then, thoroughly aroused and forgetting herself entirely. "I like yours."

Jake swore and moved suddenly, making her shoot straight up in alarm. Then his mouth covered hers hard. Fireworks exploded behind her eyelids, and she made a sound of surprise, rocking back. One of his hands shot out and cradled the back of her head as he took the kiss deeper. His tongue stroked over hers, and she moaned helplessly, wantonly, leaning into him and feeling his hot, silky skin against hers.

Jake broke the kiss and yanked back, scowling hotly. "Go home."

Dazed with arousal, Apple blinked. "Excuse me?"

He thrust her glasses into her hand. "I said go home, Apple."

She forgot they were naked as her mouth dropped open. "But my questions, my book?"

Jake began pacing, every inch of him masculine, turned-on male. She couldn't stop staring. "Another time."

Apple reached for her shirt and quickly put it on. "But—"

He stopped pacing. "If you know what's good for you, Apple, you'll leave right now."

She gathered her things and put on her glasses, her bra bunched in her hand. "Why?"

He pegged her with a smoldering stare. "Because I really fucking want you."

Holy shit.

Apple swallowed hard. *That* wasn't anywhere in the rulebook. "I think I'll, um, just go."

"Smart woman."

She backed away, stumbling down the first porch step and laughing nervously. "Clumsy me," she said before descending the rest. Hitting the grass, she couldn't help from glancing over her shoulder and wondering about his final words.

Was she smart? When Jake was there with his feet planted wide and muscular arms crossed—*complete* sex on a stick—and ready for *her*.

Did smart women just take their bras and run?

Chapter Eight

"HERE, LET ME get that," Jake said to his father a few days later. Early that morning he'd arrived at Harvey's place so the two of them could sort through his things. Jake had been encouraging his dad to do it for months now, but his old man had resisted so much as touching any of Harvey's things. Though Verle had lived in that old miner's shack along with Jake's grandpop for going on fifteen years now, to him it would always belong to Harvey. Funny how that was.

Now, three months after Harvey's death, he'd finally managed to convince Verle to let go. At least a little bit. Starting with Harvey's clutter was a good sign his pop was starting to process the grief and move forward.

Jake looked over to see that Verle was boosting a fifty-gallon wood barrel on his shoulder and was in danger of falling over. "You know your balance is terrible, Pop."

His dad wobbled, and instantly Jake was right there next to him, taking the barrel out of his trembling hands. "Sorry, son. Thought I had it." But he handed over the barrel with a grateful smile.

"No problem." Jake patted him on the shoulder once he set it down. "Why don't you start inside sorting through Grandpop's old books? If you see anything you want to keep, put it in a separate pile."

Verle inhaled deeply, looking around. "Still can't believe he's gone, Jakey." His lips pressed tight, and his chin began to quiver.

"I know, Pop. I miss him too." That was the truth. Harvey Stone had been a good man. A loving one. And he'd been the rock in Jake's turbulent youth.

Together they surveyed the humble dwelling tucked in among the pines on Jasper's Peak. Appreciated it for what it was and what it represented. Maybe most important, for what it had taught Jake about living simply and finding peace in modesty.

"If your mom was still alive, I'd fix this place up and move us here. She never liked living in that trailer on the edge of town anyway." Verle shook his head, smiling fondly. "Always did fancy herself more of a country girl."

An old familiar ache started around Jake's heart, and he pulled his dad in close with one arm and kissed him on his unkempt gray hair like a child. His dad was in one of his moods today. They tended to show themselves most when he was in a sober state—which was rare. Still, Jake would take it. It wasn't often these days he got to visit with his dad when he wasn't drunk, so when he did it was like a small miracle.

"She sure did, didn't she?" he said, his mind only on love and support for his father.

Besides it didn't do any good to remind his pop that Sonia Stone wasn't dead, that she'd left them right before Jake had started kindergarten. Her last words to him as she'd flung clothes in a crappy yellow suitcase were, and he quoted, "You better hope like hell you don't turn out like him." Then she'd hopped in her B-series Datsun with the duct-taped muffler and vanished into the sunset.

But in Verle's mind, she was dead and buried. Wasn't anybody going to change that, Jake knew.

"Hey, Pop," he gently urged. "Let's head inside and get started."

Verle looked at him, his brown eyes glazed and slightly unfocused. But he didn't smell like Jim Beam. Jake had grabbed him that morning straight from bed before he could start drinking.

Feeling that tug on his heart again, Jake pressed his lips together and forced it back. But it was hard, knowing his dad was having an episode and was disconnected from reality. All the straight talk from Jake wouldn't help—it was just wasted breath.

But, Harvey had also taught Jake a thing or two about compassion, so he kept his mouth shut and let his dad have his beliefs.

"She was the love of my life, you know," Verle said. Pushing away from Jake, he began spinning in a slow circle, smiling freely. "Being with her felt exactly like *this*."

He began twirling faster and faster, giggling when he fell to the soft grass.

Love and acceptance, along with that old familiar sadness, settled over Jake as he watched his father behave strangely, knowing it wasn't his fault. It wasn't even the alcohol. It was just the way he was made. Fucking familial glioma. "I bet it was. *Just* like that. Felt exciting, didn't it?"

Resting back on his elbows on the small grassy hillside, Verle squinted up at him, his unruly long hair barely contained in its ponytail. Wiry gray hairs sprouted up all around his head. "You ever been in love, boy?" he said, sounding suddenly authoritative.

Youthful one minute, something else entirely the next—that was Verle Stone. The change in him would have been disconcerting for anyone else. They'd have blamed it on him being a drunk.

But for Jake, it was just normal. "Never have." He shoved his hands in his front pockets and kicked at a clump of dirt, muttering under his breath when an image of Apple topless and perfect popped into his head. It was the very same mental picture that had haunted him every second last night before becoming a full-on fantasy—one that had driven him over the brink before dawn.

Yanking his dad out of bed at six in the morning to clean his grandpop's place hadn't been altruistic in motive. It had been a desperate attempt at distraction. He'd have done anything to take his mind off Apple.

"Took you a while to respond," Verle mentioned, a twinkle in his dark eyes. "You sure about that?"

The man chose the oddest times to display lucidity and intuition. "I'm sure." The minute the words left his lips a voice in his head called Jake a liar. He told it to shut up. "No woman's ever gotten her hooks into me." He smiled lightly.

Verle scratched his ZZ Top-style beard and laughed. "Then I feel bad for you, boy. Ain't nothing like a woman's hooks, that's for damn sure. Count yourself lucky if one decides to sink hers into you."

Apple leapt straight to his brain again, torturing him with her amazing curves and sweet, sexy face. He'd been almost close enough to touch her beautiful pale skin last night. A mere twenty-four hours ago—less than, actually. It was testament to the strength of his willpower that he'd been able to keep from caressing her gorgeous, perfect breasts when he'd been close enough to smell the heated scent of her skin.

Jake sighed long and heartfelt as arousal stirred in his belly. Lowering himself to the grass next to his dad, he leaned back on his elbows too and took a look around the hillside property. From where they were lounging, the squat weathered shack sat to the left. Its tin roof was showing more than a little rust, and the front porch looked like it was beginning to settle on one side. But there were two wooden rockers on the front porch, and a few hand-carved wind chimes hung from it.

It had a homey feel to it, even if it wasn't what most people would consider a home. It didn't have a dishwasher, an automatic garage door, or a jetted Jacuzzi tub.

And it wasn't a twenty-five-hundred-square-foot, three-bedroom "American Dream."

Thank fucking God.

"Well, there is one woman. Though she doesn't have any hooks in me. Claws, maybe. But she's been harassing me for a while now about something I want to talk to you about."

Verle dropped all the way down to the grass and stretched out long, his hands cradling the back of his head. "You talkin' about the Woodman girl?"

"Yeah, that's the one. Apple." Just saying her name made his gut tighten.

His dad plucked a blade of grass and stuck it between his teeth. "What'd you do?"

"Nothing, Pop. She's writing a book about Fortune, is all."

Across the clearing at the edge of the trees just down the hill, two elk does stepped out of the shadows, their ears twitching as they braved the open space for some tender green grass. Jake smiled. The rut was beginning. One of the coolest things about Harvey's place was that elk moved through it coming down the mountain for mating season, and then again on their way up. It was part of the herds' migratory pattern. If he and his dad were in luck, a bull elk or two would come wandering through and they'd get a show.

"Remember that time when I was ten and you, me, and Grandpop stood on the porch and watched those bull elks fight right there?"

Verle squinted over at the spot Jake had pointed to, grinning. "They stomped the hell out of his spaghetti squash."

Yeah they did. In fact, they had demolished his entire garden. Harvey had been so pissed. "He cussed a blue streak over it. That was a fun night." The three of them had grilled dogs over the fire pit, and Harvey and his dad had taken turns telling Jake ghost stories until he'd fallen asleep under the stars. "We had some good times, the three of us."

Tears welled suddenly in Verle's eyes. "What am I going to do without him, Jakey?"

That was the very question Jake had been asking himself for the past few weeks. The two of them had taken care of each other—the recluse and the drunk. And now that Harvey was gone, he had some very real concerns about his father being able to care for himself alone up here.

Maybe it was time. "Do you still have those brochures I brought last week from that place I told you about? The one with the apartments?" Sweet Brook was essentially an assisted-living community for people with special needs like Verle. He could still be independent and have his own place; he would just be looked after by a professional full-time staff. "I think you and I should go for a visit. Check it out in person."

Verle swiped the back of his hand across his eyes. "You know I'm never leaving this place, Jake. Stop trying to get me to." His voice was small and shaky, like it was coming from far away.

Frustration tried to rear its head, but Jake forced it to stop. It was the same argument he'd been hearing since Harvey had died three months ago. And getting aggravated didn't help anything. Verle Stone was a stubborn son of a bitch when he wanted to be.

"Look, Pop. I worry about you up here all by yourself. At least when Grandpop was alive you had someone looking after you. But he's gone, and I can't fill his shoes. I have my brewery to run. What if something happens to you?"

Clearly agitated now, Verle sat up, pulled his knees to his chest, and started wringing his hands. "You can't make me go, Jakey. I won't let you. You'll be prying my cold dead fingers off the front door, because I ain't leaving." He turned to Jake, his eyes bright and darting about wildly. *"You can't make me!"*

Feeling his father beginning to unravel, Jake took a deep breath and said in a soft, gentle voice, "Easy, Pop. Nobody is making you leave, okay?"

"What about the librarian?" Verle began to breathe heavily, almost panting. "She knows, doesn't she? *She* wants me gone."

A frown tugged his brow. "Why do you say that? Apple just wants to know about what really happened to our ancestors when they first came here to mine for gold and founded the town."

Verle's whole body began to visibly tremble now as he shook his head emphatically, his jaw set in stubborn lines. "I'm not telling her anything."

Jake looked from his dad to the late summer wildflowers carpeting the ground nearby. "Why not? It wouldn't really hurt anything to let her know what happened, would it? It was a long time ago, Pop, and nobody is going to blame you or me for what our ancestor did. He was the crazy cannibalistic bastard, not us."

Verle leapt up and began hopping from foot to foot, his eyes bulging. "No, no, *no*. They *will* blame me when they find it! They'll want it for themselves, and they'll say I'm just like him to get it. They'll say I'm dangerous too and lock me away. Make something up. Lie. Nobody but us knows anyway. Do it and she'll take it—they'll all take it!"

He was confused. "Take what, Dad? What would Apple take if she knew what happened?" Sure she'd be horrified, but she'd never take anything. She'd just never see him in the same way again. And that would really suck. Because sometime around three in the morning he'd finally submitted to his higher nature and got honest with himself. He *needed* her belief in him. Her light and sweetness. Her faith in the goodness of him. It kept him going.

And he was willing to do almost anything to keep it—like avoid giving her straight answers to her questions for fear of her rejection no matter how guilty it made him feel.

Why, he hadn't yet figured out. And honestly he was afraid to. This was some significant shit. And like a pussy, he wasn't exactly ready for significant.

Now his father was shaking his head frantically and tugging at his hair, concerning Jake. "She can't have it! It's mine. *Mine!*"

Sadness fell over him, having been through this so many times before. Rising to his feet, he pulled his father in for a tight hug, knowing that's what he needed. "Shhh, Pop," he said into his hair, cradling Verle's head under his chin, feeling every bit of the love and weariness that went with being his son. "It'll be okay. I won't tell her, I promise."

Verle hiccupped, his body hunched and feeling small to Jake, but calmer. "What will you say?"

"I don't know," Jake said with a sinking feeling, hating this new predicament. "But I'll think of something." Squeezing his father's shoulders gently, he turned them toward the shack. "Hey, let's get some work done, okay? Help take our minds off things by working with our hands. That always cheers you up."

His dad nodded and hiccupped again. "Does, yeah. I like that."

Relieved to see Verle perking up some, Jake added, "I was thinking we'd start simple with Harvey's old book collection."

"He has a first edition of *Moby Dick*."

"No shit?" That was impressive. Harvey had always been full of surprises. Apparently he still was, even after his passing. "You want to keep it?"

"Yep. Want *Huck Finn* also. I like that story. *Tom Sawyer* too. Oh! Want all the Harry Potter series too. Make sure we keep those separate. I ain't lettin' those go!" he finished with a good-natured grin, coming back around.

"That's my pop." Jake smiled back and pulled him in for a hard squeeze as they climbed the rickety front steps. "You know I love you, right?"

"Sure as the sun comes up each morning," Verle replied, patting Jake's hand on his shoulder. "You're a good boy."

"Sometimes."

"All the time." He squeezed Jake's hand, held it briefly before dropping it and stepping away. "Now let's get to work."

And apparently that was enough cheesy sentimentality. Amused, Jake pushed open the front door and was instantly transported to a simpler, earlier place in time. The only concessions to modern living were electricity, a tiny kitchenette, and a compostable toilet that had been attached to the house through a door in the far wall. It made going in the winter a real adventure.

They crossed the single-room dwelling, navigating around a rough-hewn wooden table and between a set of twin beds until they were standing in front of the bookcase. As tall as the ceiling and twice as wide, it spanned the entire shack wall and was crammed well past full with books in varying states of condition. Several were tossed on top of the neat stacks with loose pages sticking out, like Harvey had run out of places to store them and had made them fit, come hell or high water.

Jake smirked as his chest warmed at the thought.

"Hey, I'm going to start on this side," he said to his dad, shifting to the left side of the case and reaching for a random book up top. "Why don't you start on the other? Anything you want to keep, toss it gently on the bed behind you. We'll make sure those stay."

"What about the ones I don't want to keep? Where should I put them?" Verle asked, holding a worn copy of *Turn Gold into Cash*. He gave it a frown and thrust it out toward Jake. "You take it. I don't like that one."

Confused, Jake brought his hand down from the shelf, a book in his fingers. Without looking at it, he took the how-to from his pop. "What's wrong with this one?"

Verle made a face and growled, turning his attention to the shelf in front of him. "Gives away trade secrets."

Whatever that meant. Shrugging it off, Jake placed it on the other bed and said, "Gotcha. So just use this bed for the donations." The library could probably use some of them.

Apple.

It was like the two things were conjoined: Apple and the library. He couldn't think of one without the other. Which was disconcerting when just a thought of the place gave him a damn semi now.

Shaking his head, Jake looked down at the book he was still holding. In his hand was an old ratty Bible. He went still. Then he brought it to his face, scanned the cover. Flipped open the front page.

And came face-to-face with his ancestor's handwritten signature and a date.

"Fuck me," he said on a heavy breath.

A real artifact of history right here in a dilapidated old miner's shack. Harvey had kept it here the whole time. An actual relic from the first founders of Fortune—from his family.

Apple *had* to see this.

Jake's slightly trembling fingers curled around it protectively. Jitters started in his stomach, equal parts excitement and nerves. God, she was going to love this. Just truly love this tangible piece of history. He could just so perfectly picture the smile that would sweep her pretty face.

"Hey, Pop. I've got to run to the truck. I'll be right back."

Jake left his dad grumbling to himself in front of the bookcase and tucked the old book safely in the front seat of his pickup after wrapping it gently in an old flannel shirt. When he was done he took a deep, reassuring breath and looked up at the brilliant blue sky. Was it wrong that he just sincerely, really wanted to make Apple happy?

"Of course it's not wrong," he mumbled to himself, kicking at a rock by his feet and feeling suddenly insecure.

It was just scary as fuck what it meant.

Chapter Nine

A FEW DAYS later, Apple was busy shelving books in the nonfiction section of the library when a shadow fell across her vision. It had been a particularly bustling morning, unusual for this time of year. With school recently started up again, most of the summer reader foot traffic had died down. Still, it did her heart good to see so many people coming through. To her it was just more proof of the one true fact she held dear: libraries were awesome.

"Can I help you?" she asked as she placed a historical account of the British Isles back on a shelf.

"Actually, I came to help *you*, my dear."

Spinning on her flats, Apple came face-to-face with one of Fortune's biggest and most notorious gossips. Her mood plummeted right through the floor. And it had been such a lovely morning. *Sigh*.

"Good morning, Mrs. Browley. Pray tell, what is it that I am in such dire need of assistance with?" She loved to channel Jane Austen when annoyed.

"Sound womanly advice…and maybe a bit of a well-intentioned warning as well," the old helmet-haired busy-body stated matter-of-factly. Her bifocals slipped down her nose, and Apple could swear the woman sniffed them right back into place. Literally. And with a whole lot of unconcealed disdain. What had she done to make the woman so ill-tempered? Fail to keep all the seasons of *Murder She Wrote* in stock in the DVD rental section?

"I'm all ears," she said with a smile, clasping her hands politely in front of her and remembering to play the professional. "Advise away."

"I'd so hate for your reputation to be sullied, you know. Or for you to lose your job." Mrs. Browley was nodding emphatically, her blue-tinged fluff of curls rigidly holding in place from probably about a liter of Aqua Net. "Good girl like you needs to be warned about such things, about making unsavory pacts with men."

Agitation began to creep under her skin, and her smile turned a notch tighter. She just knew this had something to do with Jake. In the past week she'd overheard enough rumblings to know she was on the local gossip radar. Why? She still really had no idea. "Thank you for your concern. I promise you there's nothing untoward going on here at the library or elsewhere."

"You work for a public, government-run institution, young miss. Misappropriation of property is grounds for firing, you know. I'd so hate to see that happen, as you've been such a gold-standard role model for the town's youth to date."

Now she was grinding her teeth. "Is my job in jeopardy here, Mrs. Browley? Can you tell me exactly what you're accusing me of?" Feeling herself start to amp up, Apple took a deep breath and said baldly, "Is this about Jake Stone?"

"Of course it is!" the old woman hissed. "There's a lot floating on the wind about the two of you as of late."

Apple had enough. Gripping the shelving cart like it was her lifeline, she was about to push past the old woman and thought better of it. Instead, she looked Mrs. Browley square in the eye. "The only thing going on between me and Jake Stone is words. I'm talking with him about getting the Bachelors to do an event here at the library. That is all. Now if you'll excuse me, I have books to shelve." Damn busybody.

The old woman just gaped at her with wide blinking eyes behind her bifocals as Apple brushed past, chin high in the air.

Yeah, that's what she thought.

Four Weeks until Deadline

APPLE STARED AT the words typed in bold on her laptop screen and fought the urge to scream. Though it was after hours at the library and she was busy making headway on her book, it still felt somehow profane to do such a thing. Unruly noises in the public library? *For shame.*

Sighing, she reached for the number two pencil she'd shoved into her thick bun and began jotting some notes down. Mostly she was fact-checking dates at this point about Fortune's settlement timeline. Because of the way things had gone down with Jake, she still didn't have any answers to her biggest questions.

But she sure did have a whole new slew of them. And none of them were about Fortune. They were all about Jake and that comment he'd made about wanting her. Part of her couldn't help wondering if he was just trying to intimidate her. But why would he do that?

It didn't make sense.

And *now* she was officially distracted from her task. She blamed it squarely on the memory of how Jake's eyes had blazed so hot and intense when he'd been naked and mere inches from her bare breasts. There'd been such a charged energy. Sure she'd known he was interested in seeing them, but the heat of his response had been completely unexpected.

Standing up, Apple walked barefoot across the wood floor toward the entrance, having kicked off her shoes to stretch her toes the minute the doors had locked. It was one of her quirks—going barefoot. Every chance she got. It made her feel happy and carefree like a kid. And well, she figured that everyone needed to feed their inner child.

Speaking of which, having the library at her fingertips for research sources was great. She was heading to the reference section to see if there was anything good she could dig up, since she and Jake had been distracted the other night and she hadn't gotten any more answers.

Deep down she secretly hoped like crazy that she'd get another chance, at both the questions and his nakedness. Wow, that had been something to see.

She had just crossed in front of the entrance doors when a knock scared the shit out of her. Apple gasped and spun toward the sound. Through the glass in the door she could see it was Jake. The sun was just starting to set, and he was backlit by a warm glow, making his hair shimmer bronze and dark gold.

She reached for the door, unlocked it, and swung it open. "You scared the crap out of me."

"And a good evening to you too." Jake stepped over the threshold.

The very sight of him had butterflies taking flight in her tummy. Which was funny because she'd never really considered herself the mountain man type. "You need to shave." His stubble had almost reached the tipping point into beard.

"Don't knock the beard, juicy fruit. It has its uses." His eyes lit with a wicked glint.

She scoffed. "For straining soup, maybe."

He took a step toward her, his broad shoulders swallowing her view of the entrance. "Among other things." His gaze dropped to her just-visible cleavage.

"What, like rug burn?" She was missing something, obviously. What good is a beard? And then it hit her. "Oh!" *Friction.* Duh.

The raw sex appeal in his smile then had Apple taking a step away nervously. But he only leaned his butt against the circulation desk and crossed his arms, making his pecs bulge beneath his navy blue Two Moons Brewery and Pub T-shirt. "Now you're thinking."

He hadn't given her that dark angst-filled look again, but she was suddenly feeling agitated and out of sorts anyway. She crossed her arms and demanded, "What are you doing here? I haven't seen or heard from you since you kicked me out last week."

"It's hardly been a week," he scoffed.

Eye roll. God, men just loved their technicalities didn't they? "I said *last* week, not that it's *been* a week. And that's not the important part of what I said anyway."

He broke eye contact, looking at the window behind her where the sunset was framed gorgeously, all bright orange and fuchsia and purple. "I'm sorry that I got edgy."

She cocked her head and studied him. "Yeah, why did you? What was that about?"

He slid her a look. "You really don't know?"

"I never claim to understand the workings of the male mind. I just end up looking like an ass when I do." Like the time junior year she'd been convinced Tyler Bradshaw wanted to ask her to the prom, so she'd tried to beat him to the punch. Only she'd been humiliated in front of the entire class when she passed him a note and he shot her down in front of *everybody*. It had been mortifying.

"I'll save you the trouble then." Jake smirked, one corner of his sculpted mouth lifting.

He took a step toward her, and Apple spun around, suddenly excited and nervous and unsure. Only she didn't really know where to go, so she just ended up doing a full circle, stopping when she was facing him again.

"Well, that didn't work out *at all*," she grumbled under her breath.

Jake gave a short laugh, taking another step. "Problems, juicy fruit?"

"Well, *yeah*." She tossed him a look full of consternation.

"I can help you with that."

"You could *help* me with my damn book too, you know. Why are you making it so hard?"

Something that looked a bit like regret flashed across his eyes before they shuttered and went unreadable. "I'm sorry, really I am. I have family commitments."

Apple's own gaze narrowed, and she stepped away, moving toward the big picture window overlooking the river. "I don't understand that. How could there be family commitments that keep you from talking about your family? If that were true, wouldn't that mean—" She broke off. "Wait, are you hiding something?"

Again something shadowed his gaze briefly. "It's complicated."

So yes, yes he was.

Perfect. "What's so difficult about helping someone else out?"

"You'd be surprised."

Apple planted her hands on her hips, the large window at her back. "Try me."

"I can't." He looked upset about it. "But I did come here to bring you something."

She ignored his last statement and pressed, "Why not?" She really wanted to know. There was under a month left until her deadline, and she still didn't have what she needed. It was stressing her out like crazy. And now this late in the game, it was just dawning on her that he might be hiding a secret from her too. Aneurism anyone?

He didn't answer.

So she pressed on. "If I agree to do another thing with you, will you talk?" At this point there wasn't much she was unwilling to do.

His eyes changed, lighting with humor and something else, something entirely naughty. Then he smiled. *Phew*. There went her brain function.

"Wait a minute. You never showed me what you brought." She darted a glance over his shoulder at the encroaching darkness outside. It was getting late. More to the point, it was *after hours*. At the library.

Jake didn't hang at the old mill just for kicks.

"No, back that up," he said, his gaze roaming over her face, pausing on her lips before trailing slowly to the valley between her breasts. "I want to hear more about this thing you're willing to do."

"I want to finish my stinking book, but that's not happening today, now, is it?" Apple looked him square in the eye.

Jake seemed to consider and rubbed his chin, looking thoughtful. "Well, now, it's quite the pickle, us wanting different things."

"It is not!" she exclaimed. "It's easy, it really is. You and I made an *agreement*. As in, you *agreed* to tell me some key information that I need."

"And I will." He took a step closer.

Recalling a particularly unpleasant conversation that morning with Mrs. Browley, the judgmental old busybody, Apple frowned right at him.

"Do you have any idea how quickly word is spreading around town about our conversation at Two Moons?"

Jake looked like he was biting his lip to keep from laughing, the dirty rat. "No, I don't. Want to enlighten me?"

Getting worked up about it all over again, Apple planted her butt on the windowsill ledge and crossed her arms, raising one hand to adjust her slipping glasses. "Everyone is expecting the Bachelors to do some event here at the library now."

He moved closer, just a single step, but she could feel his energy increase exponentially. "I recall, yeah, but we didn't agree on it. So why the expectation?"

This was the part she had been hoping not to have to explain. "Because I kind of told Mrs. Butler and Mrs. Browley that you guys were?"

If he laughed at her, she was going to kick him in the shins. Guaranteed. Luckily for him, he kept it together—barely. His lips were twitching bad. "And I suppose now you want us to really do something. To save your pristine reputation from being tarnished, I'm sure."

Why did it sound like there was an edge in his voice on that last bit? "I would, yes. Call it whatever you want, but I do have a certain keen desire to keep my job. If word got out that I made a sex pact with *you* in regard to the library like Mrs. Browley inferred…well, I'm worried about my position here."

Again, something flickered in his gaze. Something deep in the shadows. Her belly tightened in response. "Right. It wouldn't do well for the good town folk to think you might have something going with me. Underneath the Bachelor of Fortune label and the heaps of money, I'm still nothing more than Crazy Verle's misfit son."

Apple's heart sank, and she instantly felt terrible. "That's not what I meant, Jake. You know me better than that. I don't feel that way. I never have."

He stood quiet for a moment and then seemed to come to a decision, shaking it off. "Don't worry about it. If you need the guys and me to do something for you, let me know. I'd hate to see your reputation ruined by the likes of me."

Though he tried to say it lightly, Apple could hear the underlying emotion and knew he wasn't really joking. Still, if he was offering…

"I would very much like you guys to do something for the kids. Perform a concert, put on a play, do puppetry—*anything*. The town's biggest gossips have already been bugging me every other day for info, and I've got enough on my plate as is. I could use the help if you're really offering."

Jake looked out the big window as dusk slowly fell on the far river bank, and Apple's heart skipped a beat at the sight of him in profile. How one man could be so gruff and rugged, and yet so incredibly sexy at the same time, boggled her mind. But more than that—and this was what really got her—he had a steadiness, a centeredness that had never waned. For as long as she she'd known him, he'd been like the Rock of Gibraltar. How he'd wound up like that with a recluse grandfather and drunken dad was beyond her.

However he'd done it, it said a lot about Jake.

He'd moved to stand directly next to her. "You've got it. The guys and I will figure out something fun for the kids. When would you need us?"

She hadn't actually expected him to agree so readily, so she wasn't sure. "Can I take a look at the event schedule and get back to you?"

He nodded, his arms crossed. "Sure, sounds good."

Feeling oddly bereft, Apple glanced at her bare toes. "You still haven't told me why you swung by."

He reached into the back pocket of his faded jeans with the ripped knee and pulled out a small leather-bound book. "I did, actually. I said I came here to give you this. I was up at the old man's place going through some of Harvey's things, and I found this on a shelf mixed in with a bunch of books. I thought you might like to have it for your project."

Apple took the small brown book, read the cover, and raised a brow at Jake. "The Bible, Jake? Really?" If he was making some sort of commentary about the state of her virtue, she was *not* going to be happy.

"Somebody's got to look out for your moral integrity, you little hussy." He grinned down at her and winked.

Her mouth dropped open in immediate outrage until she noticed the twinkle in his chocolate-brown eyes. "Shush," she said, instantly blushing.

Jake must have decided to take mercy on her because he tapped the book, turning the topic. "But seriously, take a look inside the front flap. You're going to like this."

Apple tossed him a skeptical look, but did as he suggested and opened the cover. Inside was written in jet-black ink on the blank page: *Jesse Stone, 1875.*

Jake's ancestor. One of Fortune's first settlers. Oh, she loved having the real-life artifact in her hands.

Oh, she could just kiss him!

Elated at the unexpected gift, Apple beamed up at Jake and rose on her toes and kissed him. Right smack on his firm, stubborn mouth.

"Oh my God, thank you!" she said as she dropped down to the flat of her feet, hugging the worn little piece of Fortune's history gently in her hands.

But before she could do so much as peek at the almost-150-year-old signature again, Jake grabbed her chin with his hand and demanded, "Again."

His mouth covered hers, hot and restless. Taken by surprise, Apple gave a muffled sound. But then Jake's big warm hands were cradling her head, his thumbs on the underside of her jaw, and his tongue brushing hers once, twice. When she moaned breathlessly, he smiled against her lips. "I've been thinking about the taste of you for a week now." He brushed his lips against hers again. "This is better."

Totally.

Because she couldn't help it, Apple flung her arms around his neck, the old Bible dangling precariously from her fingertips before it dropped to the floor with a *thud.*

Throwing herself into the kiss, her body went pliant when his big, hard hands gripped her hips and slowly stroked down. Trails of heat marked her, making her body go soft and hot all at once. And when his hands cupped her ass cheeks, squeezing with barely restrained strength, something rather feline rose up inside her—something that made her arch into his palms, silently asking for more. She let out a little sound that was suspiciously like a contented purr.

She couldn't help it. Jake's hands were magic. Hot and hard and confident.

Just like she'd always known they would be.

Streaking her hands into his luxurious hair, Apple sighed against his lips at the silky feel. Finally, after all these years, she knew how it felt. And it was just as good as the rest of him. Teenage Apple melted into a pile of giddy hormones.

Adult Apple embraced the heat in the pit of her stomach and craved more.

"I love the feel of you," she whispered, lost in the size and heat of Jake's sensational body. His chest was hard; his thick cock brushing against her belly even more so.

He growled low in his throat, and his hands flexed on her ass cheeks, gripping hard before they slid down to her thighs and wrapped them around his lean waist. He tore his lips from hers and trailed his mouth along the sensitive skin of her neck, the tip of his tongue against her skin making her shiver. Surrounded by the scent and feel of Jake, Apple moaned when her core came into contact with his rigid erection. Lust slammed into her, and she went achingly, shockingly wet. She gasped and squeezed her thighs in response.

"Christ, Apple," he rasped against her collarbone. "I knew," he said, his breath coming in short bursts and filled with emotion. "I knew it would be like this with you."

Tears sprang to her eyes at the unconcealed yearning she heard in his voice, and something inside her responded in kind, knew *exactly* the longing he felt.

Because it was the same one that was in her.

"Oh, Jake," she cried when his mouth covered her nipple through the fabric of her dress and sucked, using his tongue and teeth together on her in ways that made her head go floaty and her body taut with heightened desire. His mouth was quickly driving her to the brink of explosion. Chemistry sparked like fireworks between them, pulling them into each other—their energies, their passion, their very souls merging.

Jake made a restless sound and pushed her against the circulation desk, one hand letting go of her ass long enough to yank her dress and bra down to free her breasts. Then his mouth was on her bare skin, and they both groaned—in pleasure, in desire, in something else that she couldn't define. But it rocked her.

His tongue flicked over her hard nipple. Once. Twice. Three times. And Apple felt her core start to tremble as the orgasm built, only a few sensations away from exploding. "Jake!"

The sound that came from him was one of such hungry, passionate male that her pussy quivered in response.

"Give it to me," he demanded, his mouth never stopping on her breast. "I need it, Apple." He thrust his cock into the valley between her thighs, rubbing hotly against her, and splayed his fingers under her until they just touched her crotch. Until he found the heat there and groaned, long and low. "You're so wet. God, you're so wet." He pushed a thick finger into her, rubbing her slit back and forth through her drenched panties. "So beautifully, gorgeously wet."

Never had she felt anything like this. Dropping her head back, Apple dug her fingernails into his shoulders and whimpered. What was happening to her?

"Come for me, Apple." His words coaxed, and his mouth persuaded. "My sweet, beautiful queen."

That did it. His words unlocked something inside her, and Apple felt tears well in her eyes again. Felt herself surrender.

Yes.

Her body coiled and heat flooded her, stars bursting behind her eyelids as the orgasm came, hard and intense and soul-shattering. Apple cried out and clung to Jake, holding him as the current swept her away. It was the only place she wanted to be.

For long minutes they stood there in that position, their breathing shallow, their chests heaving from exertion.

What had just happened?

Just as she was coming back to herself, or as much as she could considering her world had just been rocked three ways from Sunday, he set her feet on the ground and stepped back, his face set in tense lines. His eyes were darkly intense. "I have to go."

He didn't wait for a response. In seconds the front door was clicking shut behind him. Apple blew out a breath and let the tears fall.

Whatever had just happened changed everything.

Shaking her head, emotions cascading through her, Apple stared blankly at the entrance door where Jake had just stalked through. God, he was such an illogical, infuriating man.

But he'd called her his sweet, beautiful queen.

Her heart seized and then did a long, slow nosedive into the waters of emotion, swimming alongside those feelings of love and attachment. And that was probably not good. Not good at all. Jake was a one-way ticket to heartbreak town.

Sighing, Apple looked down at the book she'd dropped on the floor and picked it up. With unsteady hands, she opened it and gently flipped through a few pages, skipping to the end.

And she frowned.

Stared in puzzlement.

Forgot for a moment that she might have just fallen in love with Jake Stone.

Because there, in the upper right-hand corner, was a small symbol sketched in black ink of two crossing pick-axes and a bumpy rock in front of them. It was one that she didn't know but could swear she'd seen before, and it sent nerves darting down her spine. It felt so familiar—and like it *meant* something. Where had she seen it before?

Maybe if Jake hadn't just given her the orgasm of her life and left her an emotional roller coaster she'd be able to think better.

But one thing was for sure as she looked at the small unfamiliar, yet familiar symbol: she suddenly felt very much like she'd been dropped into a treasure-hunting adventure without a single guide map. Or even a damn compass.

Chapter Ten

AIDAN WALKED INTO the brewpub the next day just as Jake was struggling to carry multiple pitchers of beer.

"Here, take this." Without waiting for his friend to reply, he practically tossed Aidan a full pitcher just as another slipped from his grip. "Shit. Okay, got it? Help me get these to the party out on the patio, will you?"

"Your moves are slacking in your old age, my man," Aidan said.

Jake chuckled, but he knew someone who might disagree with that. In fact, he'd demonstrated some mighty fine moves on her just recently. He could still remember the dazed and sexy look on Apple's face when he'd pulled back from their kiss. Yeah, she might disagree all right.

Satisfaction warmed his chest. It spread up his neck until he was grinning like a fool. Then he remembered what he'd said to her and bobbled a pitcher.

What the fuck had gotten into him?

Setting the pitchers down, Jake shook off the thought and made sure the customers had everything they needed before heading back to the bar, making his way around a water fountain centered in the brick patio.

Aidan was right behind him. "Apple tells me you've finally decided to stop being a stubborn ass and answer her questions. It's about time, man."

"I do what I can." Still, it nipped his conscience that what he was really doing with Apple was stalling because he'd made a promise to his pop and couldn't share the truth. Especially now that he'd owned up to some complicated feelings for her. The guilt that was chewing at him and his feelings were the reason why he'd given her the old miner's Bible he'd found out at the shack. In his way, it had been a sort of a peace offering.

Only she had no way of knowing that.

Once they reached the bar, Jake stepped behind it as Aidan slid onto a stool. The contractor nodded toward the beer taps. "I could use one of those." His normally clear hazel eyes looked troubled. "Have you heard the news?"

Grabbing a pint glass from the shelf below the bar, Jake slid a glance at his friend, noting the tenseness around his mouth. "Depends on the news. But I haven't heard anything bad if that's what you're getting at. Why? Did something happen?"

Jake handed the pint to Aidan, who promptly took a prolonged drink. When he'd downed half the glass, he set it on the mahogany bar top with a sharp rap and then pushed a strand of auburn hair away from his face, sighing heavily. "Shirley Hardy died yesterday."

Jake went very still. "Shit, man."

"Yeah." Aidan grimaced into his beer.

Needing something to do with his hands, Jake located a bar towel and began wiping down the counter. "When's the funeral?"

"Whose funeral?" Sean asked as he pulled up a stool next to Aidan and sat down, wearing his favorite Irish wool cap. "And why do you look like you've swallowed a frog, mate?" That question was directed at Aidan.

Jake took mercy on his friend and answered for him. "Shirley Hardy. She was the librarian before Apple took over."

"I'll have a pint too," Sean said to Jake before turning his attention to Aidan. "Was she special to you?"

Jake noticed the slight tick that was starting at Aidan's temple, but his voice was carefully neutral when he replied, "Not especially. But her granddaughter was."

"Hey, man. Even if she does show back up in town for the funeral, you don't have to talk to her. Besides, she was never the type to stick around for long." Jake could feel the old anger for his friend start to bubble. He'd never forgive that granola-eating tree-hugging hippie for what she did to his best friend.

Before the anger could grab hold, he changed the subject. Tossing the towel over his shoulder, he leaned his elbows on the bar and looked from one friend to the other, his gaze assessing. "How do you guys feel about putting on a puppet show or musical performance for the kids at the library in a few weeks? Personally I'm leaning toward a play. Apple thinks it would be a great way to draw people to the place." At least that's the story he was sticking to. He'd promised her. And for some reason, it really mattered to him that he not break that promise. "I figured you wouldn't have an issue with it, Aidan, since she's family and I know you won't say no."

His friend raised a brow. "Only if I get to pick the play, man. Your theatrical knowledge is sincerely lacking, Stone. Left up to you, we'd end up doing *A Streetcar Named Desire* with Muppets to a bunch of three-year-olds."

"Now that I'd pay to see." Sean laughed, his green eyes lit with amusement.

"Hey, wait a minute," Aidan suddenly said, his eyes narrowing on Jake. "When did you talk to Apple?"

"So, it's agreed then?" he said, ignoring the question. "I can tell her yes?"

"Is there something going on with you two that I should know about?"

Looking his friend square in the eye, Jake swallowed hard and lied, "Nope, not a thing."

THAT SAME DAY, Apple stepped through the side door to her parents' house, her mouth watering instantly at the scent of cinnamon and spice that greeted her. Steady and predictable as the snow that fell in January, she'd always been able to count on something deliciously home baked by her mom. Her entire childhood was cocooned in a warm, homey glow because of it.

One day she was going to give that to her own kids. Just memories upon memories of wonderful, cozy moments of home created by her and her One True Love. Even now thinking about it, her pulse was beginning to speed up and her breath was going shallow. It was her deepest desire to be a mom, just like hers had been.

All she needed was Mr. Right.

"Hey, Mom! I'm here."

An image of Jake popped into her mind. Now, there was a perfect example of Mr. *Wrong*. Sexy and dirty in all the right ways.

He called me his sweet, beautiful queen.

"I'm in the back, darling, just finishing cleaning up. Come on out!" Sedona Woodman called from the backyard. "You just missed Nell. We had a *fantastic* kiln session today. It's amazing, really, how quickly she's taken to our lessons."

Apple made her way through the big old Craftsman bungalow that was her childhood home, noticing a few new ceramic pieces sitting on the mantel above the fireplace in the living room. One of them she could definitely tell was her mother's sculpting, but she wasn't sure about the other one. Which meant it must be Nell's.

The piece was a graceful flame dancing, sinewy and sensual at the same time. The multilayered red and orange glazes melted together flawlessly, gorgeously. Her mom was right: her best friend had the gift.

Stepping through the airy kitchen with its glass-front painted cabinets and out the back door, Apple was greeted to the same sight that had filled her with joy for most of her life: her mother's gardens. Like a fairyland, flowers sprung from the ground everywhere, creating hidden pockets of grass lawn around the yard just waiting to be discovered. Her mom had liked to place special things in the secluded spaces too. Apple's favorite tucked-away spot had a beautiful painted bench and stone birdbath underneath a peach tree that produced the most succulent fruit.

As a girl she'd spent hours and hours reading and imagining in the wonderland that her mom had created for her. She saw it now and understood the work and love—the dedication—that had gone into creating such a unique backyard world for Apple.

She only hoped that one day she'd get the chance to be the same kind of loving parent they were. "I love what you've done with the herb garden this year. They're so lush and healthy."

Her mother looked up from wiping down a potting wheel on the cement patio and smiled, her blue eyes warm and happy. And that's exactly how she'd always been, even though life hadn't always been kind to her. Happy. Her mom was a hell of a woman.

"I keep telling you that you need to go organic," she said, her bare feet smattered with dried clay dust, turning them blotchy gray. "Earthworm castings are the way to go. *Miracle*, I tell you."

Her mom was an artist through and through, and Apple adored her for her slightly hippie, earth-friendly ways. She'd learned to be conscientious and compassionate because of her, and she'd discovered the satisfaction of giving and sharing.

Besides, she'd always been darn proud of having a mother who'd never listened to the word *no* and now had pieces of her pottery in galleries all over the world. She'd believed in herself when no one else had.

"I can't stay too long, Mom. I promised Waffles that I'd take her on a hike around Moose Lake before it gets too late." Mostly their "hikes" consisted of Waffles sniffing everything within reach and then tiring out halfway through and needing to be carried the rest of the way back. Still, for a pint-sized canine, there was nothing quite like getting to pee on mountain strawberries to make her feel like a big dog. "What did you want to talk to me about?"

Sedona wiped her hands on a plain white apron tied around her waist. "Help yourself to some lemonade. Your father made it fresh just this morning."

"Is it straight or did he mix it like he did last time?" Mango, strawberry, guava lemonade had sounded good in theory. Not so good in reality.

Her mom laughed, her round cheeks flushed with health and vibrancy. "It's plain, thank goodness. Be thankful you weren't here when he decided to see if steak juice tasted as good as it sounded." She shuddered. "Made me reconsider giving up vegetarianism."

"He keeps you on your toes, Mom, and you love him for it."

"Bless my heart, I do." Moving away from the pottery wheel, Sedona came over to Apple and gave her a warm hug. "And he wants to know when you're free to come for dinner. He's been pouting ever since you had to cancel last week because you were up to your neck with research on your book."

Apple blushed hotly and looked away. The *research* she'd been doing had been at Jake's, and even though she was a grown woman she still felt embarrassed about it. Her dad certainly didn't need to know whom she'd been with during that time. Open-minded and egalitarian with the best of them, Marty was still a father, and Jake wasn't exactly someone he'd be happy knowing Apple was spending time with. "Tell him I'm free Thursday."

"Oh, he'll be so happy, honey. You know how your father adores listening to all your latest adventures."

"Speaking of, where is he?" Apple asked in an attempt to change the subject. The last thing she wanted to discuss with her dad was her "latest adventure." She wasn't sure his heart could handle it.

"He's out with Hugh hiking Jasper's Peak." Sedona plopped in a lawn chair and sighed contentedly. "So Nell tells me you've been spending time with Jake Stone for your book project."

Apple looked at her mom. "She told you that?" What else had Nell said? Man, she was just as much a blabbermouth today as she'd been back in junior high when she'd blabbed about Apple's enormous crush on Ryan Wilcox and it had gotten back to him.

And no, it hadn't ended all perfect teen-romance-movie happy.

As if that ever *really* happened.

"Should she not have said anything to me about it?" Sedona asked, wiggling her unpainted toes in the sunshine.

Apple sighed, feeling frustrated and self-conscious. "It's just there's nothing more to tell. He's finally agreed to talk to me about the first Fortune settlement. That's all."

"Mmm-hmm."

"I'm serious, Mom."

"And I'm not blind. I can see just how good-looking that boy is now that he's all grown up." She leveled a look at Apple. "How much trouble too."

"Are you warning me off of Jake, Mom? Really? Since when did you decide to become *that* parent?"

Sedona sighed. "I'm not, honey. It's just your dad and I have known Jake since you were in diapers. And it's our job to look out for you—no matter how old you are."

Right. Like she hadn't been taking care of herself for the past fifteen years just fine. "Thanks for worrying, but I can handle it, Mom." There wasn't anything to deal with anyway. It was just Jake.

He was only the man who'd given her the best orgasm of her life and called her his queen.

And who confused her, aggravated her—*excited* her.

Her heart flopped.

Oh boy.

Snatching up a glass on a nearby patio table, Apple poured lemonade into it until it almost overflowed. Then she gulped it down in one long slug. Wiping the back of her hand across her mouth, she poured another glass and said, "Parched," in an affected voice, trying to sound like the lone man in the desert.

"Ha-ha." Sedona patted the lawn chair next to her. "Come sit and tell me what's really going on, honey."

"Nothing's going on, Mom. Really." Apple feigned innocence with wide eyes.

"You're a worse liar than your father, girl. So give up the info. You know I'll get it out of you one way or the other."

"Mom—"

"Don't make me call Aidan."

"No, don't!" That got her attention. "He doesn't know anything about anything. I swear. But if you call him, he'll go sticking his big fat nose into places it doesn't belong. And that will just annoy me and cause everyone grief."

"Exactly." Her mother laughed good-naturedly and patted the seat again. "Sit."

Sighing because it was futile to argue with Sedona when she was in one of her moods, Apple slowly walked to the lawn chair and slunk into it. "I'm just wound up about my book. I'm frustrated and stressed out that it's not done. It should have been done *months* ago. And it's not my fault it's not done. Jake was a jerk for like, *forever*, and I'm cutting it really short on time."

"So Jake was a jerk before, but he's not now?"

Hadn't she just explained that? "Now he's cooperating, so yes he's not a jerk." In fact, he was a whole lot of something else. And she was still trying to put her finger on it.

"Honey, I'm going to say something, and you might not like it." Sedona reached over and squeezed her hand, smiling gently in a reassuring way.

Yet somehow she didn't feel reassured. Sedona Woodman was known for dropping some seriously big truth bombs. She saw to the heart of things with blunt precision. And she did it with no damn warning.

"What is it, Mom?" She had to fight the urge to actually brace her feet for impact. Instinct told her this was going to hit home hard.

"Follow-through has always been a challenge for you. Maybe this book just isn't meant to be, sweetie. And maybe you've been using Jake's lack of helpful information as an excuse not to finish. Not that that's bad or anything, honey. We all have our struggles. But maybe it's time to ask yourself why that might be."

Apple felt her stomach tank. "Not the follow-through speech again, please." She refused to acknowledge the other part her mom had mentioned. It was just flat wrong. She *was* meant to finish this book.

Her mom leaned over and kissed her on the cheek. "Got to, babe. You need me to be your mirror."

"No, I really don't." But deep down she knew Sedona was right: she needed some Mom Vision.

"See now, this is one of those things you'll view perfectly in hindsight when you have kids of your own."

Sudden burning at the back of her eyes took Apple by surprise, as well as the longing that set off inside her like a homing beacon at the words *kids of your own*. Before she could so much as think she blurted, *"I want babies!"* Then was shaken by a sudden sob.

"Oh, honey!" Her mother scooted her chair closer to her and put a comforting arm around her shoulder. "I know you do. You always have. And it will happen, I promise. You just need to be patient."

"I'm tired of being patient!" Apple wailed and then was instantly mortified at herself for her outburst. When had she turned five?

"Wait. Is that what this is about?" Sedona tipped her head to the side like she was considering something. "This makes some sense. Is that why you've been seeing Jake, honey? Are you looking for a sperm donor?"

Apple jerked away in shock. "Oh my *God*, no! Mom, that's awful!"

"Why? It seemed a rational progression of thought. You two certainly can't be dating out of compatibility."

"And why not?" Apple suddenly wanted to know, a little offended. For her or Jake, or both of them, she wasn't sure. Jeez, the conclusions her mom jumped to! Not that they *were* dating, but would it really be so bad if they were? Besides, maybe she wanted to.

Apple went very still as the truth of her feelings sunk in just then and paralyzed her.

Holy shit on a silver platter.

She *wanted* to.

"Apple, are you okay? Honey, you've gone pale. Look at me." Her mom grabbed her chin and turned her to face her, her blue eyes filled with concern.

"What am I going to do?" Apple whispered through suddenly dry lips. Her heart was pounding and her head was still spinning from the truth.

"About what, honey?"

She almost couldn't say it. "I-I have f-feelings for him."

Sedona's eyes narrowed. "For Jake?"

Apple nodded, her chin still in her mom's fingers. "Yeah."

Her mother stared into her eyes for a long, quiet moment before releasing Apple's face. Then the corners of her eyes creased and she smiled, winking playfully. "We all make mistakes sometimes, sweetheart."

Apple's eyes flew wide. "Mom!" She gasped in indignation. But then Sedona started laughing. And soon she was joining in, instantly feeling so much lighter inside. Whatever her mom felt about her feelings for Jake, she was respectful enough to keep them to herself. And that filled her with relief.

Then her mom had to go and sober up and say, "In all seriousness, Apple, if you do truly have feelings for Jake, then maybe this book was just a subconscious attempt to find a way to be close to him. Not because you actually wanted to write it. And that's okay."

Now she was back to feeling upset.

She also refused to believe that what her mom said was true. "It's not. They're mutually exclusive things. One hundred percent." Besides, she'd wanted to be a writer most of her life. These feelings for Jake she'd just discovered recently.

Sedona stood from the chair and went for some lemonade. "All I'm saying, Apple, is that it's okay to not finish sometimes if the thing we're working so hard for isn't where our heart really lies and is making us miserable. That's all. It's not a weakness, shortcoming, or flaw in character. It's simply a truth we all should hear from time to time. Sometimes it's okay to just stop."

Apple rose too, feeling conflicted inside. "That's the thing, Mom. It *is* in my heart. I don't want to stop." And she wanted to make her dreams come true. All of them.

Her mom let out a long-suffering sigh. "Then you have to find a way to see it through."

Apple tipped her chin. "I will."

"There's that fighting spirit I love so much." Sedona grinned and began collecting empty lemonade glasses.

Darn straight it was. She was Apple Woodman, writer extraordinaire, and she was going to finish her damn book.

"Oh, and Apple?" her mom called over her shoulder as she headed inside with the lemonade pitcher.

"Yeah, Mom?"

"Be careful with Jake, will you? Your heart is too precious to break."

Chapter Eleven

THEME NIGHT WAS upon Jake.

That was part of the reason he was currently holed up in the back of the bar playing accountant. He'd wanted a few hours of calm and quiet before the storm. Last year they'd far exceeded the pub's maximum capacity, and it had spilled onto the patio and beyond. If this year was anything close to that he was really going to need his camping getaway.

Last year it'd saved his sanity.

This year he'd prearranged everything so that he could take off afterward into the backwoods of the great Rocky Mountains for five blissful days of not having to see or speak to another soul. Aidan had even agreed to look in on his dad for him, so he'd covered everything. It was going to be so sweet.

He was laying tracks out of town tomorrow.

But tonight—tonight was the *fun*.

He grinned, going back to work, and began humming along when the player tucked in the back corner of his office shuffled CDs and his favorite musical guilty pleasure, Taylor Swift, came on.

Jake figured that not too many people got excited about doing their finances—and for good reason. Before he and the guys had hit the proverbial gold mine, he'd hated it too. Of course, he'd also been living paycheck to paycheck working as a brew master for his main competition across town, Gold Nugget Brewery and Pub. Not to be confused with the Golden Nugget *Saloon* off Water Street. They served the hard stuff. And they'd permanently banned his father from the place five years back after he'd had a few too many Jägers and picked a fight with the bartender when he'd been cut off.

Still, before Jake had struck it rich, going over the accounts hadn't been his cup of tea. Now, however, he was so damn thankful every day for what he had that paying his monthly bills was an enjoyable task. It made him *happy*.

Because he was living the dream, baby.

He had just finished paying the utility bill online when someone knocked on the door, slightly jarring him. "Come in," he called out, hoping it was the bar manager, Cory Reynolds, coming to tell him they'd found a copy of Super Bowl '98 to play on the TV screens later after all. Jake had thought it would be the perfect finishing touch for the night, but so far nobody they'd asked seemed to have a copy.

"Look at you, being quite the businessman."

Apple.

Heat instantly coiled in the pit of his stomach. The last time he'd seen her, she'd been flushed and glassy-eyed with arousal. Though she looked clearheaded now, she still flushed when they made eye contact.

"It keeps me honest," he said, fighting the biggest urge to make those gorgeous blues of hers go all hazy again. He shook his head and leaned back in his chair, propping his Merrells on his scarred wood desk. Lacing his fingers behind his head, he let his gaze roam freely over her, and grinned. "Look at you, being quite the bohemian."

She had on a long gauzy white dress that hung off her shoulders and tied in a bow around her waist. Strands of her blonde hair had slipped from her bun and hung around her neck, and chunky wooden bracelets decorated her wrists. And, of course, she had those glasses.

Apple blushed even more but struck a pose with one hand on her hip and one at her head. "Do you like it?"

He liked it. "Yeah." A. Lot. She looked like she belonged barefoot on the beach in Tahiti. He could see it perfectly.

And Jake suddenly really wanted to take her there.

Something lodged in his chest, creating the biggest pang, and he gulped in air, slamming his feet to the floor and sitting up. Holy shit, what was that? Was he having a coronary?

Apple rushed to his side, crouching down in front of him, her blue eyes round and full of worry behind her ridiculous glasses. "Are you okay, Jake?"

Though he wasn't entirely sure, his heart rate seemed to be holding steady, so he must be. "Yeah, I'm fine."

Small, feminine hands covered his knees, the warmth of them branding him through his jeans. "Are you sure? You went really pale."

"I'm sure," he said, needing to change the subject.

Apple regarded him with worry for a few more seconds until suddenly her eyes narrowed and she tipped her head to the side like she was listening hard. "What are you listening to?" Her eyes were quizzical now.

Embarrassment flooded Jake when he realized the player was still on, and who was playing on the stereo. He quickly broke eye contact and cleared his throat. "Nobody. Here, I'll just turn it off." Leaning far back in his chair, Jake reached over his shoulder and slapped the stop button, the room dropping into silence. Righting himself, he tried for a disarming smile. "There. Now, where were we?"

But Apple wasn't listening. She'd pushed up to her feet and was quickly making her way around him, her floaty white dress brushing over his bare forearm as she went. "Oh my God, is that who I think it is?" Her eyes were zeroed in on his CD player.

Mortally embarrassed, Jake grabbed her around the waist, stopping her and pulling her back. "No, don't!"

But she managed to snag a CD case from his rack, quickly reading the cover. "It is! Oh God, this is awesome. It's *Taylor Swift*!" She burst into laughter.

Jake pulled Apple right down on top of him and went straight for the case, gripping her tiny wrist in his hand.

"Give it," he demanded, sure that this was somehow going to be his undoing—his goddamn secret love affair with all things Taylor. Why he suddenly felt unmanned, he wasn't sure. But it was killing him that Apple was laughing at his choice in music. Fuck, why hadn't he been listening to something like Motley Crew? That shit was manly.

"I'm going to have so much fun with this," she taunted, her eyes shimmering with mischief. "I've got you now, Jake Stone."

His heart tumbled and rocked unsteadily. The way she said it had something deep in him rising up in agreement. But he wasn't ready to deal with that. "You can't tell anybody."

"Are you kidding me? I'm telling *everybody*."

It was beginning to sink in that Apple's lush body was pressed against him. Her amazing breasts were plumped like two warm pillows against his chest, making his brain start to go fuzzy. Having her face so close to his that her breath whispered across his cheek was sincerely distracting because it put her full, beautiful lips mere inches away. Before he forgot how to think, he tried again. "You can't tell anyone, okay? It's fucking embarrassing."

Apple placed a palm against his chest and looked him in the eyes. "Fine, but you'll owe me." She pushed away a little, wiggling against him. His body reacted to her by going instantly rock hard.

But damn it felt good to hold her soft, curvy body in his arms. His gaze dropped to her bare lips. "Yeah? What will I owe you?"

She smiled then, brilliantly, and caressed his chest. "I want nudity-free questions."

His brow rose. "Excuse me?"

She raised one right back. "That's right. I want three free questions—anytime, anywhere. Or else I'm going to blab it all over town that you have a crush on Taylor Swift." Her index finger trailed over his collarbone, leaving his skin tingling in its wake. "You wouldn't want that, now, would you?"

He really wouldn't, that was the thing. Christ, he'd never hear the end of it. Especially since he used to drum for a rock band. But more than that—what really got him—was the fact that he owed Apple. Had *been* owing her for months. Guilt for keeping her in the dark about his family's history swirled in the pit of his stomach and had him blurting, "Fine, I agree. But you have to seal the deal with a kiss."

Her gaze dropped to his mouth, and she chewed her bottom lip. "And if I don't?"

Desire reared up, temporarily snuffing out the guilt, and Jake grabbed her by the back of the head gently, pulling her close and whispering against her mouth, "Then I will."

She gasped softly, her lips parting into a small smile as she melted against him. "Well, fine then. I suppose if I *have* to…"

A FEW HOURS later, Apple sat at a corner table in the Mother Lode, her laptop open and a huge-ass cup of coffee at the ready.

Inhaling deep, she tried to mentally pump herself up for about the thousandth time. She was going to do this. See her write; hear her roar. Kicking ass and taking names were the specials of the day. This book was getting *finished.*

She closed her eyes. Breathed one more steadying breath. Opened her eyes again.

The blank screen stared back, cursor blinking, mocking her.

Yeah, she was roaring all right.

Swearing under her breath, Apple snatched up her coffee and glared at her laptop. Maybe if she tried hard enough she could simply stare the book into completion on her computer through some sort of telekinesis. Taking a drink of her vanilla latte, she leveled dagger eyes on her Mac and mentally willed her book into being. *Be finished NOW!*

Unsurprisingly, it didn't work.

If you do truly have feelings for Jake, then maybe this book was just a subconscious attempt to find a way to be close to him.

"Oh, just shut up, Mom." Slapping her laptop closed as her stomach went tense and jittery—and not in the good way—Apple pushed her fingers into the bridge of her nose as her eyes began to sting. Sedona wasn't right about that. Couldn't be.

"Is this a bad time to join you?"

Apple startled and opened her eyes. Nell stood next to her looking tall, fit, and pretty in a spring green cardigan. The color on her was absolutely gorgeous. "No, not at all.

Sit, please. I need the break. I'm not getting a darn thing done on my book anyway."

"Ah, that makes sense now. You were scowling something fierce and talking to yourself, honey. Is it technical stuff that's giving you fits, or is it Jake?"

Definitely door number two.

But not for the usual list of reasons. "I have to confess something to you, and you can't tell a living soul, okay? I'm invoking the girl code oath we swore in eighth grade."

Nell's green eyes went round as she slid onto the chair across from her. "Wow, this must be serious. What happened?"

"I did a bad, bad thing."

"How bad? Scale of one to ten." Her best friend swept her arm from one side of the old round wood table to the other. "Where's it hit on the Richter scale?"

Apple didn't even have to consider it. "Twelve," she blurted and promptly took another swig of coffee. Chugging caffeine gave her something to blame for the nerves, and she was not above scapegoating at the moment. She swallowed and just went for it; put it all out there. Because she had to tell *somebody.* "I kissed Jake."

"Apple!" Nell squeaked softly, her tone filled with surprise.

"Twice."

Her friend's mouth dropped open.

"I'm just kidding," Apple said.

"Okay...well...good?" Nell replied, her expression filled with confusion.

"It was *way* more than that."

For a moment her friend just stared at her in shock before she seemed to find her voice. "Are you serious? When?"

Apple glanced at her phone. "The last time was about two hours or so ago." She looked at Nell and couldn't stop the grin. "And it was *good*."

"Wait, wait, wait! Hold up. Clearly I'm missing something important. The last time we were in here you couldn't stand him. When did that change, and how? Why?" She grabbed Apple's latte and took a drink, staring hard. "Obviously you've been holding out on me."

"Only a little bit." Apple held up her fingers, just a fraction apart. "I told you about the agreement."

"Of which you said there was to be no touching. Clearly, there's been touching."

Apple tipped her head to the side and studied her best friend. Noticed the tense lines of her face. "Are you angry at me?"

"Not angry. Worried, honey. I like Jake—you know that. But he's not the commitment type. And you—well, sweetheart, you are a lifetime guarantee." Nell brushed a strand of dark blonde hair off her face, her eyes filled with concern. "It's the mom in me. I can't help it."

"I know, and I love you for it." Reaching out, Apple gave her hand a reassuring squeeze. "Thank you."

Her friend took a breath and slowly exhaled, briefly closing her eyes. When she opened them again, the expression was clearer. "Okay, now that I had my moment of anxiety over that, tell me the good stuff. I want details." She leaned forward. "Was it as good as the rumors say?"

Apple leaned forward too, amused at their whispering. "Better."

Nell's eyes went round. "Holy shit."

"Yep." She nodded. Emphatically. The man had *skills*.

"Are you duping him with kisses into giving you information?"

"No, but man, that would have been a great idea! Maybe I could still use it..." She trailed off, thoroughly enjoying the mental image of kissing Jake into cooperation.

Nell rapped the table softly. "Hey, dreamer. Focus."

Apple looked at her best friend and blushed hard.

"Ha! That's what I thought, you perv. Get your mind out of the gutter. I have important questions to ask, and I want real answers. When and where did you two first lock lips?"

Briefly Apple wondered at how much to divulge but then realized whom she was talking to and felt a flood of relief that she could finally get it all out. "It was at his place during our agreement. I asked him a question. He sort of answered and told me to take off my top, so I—"

"He did *what*?" Nell exclaimed, turning several heads in the coffee shop.

"*Shhh!*" Apple leaned forward. "Everyone's staring."

Her friend shot her apologetic eyes and lowered her voice. "He really told you to take off your shirt?"

"It *was* a game of strip, honey. Do we need to go back over that part of things again too? Because you seem to be having difficulty keeping up." She grinned, only teasing. "I got to see him naked too."

"Ha-ha. You're funny."

"I'm serious. It was…*incredible*."

Nell just gaped at her, speechless.

"Remember the old high school rumors about his, um, anatomy?"

"I do, yeah. The cheering squad was always giggling about it."

For good reason. "It's true."

"The rumors?"

"Yep." Apple took a swig of her coffee and hid her flaming cheeks from view behind the cup. It was really warm in there. Okay, so maybe it was suddenly hot because she was remembering Jake in the buff. The image of him in all his manly, well-endowed glory was burned into her brain for all eternity.

"*Really?* Wow, am I having a hard time keeping up. This is completely unexpected news." Nell raked a hand through her hair and stole Apple's coffee again. "Give a woman a break, will you? You and Jake playing hanky-panky together isn't the easiest information to digest. Especially since I've spent the better part of twenty years listening to you complain and go on and on about him." Nell froze then, her green eyes going round. Like a statue she sat for several heartbeats. Then she gasped. "Oh. My. *God*."

Apple darted her gaze around the café. "What? What is it?"

Tears began to well in her friend's eyes, and their expression went soft, emotive. "Oh, honey, you've been *complaining* about him for twenty years."

She didn't get it. "Um, *yeah*. Because he's been a pain in my ass for that long."

Nell slid a hand across the table and gripped hers gently, briefly. "That's not why," she said with a tender smile. "It's just the opposite, actually. I recognize the signs now and can't believe I missed them before. Oh, sweetie, it's written all over you."

Apple had to fight the urge to wipe her sleeves all over her face to get it off. Whatever it was. She couldn't, however, fight the urge to fidget as something close to panic bloomed in her chest. It was almost like deep down she knew what her friend was going to say and she couldn't sit still long enough to hear it. She had to move *now*.

Definitely too much coffee.

"I'm not sure what you think you see in my face, but I can assure you it's nothing."

Nell grabbed both of Apple's hands now, her gaze compassionate. "It's not nothing, sweetie. It's everything. It's *love*. And I see now that it's been there most of your life."

Apple went numb. She just stared across the table at her friend. Tried to compute what she'd just said.

Her.

In love.

With Jake.

How about that?

She went from numb to a tsunami of emotions in less than three seconds flat. Feeling them clawing up her throat at a devil's pace, Apple shoved away from the table, trying to stand, and caught her heel on the bottom rung of her chair. Diving headfirst into the wall, she flung out her hands just in time and caught herself. A picture jarred loose from the wall and fell with a crack of glass to the floor. But no bones or noses were broken.

"Are you okay?" Nell asked, her voice filled with worry.

Nodding, Apple bent over to retrieve the photo. "Yeah, I'm fine. Just clumsy." She glanced at her friend as her fingers came into contact with the cool wooden frame lying listless on the floor. "Also, you can't dump something like that on me and expect me not to flip out. You know that."

"I'm sorry about that, but I had to say it because it's true. I've been in love. I know the signs." Nell's eyes went misty with memory.

Apple went nervy. That might have been because there was some truth in her friend's words, and she didn't have the ability at the moment to deny them. "Yeah, well, maybe," she grumbled and righted herself, holding the photo in her hand. Turning to look at it, she frowned at the long, thin crack that went all the way from the top left corner down to the bottom right one. Mrs. Thomas, the café owner, was going to be so disappointed. "I better go find Winnie and tell her I broke her picture."

Nell leaned across the table. "How bad is it?"

Apple angled it so that she could see. "It's bad." She slid a finger along the length of the crack. "Which is unfortunate, because I know this photo. It's the one taken during that brief gold strike in the fifties. Fortune was flooded with out-of-towners trying their hand at prospecting. This picture is of the group of Fortunites who started that short-lived craze." She smiled fondly at the faces in the old black-and-white. Most of them she was able to pair with names, thanks to her research. All six of them except for one.

She handed the photo to Nell. "Hey, you don't happen to know who this is, do you?" She pointed to the young teenaged man wearing prospector's clothes and a huge, proud smile. Ugh, it nagged at her, not knowing. She was usually so good at this kind of stuff.

"I don't personally recognize him, no. But he does look a lot like Jake did when he was younger, don't you think?"

Apple snatched the photo back and squinted her eyes, drew the picture close. And her eyes flew wide when she realized Nell was right. "Holy crap, that's Harvey!" She shoved the photo under Nell's nose. "See? He's holding a bag with the initials H. S. on it. How have I missed this? Gosh, he couldn't have been more than sixteen, seventeen when this was taken. Wasn't he handsome?"

Before Nell could answer, Apple pulled the picture back and scoured the photo again. "I love all this history. It's so fascinating!" And it was incredible. All of it. Every single thing she could see in the old black-and-white. From the metal pans piled at the successful prospectors' feet, to the rubber waders they all wore, to the stake in the ground just behind them near the river shore that had a carving notched into the top. Squinting even more and pulling the photo close enough to fog it up with her breath, Apple stared at that carving until the symbol became clear. When it did she promptly sat her butt back down in her seat.

Man, it had been one roller coaster of a day.

"What is it?" Nell immediately demanded.

"I've seen this design before," Apple replied and tapped the glass over the stake in the photo.

"What does it mean?"

"I think it means 'gold strike,' given this picture and the history I know associated with it. Don't you think?"

Nell looked at the whole photo, from the background to the foreground. "That makes sense, yes. Like the stake marked their panning sight or something."

"Exactly." Why had Jake's ancestor drawn it on the inside flap of his Bible? Had he considered the book to be his treasure? Or had he put it there because he'd found a real gold strike? "It looks that way."

Did this have anything to do with the first settlers and what actually happened to them?

Before she could ruminate any further, Nell broke into her thoughts. "Crap, it's late!" She frowned at the clock on the wall and then grabbed up her purse and stood. "Well, that's fascinating and all. It really is. And I hate to be a jerk and cut you off, but I just noticed the time and I have to pick up Sam from practice. He hates when I'm late and he's the last one, and I promised him I'd make it on time today because I've been struggling with that lately." Nell stood from the table and came around to give Apple a hug. "Promise me you'll think about what I said, okay?"

Like she was going to be able to do anything else. "I promise." She watched her friend go and gently placed the photo back on the wall. Then she turned to find crotchety old Mrs. Thomas to tell her about the crack.

Nell thought she was in love with Jake. Had been for a long time. Well, what did *she* think about that?

Turned out, she didn't know.

But she *felt*.

Oh man, she most definitely felt.

Chapter Twelve

NINETIES NIGHT WAS in full swing by the time Apple pushed through the saloon doors to Two Moons and was hit with *a lot* of noise. Jake sure knew how to throw a party. And by the looks of things, pretty much every citizen of Fortune over the age of twenty-one was in attendance.

"I was hoping you'd come," came a female voice from her left.

Swiveling her head, Apple grinned. "Wow, now *that's* an outfit, Shannon." Fortune's newest resident had gone all out for the night, wearing platform lace-up boots, a plaid miniskirt and fuzzy crop-top sweater. To finish the look, she'd added white knee-high socks. "I'm very impressed."

Her friend gave Apple a once-over. "Not nearly as much as me. Where on earth did you find that dress?"

Apple hooked an arm through one of Shannon's, and they began pushing through the crowd to the bar. "I'm not sure if I should admit this or not, but I found it in the back of my closet. Apparently a part of me had always known it would someday make a comeback." Didn't floral dresses with oversize buttons up the front always come back into style? What about her old Doc Martens? No?

Well, tonight they had. And she was rocking it all proudly, right up through the cropped jean jacket and hot pink scrunchie. And yes, she had found a shoebox full of them stuffed on her closet shelf. So what?

Shannon tossed her auburn hair over her shoulder, laughing. "Oh, honey, you don't even want to know how many clothes I had in my closet before moving here and how old some of them were. It took a solid week of purging and donating to charity to get it to a reasonable level. As it is, I still had to take over the closet in the guest room, much to Sean's dismay."

"What do you mean? That man looks downright elated every time I see him nowadays. You know he's thrilled to share his closet with you."

Warm, cognac-colored eyes smiled at her. "Oh he is, definitely. It's just that he's still adjusting to the reality of how much *stuff* a woman comes with. I don't think he was prepared for twenty-some pairs of shoes and half a dozen face creams."

"My mom swears that the only moisturizer a woman really needs is extra-virgin olive oil."

Shannon gave her a quizzical look. "Really?"

"Yes, really. And considering she has the most flaw-less, luminous complexion and she's in her late fifties but easily passes for early forties, I'd have to agree. I've been using a cold-pressed organic variety that I pick up at the co-op for years now and love it." Apple stopped walking and leaned toward her. "Feel my cheek."

They'd just reached the bar and Jake must have over-heard her, because he started laughing and shook his head, giving her a mischievous look. "Don't tempt me."

Not *that* cheek. Jeez. "This place is nuts tonight. You've got another great turnout," she said, ignoring his comment even though she had butterflies because of it.

Jake waved a white bar towel at the crowd, a wry, crooked smile on his face. "You can thank Fortune's dear residents. They make it what it is."

It was more than that, but she let it go. Instead she looked up and down the bar and squeezed between two occupied bar stools when it was the only opening she found.

"By the way, nice grunge look." He'd gone all out for the night, or so it seemed. But one never really knew with Jake. His T-shirt with the black-and-white image of Eddie Vedder from his Pearl Jam days smoking a cig and looking soulful while he gazed off into the distance and the blue plaid flannel he'd tossed over it might have been his everyday wardrobe.

If Apple was a seventies-throwback queen, then Jake owned the nineties. Or was it that the nineties owned him?

He shrugged his broad shoulders. "I figured I could dress for the occasion since it was as easy as opening my closet." He raised a brow, giving her a quick up-and-down. "Looks like you did the same."

Shannon tapped Apple on the shoulder, turning her attention. "I just spotted Sean, and there's a seat in front of him, so I'm going to snag it before someone else does."

She waved her friend off and watched as Shannon made her way to her man, who was also busy behind the bar, pouring pints and looking like he was having a grand time—wearing what else but flannel. The signature trend of the nineties.

About to move off and find a seat somewhere away from the bar, she had a quick change of heart when a man in his late fifties in MC Hammer–style pants and a sleeveless hypercolor T-shirt slid off the stool next to her and slipped into the crowd. Before anyone else could move in, Apple claimed it.

"I think I'll have a drink," she said to no one in particular—least of all Jake. He was down the bar halfway leaned over it, grinning at a group of what could only be co-eds from Archer as they fawned over him.

Ignoring the annoyance trying to rise inside her, Apple focused her gaze past him, finding Aidan all the way down the other side. Like the other Bachelors, he was wearing a T-shirt and flannel, only where Jake was sporting a navy blue ski cap along with his signature face stubble, Aidan's shaggy auburn hair was hidden underneath a Booker Construction ball cap and he was clean shaven. For a brief moment she stopped to appreciate how handsome they all were.

The Bachelors of Fortune really were something.

Hooking her Docs on the bottom rung on her bar stool, Apple took the opportunity to scan the brewpub, noting that an awful lot of women were cozied up to the bar. A disproportionate number, in fact. Not that she could blame them really. Three hotter guys had never graced Fortune in all its history.

The rest of the crowd was either out on the makeshift dance floor cutting loose, or they were outside on the brick patio socializing around the water fountain. Apple was impressed that Jake had kept the flowers surrounding it alive, but he had, and it made the whole patio space relaxing and beautiful.

Interesting that a guy like him had created and cared for a thing like that. She wondered for a second what that said about him. What it meant.

Then Jake threw back his head on a howl of laughter, his smile out in full force for those barely legal college girls, and a stab of jealousy almost gutted her when one kissed him enthusiastically on the cheek. Reacting swiftly, Apple shoved away from the bar, leaving him to his flirting. It's not like she should be surprised by it. Just because earlier that day he'd kissed her stupid and then reluctantly shooed her out to finish his work didn't mean anything. Not to him. Even if he had called her his queen. God, she knew that. She really did.

Still, Apple glared at him over her shoulder, but the jerk was too busy getting his ego stroked to notice. Why had she even bothered to come tonight?

Oh that's right, because he'd asked her to. Maybe somebody should remind him of that little fact? She supposed she could, but at that moment she was just too mad. How could he have been so passionate with her just last week and so flirtatious with other women now—just like his giving her that incredible orgasm didn't matter one single bit?

Hard, cold reality splashed her in the face like ice water. Maybe it really hadn't mattered to him. Wasn't this who he really was? Everybody said so.

Should she just go home? Really, what had she hoped to gain by coming tonight? She didn't know what was going on her between her and Jake—or if there was anything going on at all to begin with. Jake Stone was *not* a one-woman man.

Had she actually thought he was? Or could be? More scarily, did she need him to be because Nell was right: She was in love with Jake?

Just then a commotion at the far end of the bar caught her attention. She moved through the watching crowd to get a better view, and her stomach squeezed at the scene that greeted her, all thoughts of her predicament disappearing instantly. Aidan had his back to her, and his arms were crossed and his feet planted in a wide stance.

And there in front of him, giving him the dressing down of a lifetime was someone Apple had thought she'd never see again. Someone she knew Aidan had hoped not to.

Megan Hardy.

Shit, she'd forgotten that the woman's grandmother had just passed away.

Apple pushed through the crowd farther as her heart leapt into overdrive. Aidan was a big boy, but his ex-fiancée had gutted him like week-old fish back in college. It had taken him forever to heal and move on. And she…well, she felt damn protective.

She'd just reached them when Aidan said, "No, I didn't expect you to show up. Figured it'd be too inconvenient for you."

"My grandmother died, you ass. Of course I was coming back for the funeral. What do you think I am, a monster?" Megan said. "Why do you always have to be so nasty?"

"*Always* is quite the overstatement, Meg, considering I haven't seen or heard from you in over ten years," Aidan practically growled.

Apple was about to interrupt but was waylaid by Jake when he latched onto her elbow and began dragging her away.

"What are you doing?" she hissed, craning her neck for one last shamelessly voyeuristic view before he tugged her out of sight.

"Letting Aidan have his moment. I suggest you do the same. He's waited a long time, Apple."

She *hmphed* and tried to yank her elbow out of his grip, but he held tight. "Clearly I know my cousin better than you. He needs moral support right now, not to be left alone with that, that heartless *tart*."

"Leave it be, Apple."

"But—"

"He doesn't need you interfering."

"But—"

"*Or*, offering unsolicited opinions."

"I wasn't—"

"You were going to, and you know it."

"Okay, but—"

"Christ, you're an aggravating woman."

"Thank you."

"That wasn't a compliment."

"Sure it was. You just don't realize it yet."

"Are all females born as stubborn as you?"

"Only the really lucky ones." Apple smiled sweetly, batting her eyelashes.

He growled low in his throat. "You drive me crazy. You know that, right? You drive me absolutely fucking bat-shit crazy."

"You're welcome."

"I wasn't thanking you."

"Sure you were," she said again, enjoying the frown on his face.

"You just don't give an inch, do you?"

"Why would I?"

"To let a guy make up his own damn mind about something—*anything*?"

Raised voices came from over her shoulder again, and she tried once more to stop when she recognized Aidan's tense voice. "Let me go." She was already turning away from Jake and back toward her cousin, fully expecting him to release her.

"*Leave it be, Apple.*" His voice had a razor-sharp edge this time.

Surprised by the emotion in his voice, she darted a glance up at him. Her stomach flopped at the dark expression on his face. What in the world had happened to put it there?

Voices rose again, turning her attention back to the confrontation happening by the bar before she could ask him.

"I know what Aidan needs, Jake. I need to help him."

Jake stopped then, rounding on her. "Why can't you just leave the guy alone, Apple?" The fierce scowl on his face had her wondering if it was actually Aidan he was talking about.

Tipping her head back to look him square in his gorgeous brown eyes, Apple planted her hands on her hips, frowning right back. "Maybe it's because you men are all emotionally inept and need guidance."

"Is that so?" He took a step toward her, effectively pushing her back against the wall in the darkened nook.

"Yes, it is," she said, suddenly short of breath and trying to bluster her way through.

Jake planted both hands on the wall behind her, pinning her in. "Maybe he was just fine, doing good even. Maybe he had everything under control until you came swishing by in your sexy short dresses and your huge damn glasses, driving him nuts and making him wonder about things he was better off leaving alone." He leaned down and nipped the delicate skin just below her ear. "Ever consider that?"

Apple swallowed hard as heat poured between her thighs and she began to throb. God that man and his mouth. It was *amazing*. And doing funny things to her as he worked his way down her neck. "What am I considering?" she asked, all rational thought draining from her brain as arousal took over.

"Why you drive me crazy, woman," he ground out between clenched teeth. Then his mouth was on hers, hard and demanding, his tongue brushing against hers impatiently. One of his hard, muscular thighs pushed between her legs, rubbed her there, and she burst into flames.

Throwing caution to the wind, Apple flung her arms around Jake's neck and kissed him back passionately. Exactly the way she'd been daydreaming about for days, ever since their last encounter in his office. And *exactly* the way she'd been fantasizing about at night.

When his big, hard hands stroked boldly up her rib cage and cupped her breasts through her dress, she moaned and pushed against his muscled thigh. He groaned in response and took the kiss even deeper. She was floating, lost on a haze of desire so strong she wasn't sure she'd ever regain her senses. Wasn't sure if she wanted to.

"I can't get enough of you," he gasped raggedly after tearing his mouth from hers. "Fuck, why can't I get enough?"

Lost in the moment, she tugged his hair and arched into him. "Again," she demanded.

And he did. He branded her with his mouth, tongue, and hands as they roamed impatiently over her body. Like he was memorizing the shape of her, he stroked over her every dip and swell. "Jesus, Apple."

Feeling bold, she slid a hand down his chest to the waistband of his pants. His erection strained against the front of his jeans, and she traced her fingertips up and down the length of him. "Yes?"

He hissed between his teeth and leaned into her touch.

But just then, a crowd of rowdy pub-goers came crashing around the corner, a brawl in the works. Apple jerked and dropped her hand, pushing at Jake's chest instead.

He swore under his breath, and his hands gripped her hips, squeezing once before he dropped them slowly from her body. "Hey, jackasses, take it outside," he demanded over his shoulder.

They didn't appear to be in the mood to quit, but they shifted away from the two of them, giving momentary reprieve. All kinds of keyed up, Apple tried to duck out of his grasp, but Jake grabbed her wrist, stopping her.

"I need to get home. It's getting late," she said.

"Come with me tomorrow," he demanded suddenly in his deep, gravelly voice.

She blinked. "What? Where are you going?"

The brawl became official then as a guy in white high tops took a swing and clocked the other man square in the jaw, dropping him to the ground. Jake scowled and swore again, taking a step toward the ruckus and then spinning back to her.

"Just say yes," he urged again, sounding surprisingly earnest. He blew out a breath, looking momentarily torn before his eyes cleared and he said on a rush, "I'll answer your questions if you go."

She just kept looking at him, not knowing what to say. It was so unexpected. Such a sudden change of events.

"I swear. An honest game of strip—no hedging. You ask and I'll answer." He scooped her up for one more hard kiss on the mouth. "Just come." He set her back on her feet. "Please."

Confused and aroused like crazy, but not dumb enough to pass up that opportunity and unable to resist his plea, Apple nodded, unsure of what she was agreeing to. "Okay."

She just hoped like hell it was something good.

Chapter Thirteen

IN THE END, Jake took her camping.

Luckily for her, that *was* a good thing.

He'd just shown up at her house the next afternoon with a bunch of outing gear tossed in the bed of his truck and informed her they were splitting town. No warning, no chance for her to do more than quickly toss some stuff in a bag and grab Waffles.

Sure, she could have said no, but there was less than a month until her book was due, and she needed answers *now*. It was quickly reaching the critical point where even if he did tell her, she flat wouldn't have enough time to write it the rest of the way out. So when he'd shown up with a big, sexy smile on his face and told her what they were doing, she'd made a split-second decision to join him. No way could she afford to waste another minute.

Besides that, if she were totally honest with herself, she was excited at the idea of spending time alone with

Jake. Uninterrupted. Maybe she could finally figure out what was going on between the two of them, if anything at all. Decide if there was something to what Nell and her mother believed.

When he kissed her, something stirred deep in her soul. And it had her wondering how honest she'd been with herself regarding Jake her whole life.

She'd always told herself that he was just her cousin's best friend, somebody who'd never particularly liked her but had mostly tolerated her. However, if that was truly the case, why was he locking lips with her every chance he got lately? And why were the most important women in her life telling her what her feelings were, just like they were tarot cards laid out on a table.

Thoughts about Jake kissing her had run circles in her head the whole drive up Jasper's Peak, and then on the two-mile trek in from the trailhead to a spot that Jake had picked out. If it had been any other person than Jake, she'd have said the preselected spot was evocative, romantic even. Tucked deep into a grove of lodge pole pines and on a flat bank near a crystal-clear alpine river, the camping spot heralded an unspoiled view of high mountain peaks, cresting one upon the other in a majestic display against cerulean skies. Apple slid a look at Jake in all his rugged splendor, appreciating the scenery with a deeply satisfied smile on his face, and her heart tumbled a little.

So yeah, maybe she really was just a tiny bit in love with him.

But, only a tiny bit.

So microscopic it didn't really even count.

"We should get the tent put up before it gets dark. Why don't you set your backpack down by that rock over there and we can get started?" Jake's masculine voice cut into her musings, and she shot him a slightly startled glance, like the guilty kid caught with a hand in the cookie jar. And she blushed. She *actually* blushed.

"You okay?" he asked, his eyes narrowed on her.

"Ah, um, yeah," she sputtered, jolting into motion and quickly setting down her bag. "I was just spacing a bit and you surprised me, is all." Pasting a bright smile on her face, she rubbed her hands together. "Let's do this."

He gave her a quizzical look but didn't say anything. He just got to work.

It was a surprisingly pleasant time setting up camp with him, Dregs and Waffles acting as an avid audience. Granted, it helped a ton that he was Mr. Wilderness and had such a routine with everything that all she'd really had to do was help slide a few stakes into the ground. Which for her, was just fine. As much as she adored *nature*, she wasn't the most adept at doing outdoorsy *stuff*. She was, um, not especially skilled or graceful.

So she, Waffles, and Dregs had watched while Jake maneuvered around the campsite under the massive old pines. She enjoyed the views and chatted with him about small, inconsequential things. If there had been any undercurrent of tension or anything, she couldn't tell. Mostly the man just looked so darn happy to be playing Bear Grylls out in the wilds of the Rocky Mountains. He'd had a lightness about him, a contentment, puttering around in nature as he was.

It made her smile to see him like that. "Who taught you how to do all this stuff?" She gestured to the expertly constructed campsite. "Which, by the way, I'm deeply appreciative for," she added with amusement in her voice.

Busy securing their temporary home from bear raiders, Jake sliced a piece of neoprene rope and slid his pocketknife back into his jeans before answering her. "Harvey mostly, but my dad too some. Before he really lost it, back when I was a kid. He used to take me on these treks that would take us days into the San Juans before we'd turn back." His eyes went soft with memory, and he grinned, big and open. "We'd pan every creek we crossed, no matter how small, looking for those nuggets he loved so much."

Apple found herself smiling back. "Did you ever find any?"

Jake shook his head and laughed. "Not even close. But damn it was fun." His smile grew tender. "Those were some good times." Then, shaking his head, he looked at her and raised a brow. "What about you? You ever gone panning for gold?"

Apple was sitting cross-legged on the ground, tracing patterns in the dirt with a finger. At his question she tilted her head and responded, her hand stilling, "You don't remember?"

"Don't I remember what?" He tipped his head, studying her.

She gave him a look like, "Duh." "Really? You seriously don't recall the one and only time I went gold panning even though you were there? Fine. I was sixteen, and it was during the Bensons' annual Fourth of July picnic. You saved me from washing down current when the skirt of my dress got caught on that enormous floating log and I couldn't get free. Ring any bells?"

"That does sound familiar," he drawled, appearing hazy on the memory.

"I almost drowned!" Apple shot him an incredulous look. "How can you not remember that?"

"Wait, I do remember that." Jake shook his head, his dark eyes somber. "That must have been tough."

Finally, she thought. There's the appropriate sympathetic response. "*Thank* you. Yes, it was, as a matter of fact."

His eyes were steady on her, flat serious. "You know what I remember most from that day?"

Her fingers began doodling in the dirt again. "No, what's that?"

Wickedness cut through the serious in a blink, and his eyes went bright as the full moon at midnight. "Your see-through, soaking-wet panties."

Apple gaped at him. She tried to speak, but it came out only as a pathetic little squeak. And then there was the giant lump that was suddenly blocking her throat, making swallowing nearly impossible. Yeah, speech wasn't going to happen.

"They were this peach fabric with a small bow on the front and a rose in the middle."

"Y-you remember that?" she croaked, completely flummoxed.

"Of course I do," he replied, simply and matter-of-factly.

"W-why?" Of all the panties he'd seen in his lifetime, why did Jake remember hers?

He looked her dead in the eye. "Because they were yours."

Apple's heart seized for a beat. Then two.

Until he added with an unrepentant grin, "And because a hormone-ravaged teen boy doesn't forget his first pair of wet underpants. It was like a wet T-shirt contest, only a million times better."

Then she was laughing. "Pervert."

"Aren't we all, baby? Aren't we all?" He chuckled, turning his attention back to the work at hand.

But she stopped him. "Hey, thanks, by the way."

"For what?" His hands were busy securing a complicated-looking knot.

"For saving my life that day."

"Anytime," he said quietly after a few moments, glancing at her with an unreadable expression.

Though she couldn't read it, Apple could feel it. Wow, how she could feel it. She let out a breath to steady herself. Incredible, that man's energy was. Simply incredible sometimes.

When the site was fully set up, Jake went about starting a fire. Using a piece of flint and a practiced flick of his wrists, he had flames bursting to life and lapping hungrily at the scraps of wood in no time. Then he simply rocked back on the heels of his hiking boots and grinned at her over the fire, looking thoroughly satisfied with himself.

"What is it with men and fire?" Apple said, laughing.

"We like the flames. Makes us feel alive and manly."
He ran a hand inches over the top of the red-hot logs.
"Kinda like a woman."

She snorted at that and looked into the thick stand of
pines that surrounded them, enjoying the rich, pungent
scent. "You would know."

Whoa, where had that sudden snark come from?

Jake slid her a look through his spiky black lashes,
still crouched before the fire pit. "Funny, Apple, you've
mentioned the women I've been with a lot lately. Sounds
like you're jealous. But that can't be right because you
couldn't be, could you? Not over me."

As if. Apple rejected that idea immediately. But then
she felt a tug of something—a *lot* of somethings that
forced her to reconsider. Okay well, shit. *Maybe.*

"I'm not jealous," she muttered, not knowing what
else to say.

His smile cranked up a few degrees, and she had a hot
flash. Wow. "It's not a mark against your moral character
if you are, you know. It's allowed."

Suddenly agitated, Apple stood up and paced, before
plopping into a red camp chair. She picked up Waffles
and began to pet her rather enthusiastically. Narrowing
her eyes on Jake, she had a sudden suspicion. "Do you
want me to be jealous?"

If she'd been expecting him to be demure and modest, then she was clearly delusional because he laughed
outright and winked at her. "Maybe."

Really?

Unsure what to make of that new bit of information—was he joking?—Apple studied Jake over the flames. He was so darn good-looking that she was sure he'd had his fair share of jealous women fawning over him. It was his bedroom eyes, his potent smile—his big, virile body. And it was that simple, grounded, competent energy of his that promised safety and security would be found in his arms for the right woman.

Problem with that was that he was too busy sifting through women like flour through a strainer to notice if she'd arrived.

And for some reason, knowing that *did* make her a little damn jealous. What the heck? Had receiving a few kisses from him made her lose objectivity?

Her heart whispered that it was more than that. That it was *exactly* what she'd been warned about.

Apple sighed. *Great.*

"Why did you bring me out here?" she blurted, having meant to ask that for hours now. "What's the purpose of all of this?"

Jake brushed his hands on his pant legs and moved to the blue cooler near the low-slung tent. "I thought you'd enjoy it. You were always bugging me and Aidan to take you on our backpacking trips when we were kids, remember?"

That's right, she had been. They'd always seemed to have so much fun. "I remember."

"Honestly though, I've been coming here for the past few years to recharge my batteries after all of the chaos of Theme Night. Usually I spend about a week, but I've decided to cut the trip from my usual five-day trek to an overnight in-and-out. Figured I'd go easy on you. I remember what happened the last time Aidan caved and tried to take you camping."

"Hey, that wasn't my fault! I didn't ask him to bring enough gear to throw out his back and make him miss senior-year football tryouts."

"He said you carried him piggyback-style out of camp and back to the car like a real champ. Like a wild Amazonian warrior, I believe were his words." His lips were twitching hard by the time he'd ended the sentence.

"Gee, thanks."

"I do what I can, juicy fruit."

Apple eyed him skeptically. "Is that really the reason you brought me out here? You wanted me to enjoy it? Or did you actually bring me out here as a stalling tactic? Need I remind you that you specifically said you'd answer my questions?" Speaking of, she reached for the notebook and pen she'd set on the ground next to her earlier and placed them in her lap.

He raised one of those brows at her. "I'm not stopping you from asking anything, Apple, so long as you remember the rules." He grabbed a beer from the cooler and waved it in front of him, gesturing to the fire and the forest around them. "The night is your oyster. Ask away."

When put that way…She opened her notebook to a blank page. Why not jump right in? "How did they all die, those first settlers?"

Jake gave a laugh, flicking her a glance. "Wow, right to the point, aren't you?"

"You'd prefer me not to be?" She reached for her shoes with a hand and pulled them off. "Shoes off, Stone." One article of dress down. She did a mental tally of her outfit. That made six questions to go before she was naked.

Jake toed off his shoes and strode over to the tent in his bright white socks. He unzipped the flap, and his head disappeared inside for a minute. When he reemerged, he had a camping mat and dark green sleeping bag in his hand. Bringing it right in front of her, he quickly laid the mat down and spread the sleeping bag over it, creating a cozy place in front of the fire. "Here, since you took your shoes off and the soil is rocky." He tossed her a flirty grin. "You could have just taken off your bra again, you know. Saved me the hassle of getting this."

Apple's mouth dropped open a little at his unexpected thoughtfulness. Her parents had taught her that people's characters were made up of the little things they did, the small gestures. "Thank you," she whispered around the tightness in her throat. He'd even made it close enough for her to step directly onto without having to risk walking on a single stone to get to it.

Dregs and Waffles must've thought it looked comfy too because they made a beeline for it, but Jake shooed them away. "Nice try, dogs. Off." With tails hung low, they gave him sad, mopey eyes and slunk off to find a spot to lie in the grass nearby.

"Don't you just feel like the meanest person in the world when they look at you like that?" she said. She always felt like a big fat meanie. But that was straying off topic. "Seriously though, Jake, how did they die, the settlers?"

What she really wanted to ask was why he was being so *nice* to her. But she didn't have the courage. Not yet.

He scratched his stubbly chin like he was actually thinking about how to answer. "Some of them died of natural causes, and some didn't."

Sigh. "Why are you tormenting me?" Sliding onto the cushioned sleeping bag, Apple listened to the familiar sound of the slick fabric rustling underneath her as she settled in more comfortably. God, she'd loved having campouts in her backyard as a kid and had done it all the time in the summer months. Being with Jake in the forest at dusk now reminded her so much of that—of how much fun it had been to sleep under a blanket of stars, listening to the earth breathe.

Jake, on the other hand, wasn't playing a game of fun. It was more like a perpetual game of frustration, and she was pretty over it. "If this is how it's going to go all night, I'd have rather stayed home and freaked myself out with a few episodes of *House* and a glass of wine. At least then I'd have accomplished something," she ended, grumbling. And then she took off her socks before he could remind her, not even bothering to voice a complaint about the suspect legitimacy of his answers. "Off with your socks too, though I don't know why I took mine off. It's not like you gave me a real answer or anything, and you know it."

The fire popped suddenly, spitting flame high into the air, and Apple reeled back, gesturing at it and saying, "See? The universe agrees with me."

Jake was silent for a moment as his eyes grew dark and intense, making her insides flutter. Just when she thought he wasn't going to respond, he said in a voice that was barely audible, "Maybe it's not agreeing. Maybe it's a warning that we're playing with fire and should stop."

She tipped her head to the side and considered that, feeling something inside her shift and grow restless at his words. "Maybe I like the heat."

Why had she just said that?

Because she was ready, she realized. Heart, body, and soul.

Ready for *this*.

Jake had the beer bottle at his lips, about to take a sip. But at her words he lowered it slowly and leveled his intense gaze on her. He looked her over from her head to her bare toes, and leisurely back up.

"If you mean that, then you better be ready to go up in flames, Apple."

Chapter Fourteen

APPLE WAS KILLING him.

Slowly and with so much ease on her part. In fact, the woman didn't know what the hell she was doing at all, which made it all that much more torturous to him.

Why had he brought her out to the wilderness, alone and secluded? Jake still didn't know. All he knew was that he'd needed to be with her where there could be no distractions. No interference.

Where he had her exactly where he wanted her.

Because the truth of the fucking matter was that Apple had been under his skin and in his head for the better part of his life—and he'd had it. Playing with her and stalling had been necessary and also a bit fun, until he'd woken up late last Friday night in cold sweats because of a dream he'd been having about Apple being with another man. The damn thing had had him so upset he'd gotten up and showered at 3:00 a.m., hoping that would settle his wayward emotions.

But it hadn't, and he'd been left waiting on dawn to come with an ass-ton of heavy questions weighing him down.

"I'm willing to risk it if you are," Apple said, shifting to sit cross-legged on his sleeping bag. Though she was wearing khaki hiking pants and a T-shirt, it wouldn't have surprised him in the least if she'd decided to wear one of her dresses. The woman lived in those things.

Which he liked, way more than he should admit. They were feminine and sexy as shit. And they'd fueled his teenage imagination to no end. Christ, even now he was starting to react.

Tearing his gaze away from her, he sucked in air and thought about how to proceed. But then she reached for her hairband thing and shot him a coy smile as she pulled it and let her hair tumble loose. Lush blonde waves cascaded down her back and over her shoulders. "Sometimes I get headaches from all that weight on my head." She leaned back, exposing the delicate line of her throat, and shook her head gently. "I've been wondering if I should just cut it off."

He tensed, reacting physically with a coiled stomach at the thought of her doing anything to alter her appearance. And he realized he didn't like it one bit. He didn't even have to think very hard about why.

Apple was perfect exactly as she was.

"Ask me another question." The words were out of his mouth before he knew they'd even formed in his brain.

But he didn't want to take them back. He wanted her to ask another question. Looking at her sumptuous hair loose around her shoulders, hugging the lush curve of her breasts like he'd pictured thousands of times in his head as a kid, made his heart pound slow and heavy in his chest.

"Forget it." She smiled sweetly, beautifully. "You haven't even come close to answering my first one."

Tension coiled between his shoulder blades. His conscience wanted to tell her the truth. Yet, there was the promise he'd made to his father. And Verle Stone, well, he may not be much, but he was all the family Jake had. For all his faults, nobody called him out for a lack of loyalty. It was bred deep into his very bones.

Fuck, but it was a hard spot to be in.

Hedging as close to the truth as he could, and hating the situation he was in, Jake replied, "The settlers were wiped out, pretty much in one night. They were all killed, Apple, in a very unpleasant manner, by a very, very destructive disease."

Sitting down on the ground across the fire from her, Jake took a drink of beer to soothe his suddenly parched throat and waited for her. Impatiently. Christ it felt like he'd always been waiting for her.

Would he ever just have her like he needed her?

She gasped, "That's awful!"

He smirked. "Like I said, people tend to think dying often is."

She pulled a face and threw a small twig toward him. "Ha-ha." Then she shook her gorgeous hair back and said, her tone back to serious, "I want to hear details about that, but another question first: What year did they come to Fortune?"

"What did your research uncover?"

She glanced up from her notebook and leveled a look at him. "I'm not asking my research, I'm asking you."

The way her hair whispered around her face was slowly driving him mad. Arousal stirred inside him, pooling in his groin, and his cock began to fill, pressing against the fly of his jeans. Knowing it was probably a bad idea, but quickly losing his ability to think coherently, he raised a brow and egged her on. "In that case, I have no idea."

"Damn it, Jake!" Apple exclaimed and thumped the heels of her hands against the green sleeping bag. "I've had it." She stood up and began unbuttoning her khakis, her movements jerky. "I'm done playing."

"What are you doing?" he asked, even though it was obvious she was taking off her clothes. It was just that his brain had stopped functioning at the sight of Apple's hands unzipping her fly. And every last ounce of blood had gone straight to his cock. The way it was straining almost painfully in his pants was proof of that.

"I'm sick and tired of your half-assed answers, Jake. We had an agreement. I know that this doesn't matter in the least bit to you, but it does to me." She seemed to be getting angrier as she talked, her movements even more erratic as she yanked off her T-shirt and threw it onto the grass several feet away.

His jaw dropped a little, but he recovered quickly. "Isn't this the opposite of how it's supposed to go, honey?

Question first, then clothes?" Not that he was complaining. He was all for Apple's nudity. Grabbing his shirt, he followed suit and pulled his over his head and tossed it aside.

She didn't answer; only shot him a warning look before yanking her pants down her very shapely legs and kicking them off in the same direction as her shirt. But before he even had time to register that, she'd stripped off her bra too. Grabbing her hair and pulling it forward, she hid her breasts from view and crossed her arms over them.

"Jesus, Apple." He breathed deeply, mesmerized by the sight of her standing in front of him in nothing but a pair of tie-dye panties. For the first time in his life her bare skin was in view before him—every exquisite dip and sumptuous curve, every satiny inch.

Christ he ached for her.

"What are you doing?" he tried again, a little helplessly, entirely forgetting to lose his own jeans.

She took a deep breath and planted her hands on her hips, revealing tantalizing glimpses of bare breast through her silky hair, killing him further.

"Giving you everything you ever dreamed." Her eyes flashed like sapphires in the firelight. "You tell me right now when your ancestors settled Fortune, and I'll drop my underwear. Right here in the middle of the damn forest like a wood nymph." She met his gaze. "Are you ready?"

His life came down to this one pinnacle moment. This one moment that he had been hoping for most of his life.

A part of him recognized the danger of not proceeding cautiously and with a clear head. But every other fiber of his being demanded that he seize this moment. Rational thought was swallowed by this primal, hungry desire to take what was being offered, regardless of the potential consequences and the no-way-out position he was in.

Jake swore and was on his feet, pacing away before rounding on her and taking a step back toward the campfire. And he stopped dead in his tracks at the sight of her. The power of Apple blew through him, leveling him.

There she stood, like a gypsy goddess, her voluptuous body cast in dancing light and shadow by the flames. An expectant look was on her face.

"What's it going to be, Jake?" Her voice was soft, coaxing.

A wave of lust and yearning and some other feeling that rose up like a tsunami—powerful and terrifying and mysterious—crashed into him, and he lost his ability to think. Passion surged up, along with this absolute *need*.

Because now, he didn't just want to touch.

Now he needed to *claim*.

Lost to the visceral calling, the one that had never disappeared, but he realized now had only been banked and on slow-burn for years, Jake stared hard at Apple's body, barely able to tear his gaze away to look at her face long enough to say "1860."

The words rushed out like an avalanche. Because that's what it felt like to him just then. An avalanche. This huge, rushing, thundering crush of need/energy/*something* that made him forget the situation, forget his promises,

and forget to care that he was stalling—made him willing
to risk that potential problem—to finally just…

Fucking.

Have.

Apple.

To feel her. Taste her. *Worship* her.

It had been a lifetime of wanting and waiting. Of
dying inside, knowing she could never be his. Of needing
her to be. And knowing that even if she somehow could,
that he would never be able to give her what she needed,
and in the end he would leave her brokenhearted. Knowing that made him resist, hesitate.

But then Apple began to smile, slowly at first and
growing brighter and bigger by degrees, until she was
absolutely beaming. "Oh. My. God. Finally! You gave me a
straight answer. You told me, and I finally freaking *know*!"

But he barely even registered that she was talking
because in her excitement she'd placed her hands in the
waistband of her underwear and shimmied right out of
her cotton panties, kicking them off to the grass with the
rest of her things with a delicate flick of her ankle. Then
she reached for the blonde waterfall of hair covering her
breasts and, in an absentminded gesture, tossed it over
her shoulders.

And there. It. Was. The culmination of everything
he'd ever thought, wished, or dared hope for: Jake's deepest dream come true.

Apple stood before him, her naked body more exquisite than anything he'd ever seen or imagined. He raked
his gaze over her, like a hungry man on death row who'd

finally been presented a feast, memorizing the way her hips flared so femininely, the curve of her beautiful full breasts, the thatch of dark blonde curls covering her gorgeous, perfect pussy.

He couldn't handle it. His heart squeezed painfully as unfamiliar emotions tore through him, drowned him. Blinded him. So he reached for the only thing he knew could stabilize him. He reached out for his anchor.

He reached for *Apple*.

Wrapping her in his arms, he kissed her, not knowing whether it was smart, or whether she'd hate him later when she found out the full truth about his family.

He only knew that he *had* to.

"I need you," he rasped after he yanked his mouth away, panting heavily. His hands streaked over her body, desperate to know the feel of every dip, every curve, every silky voluptuous inch. When they came to the underside of her breasts, she moaned, and his cock jerked, hungry for her. "Apple, my Apple," he whispered against her neck, losing himself in his feelings for her. "I've always needed you. You're my only cure. Tell me *why*," he said with a heavy breath, nipping her skin tenderly.

She shivered beneath his touch, and when his hand slipped down over the gentle curve of her belly and split her blonde curls with his finger, he found her wet and so very hot. "Fuck, baby. You're so wet." He smiled darkly, something inside him deeply satisfied. "You *need* me."

"Jake," Apple cried out, her nails digging into his shoulders, her head falling back in ecstasy. "I've always needed you."

The sultry whisper cut straight to his heart. Hungrier now than he'd ever been, Jake kissed her, nipped her tender skin as he trailed a path down to her gorgeous, perfect breasts. He found her nipple puckered and tight, and a groan ripped from his throat as he took her peak into his mouth, rolling his tongue around it and sucking passionately. "Say it again," he demanded, his mouth against her creamy skin.

Suddenly hands were in his hair, gripping and tugging, pulling him from her. He raised his gaze in question, only to be sucker punched in the gut by the sight of Apple turned on and flushed with arousal. It took his knees out, but he recovered quickly, giving in to the inevitable truth: Apple had him. Completely and totally.

"Look at me," came her soft, coaxing voice.

He did, his heart stumbling a little.

"I know that now. I've always needed you, Jake," she said, her eyes filled with heat and tenderness. "Always."

He couldn't take it. Her words and the expression in her eyes undid him. Unraveling as a growl tore from his throat and his heart burst into a million pieces, Jake dropped to the ground in front of her. Breathing heavily as emotion stormed him, he wrapped his arms around her hips and placed his cheek against her abdomen, closed his eyes.

Thank you.

It was all he could think.

"It's always been you, Jake."

Opening his eyes as heat poured heavy in his veins, Jake slid his hands down her hips and around her legs until his thumbs were caressing the sensitive skin of her inner thighs. When she sighed and rolled her pelvis toward him, he smiled and slid a thumb up her thigh until he'd reached her dark blonde curls. Brushing her fold lightly and finding the curls damp there, Jake said as his mouth lowered to cover her, "Tonight I will be your king, and you will be my queen." He flicked his tongue over her slit and heard her gasp. "I will explore all of you." His tongue pushed farther until he found her clit and circled gently. "*All* of you, Apple. I feel like I've been waiting all my life."

And he did. He took her in his mouth, using his fingers to spread her for better access, and licked her, sucked her pussy until she draped a leg over his shoulder and was alternately fisting her hands in his hair and caressing it as she moaned and rocked against him. Knowing she was close to coming, but not ready for her to find release from the tempest yet, Jake pulled her leg down and spun her around and bent her forward. Before she could protest, his mouth was on her juicy ass, his tongue searching for the core of her while his hands kneaded her firm flesh.

"Jake!" she gasped when he found her and thrust with his tongue.

"Want me to stop?" he pulled away and asked.

"No!" She rotated her ass toward him and dug into his hair with a hand, urging him back. "More. Just. More."

Taking her pussy in his mouth again with a growl, Jake lapped and licked until she bucked against him. "Not fair!" she gasped raggedly.

"How's that, baby?" he said, his cock throbbing against his fly, begging to be touched.

"Because," she cried softly, her body beginning to tremble against him. "I want to taste you too."

Jerking painfully, his cock filled to impossible fullness. Unable to take it anymore, but not willing to let it end just yet, Jake used his hands and tongue on her body, exploring every dip and luscious curve as he rose to his feet. When he reached the back of her neck, he brushed her hair away and gave her an openmouthed kiss there. And when he turned her back around to him, his breath seized in his chest at the dazed, passionate expression in her eyes.

"Take me, Jake," she demanded softly, raising her arms and draping them around his shoulders. "Take all of me."

I will, every single beautiful part of you, his heart replied.

"Fuck," he growled, knowing what it meant, and not knowing if he was ready for it. But he did know one thing. "You're mine, Apple."

"Yes," she said on a sigh as his hands stroked boldly, hungrily over her. "I'm yours."

When he reached her, he parted her swollen folds and found her clit, rubbed it slowly, teasing her tiny plump bud before sliding his finger into her, filling her. "Come for me," he urged roughly. "*Now.*"

He needed to know the sight of Apple coming.

For him. Only for him. *Ever* for him.

She began panting softly, rocking her hips rhythmically as he brought her higher. Kissing her again, he took his time tasting her as he felt her orgasm build. And when she tensed, finding her peak, he stroked his tongue slowly over hers and took her moan of release into him, feeling it in his very soul.

Apple shuddered, and her knees buckled. Jake tightened his hold on her and lowered them both to the sleeping bag, laying her on her back. Impatient now, Jake stood back up and reached into his pocket. Ripping his clothes off, he covered himself with protection, knowing that he couldn't wait much longer to be inside her.

Kneeling between her spread thighs, Jake looked at her, flushed and so very beautiful with that satisfied little smile she wore. And the fact that he was the one who put it there overwhelmed him with so much emotion and male pride that he didn't know how to process it, so he stroked his hands up her gorgeous body, leaned forward, and tasted her hot little pussy again, needing that most personal intimacy. She gasped and arched into him, spreading her legs open even farther and fisting her hands in his hair, encouraging him. "More."

The musky, female scent had him losing that last little thread of control, and he rose over her, thrusting into her in one sure movement. Jake cried out as he was enveloped in her slick, swollen heat. Grabbing her legs, he pulled them up around his waist and thrust, making them both gasp. "Look at me," he demanded, needing that connection with her.

Apple opened her eyes, her expression hazy with passion, and she smiled softly, nearly sending him over the edge. "Mmm, I'm looking," she said, pulling him down for a drugging kiss. When it was over, she looked him in deep in the eyes. "And I see you, Jake. I *see* you." She kissed him gently, and he lost a part of himself to her when she added, "You're beautiful to me."

Tears stung his eyes as those same unfamiliar emotions swelled up inside him and he came undone. Linking his fingers with Apple's, he pushed her hands into the mat next to her head and took her, thrusting deep, over and over until he felt her tense once again beneath him.

"Yes." He wanted it. *Needed* her orgasm once more. And he had to see her face as it took her, knowing it was him who pushed her over. "Look at me." She did, her eyes gone with passion, and he teetered on the edge.

"Apple!" he groaned when her inner muscles started to tighten around him, signaling her impending release. It fueled him, urged him to join her.

He went.

And he didn't let go of her hands, couldn't, when the storm took them both.

Chapter Fifteen

APPLE WAS SO in love. So totally, completely, 100 percent *in love* with Jake Stone it was ridiculous. It was amazing, really, just how much a person could feel for someone else. Amazing and awesome—and *fun*. Can't forget the fun.

Over a week had passed since their camping trip up Jasper's Peak, and when she wasn't freaking out about making her looming deadline, she and Jake were spending a lot of time together. A lot of quality naked time. Because really, that was important. Every good relationship started with a boatload of smoking-hot sex. She should know. It was in all the great works of literature. Personally, she'd rather *do* it than read about it. Handily for her, Jake felt the same. And for her, knowing that it came from a place of emotional attachment—and wasn't just a fling—made it all that much sweeter.

It hadn't taken her any real soul-searching to realize that she'd had feelings for him all along, that they'd just been misplaced. Especially since she'd pretty much been slapped upside the head by her mother and best friend about it. It was kind of hard to ignore the truth when it was presented like that. Now that she had accepted it, she couldn't wait to move forward with everything. Even being upset over knowing that Jake hadn't told her the whole story during their camping trip and was still holding back didn't change her feelings. She wanted him. Turned out it was just that simple.

And maybe Jake didn't realize it quite yet, but she knew it's what he needed, to spend the rest of his life in a warm, cozy home, surrounded by a big ol' family who gave him so much love that it made up for all that he'd missed out on growing up. Oh, the babies they could make! They'd be so stinking adorable. She could just picture it: his gorgeous brown eyes and her mouth. Ah! *Too much cuteness.*

Yep, she had it all sorted out. When the time was right they'd take that next step together.

But that wasn't happening today.

Oh no, today was for fun and lightness. Why? Because it was the last Saturday in September. And that meant it was time for Fortune's biggest annual event. The one that drew crowds of thousands and visitors from all over the globe and spilled from the huge flat expanse of Riverside Park at the base of Jasper's Peak to Main Street. The very one that filled Nell's climbing club to the gills with rock climbers from all over the world for weeks on end before it started. Tourists and residents alike entered town and were greeted with the enormous banner that spanned across the road, declaring to one and all: "Fortune's Blues and Brews Festival."

Apple couldn't have been happier.

She was rocking her favorite vintage floral dress today with a ruched waist and deep neckline. She flashed Jake a secret smile when she caught him looking at her cleavage. One would think that with as much quality time as he'd been giving her girls lately that his interest level would be starting to wane. But *no*. If anything, it seemed to be growing. And she wasn't complaining, not at all.

Turns out, she rather *liked* Jake liking her body.

She also rather liked being in love with him.

"When are you and the guys going to go play?" she asked Jake as they stood under one of the many beer tents lining the side of the grassy meadow to the left of the main stage. Of course, they were in the Two Moons Brewery and Pub tent along with Aidan, Sean, and Shannon—and two actual pub employees who were there to really work and not just socialize. A band that sounded a lot like Big Head Todd was finishing up its set, the easygoing crowd clapping appreciatively.

"We're going to be up in the next set or two." He had this happy expression that just made her heart squeeze with joy for him. It was obvious how excited he was to be playing with the band again. Even if it was just for a few songs. "It'll be fun."

That was the understatement of the century. But it was just so darn cute. "What's Heath going to play since you're taking over drums?" She couldn't remember what instrument he had played last year—mostly because she'd been too busy staring at Jake and remembering what it had been like to watch him perform in high school and how much she'd hated that it had secretly excited her and made her wonder about things she was better off not wondering.

At least this time her enthusiasm didn't have to be quite so secret.

Sean squeezed in around them to hand a plastic cup of beer to a waiting customer. Lines easily five deep stood shoulder to shoulder all up and down Beer Row as people took refuge in the shade of the oversize tents. It wasn't so much that it was *hot*, it had more to do with being over ten thousand feet in elevation and that much closer to the sun. Sunburns happened fast.

Turning back to Jake, she had to stop and admire how all three Bachelors looked so rugged and handsome in their matching navy Two Moons T-shirts while they served the smiling, laughing customers. Yes, she noticed a lot of coy female glances aimed in their direction, but she didn't get her panties bunched over it. The guys had appeal, why wouldn't they look?

They just couldn't touch. At least not Jake or Sean. Aidan, well, she didn't want to think about that. Gross. He could do whatever the hell he wanted.

Happy and content, Apple waved to familiar faces and tried hard not to grab Jake and plant a big fat kiss on him, making quite the scene. But they'd already talked about it and decided that until one or both of them had spoken to Aidan about it, that they would keep their hands to themselves when out in public.

Didn't mean it was easy though.

Suddenly the crowd broke into a huge round of applause, calling and whistling and making a ruckus. Quickly moving out of the tent for an unobstructed view, Apple waved Shannon over. "Hey, lady, come here. You need to see this."

No sooner had she finished the sentence than the woman was standing next to her. "I've been dying to see this," she leaned close and whispered like she was in confession.

They both watched the scene unfolding as the Redneck Rockstars took to the stage and greeted a cheering and enthusiastic crowd. The band's popularity was *huge*. It wasn't hard to see why. Besides killer music, every single one of the band members was drop-dead sexy. It was going to be almost too much sexiness for a person to handle when the Bachelors joined them onstage too. *Phew!*

"Hey, has Sean told you anything about the Rockstars?" Apple casually started.

"Not that much, actually. Sean said Jake played drums back in high school, but for some reason he decided to drop out when they were offered a contract with their record label." Shannon brushed her auburn braid back over her bare, freckled shoulder, looking pretty in her strapless blue maxi dress.

Apple nodded and squinted against the sun glare, wishing for an instant that she had on big-ass sunglasses instead of her big-ass tortoiseshell prescription frames. Oh well, can't have everything perfect all the time, right? "He did, yeah. It was sometime during the year after they graduated. But he's never told anybody why he quit the band." She had always suspected it had something to do with his family though.

"Sean told me they were huge. Like *really* huge." Shannon glanced at her man with an adoring expression, then back. "Jake would have been so famous."

"Ridiculously so," Apple agreed. "The band made it huge all over the globe, just like Pearl Jam back in the day. They got compared to them constantly. Which wasn't off base. Only Elijah's taller than Eddie Vedder—not that that's all that hard to be," Apple quipped and then instantly felt disloyal for making a height joke. Like she was one to talk.

I'm so sorry, Eddie, she instantly mouthed in karmic apology.

Shannon looked a little awed. "That's amazing. Why are they playing the blues fest though?" She turned her attention back to the stage where Elijah was strapping on his guitar, standing in front of the microphone, and she gestured at him. "His name is Elijah?"

"Yeah." Apple nodded. "Elijah Goldman."

"I met him this summer at the donut shop and have been calling him The Guy in my head ever since." Shannon's nose scrunched a little, and she shook her head with a small laugh. "My sister's crazy about him."

Apple snorted. "Yeah, her and every other female around the globe."

Shannon just chuckled. "Trust me, that wouldn't stop her."

"I believe you. I met that firecracker named Colleen." She glanced back at the band. "Mostly the guys play here because it's home. But also because their last few albums have been bluesier and more acoustic."

Just then the Bachelors stopped by the two of them.

"We're heading up onstage." Jake looked at Apple over the top of Shannon's head, and her stomach flip-flopped excitedly. His eyes were bright and eager. And damned if the guy wasn't grinning full out, looking downright happy.

"Go get 'em, hot shot," she said.

He winked, and she felt it down to her toes. Who knew a simple wink could have so much *heat*?

"Thank you, everyone, for coming out this afternoon to our favorite little town in all the world to celebrate music and beer. And to most importantly, have fun!" Elijah said into the mic, his rough voice full of confidence. "As some of you know, we've started a new tradition here at Fortune's Blues and Brews. For those who don't, put your hands together anyway because you are all in for a real treat. Everybody, let's welcome to the stage, Fortune's darlings and our personal friends, the Bachelors of Fortune!"

Aidan slapped Jake on the back. "It's go time, brother."

The crowd went nuts as it parted to allow them through, the guys thoroughly enjoying their time in the limelight. Or maybe it was just getting to play with the Rockstars. Shoot, that would be enough to have Apple grinning.

The Bachelors joined the band onstage to the sound of a very excited audience. And Apple couldn't help the butterflies that launched in her belly at the sight of Jake settling down behind the drum set as Heath moved off to grab the harmonica. Picking up the sticks, Jake spun them in his palms and did a quick tap on the snare, grinning wide.

Aidan took up a spot next to the bass player, Dylan, his guitar at the ready. Then he leaned into the microphone and said, "Let's hear it for the Redneck Rockstars for allowing us the privilege of being up here onstage with them." The crowd clapped, and Aidan threw back his head laughing after Dylan said something in his ear. Finally, Sean took up residence behind the keyboard.

"It still amazes me that your man plays so many instruments, Shannon."

"I know, right? But he says it's because of growing up in the Dublin theaters with a lot of time on his hands and being surrounded by artists who were keen to teach him things."

"And yet he was a bare-knuckle boxer and is now a horse breeder?" Apple crossed her arms and slid Shannon a glance, smirking. "Interesting man you picked there."

Her friend laughed good-naturedly. "Oh, I know it." But then she added more seriously as the band began to play, "And I wouldn't change a thing."

Six months ago, she would have felt a pang of envy over a statement like that. But not now. Not when the man she loved was up onstage in front of a thousand people playing music and having the time of his life. It was so hard not to jump in the air, shouting, "That's *my* man!" Apple felt like giggling, her life was so perfect and wonderful.

Suddenly a conversation that had been going on behind them began to break through her musings. "I heard Jake has a thing with the librarian."

What? Wait. That was her they were talking about! Glancing over her shoulder confirmed that it was the busybody owner of the Roots hair salon.

And she was talking to another notorious gossip. That was never good.

"Why don't you scoot up some, hon? I need to grab my shoes, and I'll join you in a minute," Apple said to Shannon, although what she really wanted was to take a step backward and eavesdrop because she swore she'd just heard one of them say her name this time, and she was instantly worried it was more of that damned gossip about her and the library. If it kept up she was in real peril of losing her job, and she loved being Fortune's librarian. Just flat *loved* it.

Shannon moved up toward the stage, leaving her to listen.

Turned out she was right.

One of them was saying, "I don't know what that Apple is doing with Jake, but it certainly isn't something for the library like she said. I mean, have you even seen an announcement for a Bachelors event?"

"I haven't, no," said the other quietly.

"That's because there isn't one, I tell you. I think I overheard those two agreeing to something else entirely. Something more like..." An extended pause. "You know. I really think she might be exchanging goods, *if you know what I mean*, for the library."

"Oh, I don't know about that. Why do you say that?"

The voice lowered to a whisper. "I've been hesitating to say anything, but my son told me he saw her through the back windows at the library late one night, with a man who couldn't be anyone else but Jake."

"Really! My, my."

"Mmm-hmm. And he said it didn't look like any business meeting he'd ever seen, if you get my drift."

Apple's stomach dipped. Great. Just what she needed.

She heard a disdainful sniff. "Well, if that's true then somebody should tell her boss. That's no way to appropriate equipment for a public institution. But beyond that, somebody should warn that girl away from that no-good jerk before he leads her on and then breaks her heart."

Misappropriation, her ass.

Apple scowled and felt her nails dig into the palms of her hands. She had to clench them because she was tempted to wring the woman's neck for talking about Jake like that. Just like he didn't matter.

"Who knows, maybe she'll be the one to change him," Apple heard the other woman say and straightened her spine. Darn tootin', she was the woman for the job.

Barbara Keeley laughed, the sound surprisingly bitter. "Oh, honey, you and I both know that if there's one thing that men just don't do, it's change. That girl's in for a world of hurt if she's messing with Verle's son. Good-looking he is and good for a fling, but love? If that's what she's after, then she's going to be out of luck."

"You speak like you're talking from experience."

She sighed, long and slow. "Let's just say there was once a time I got the notion that I could fix Verle, sober him up and give him love. I can tell you I was wrong. And, well, the apple just doesn't ever fall that far from the tree."

Tears stung Apple's eyes, and she swallowed around the hard knot in her throat, forcefully ignoring the instant self-doubt that rose in her, even as she fumed over the attack on Jake's character. Stepping away, her hands still clenched into fists, she notched her chin and went to find Shannon. While she weaved through the crowd, she told herself exactly one thing, because it simply *had* to be true: they were wrong.

They didn't know what they were talking about, so screw them.

Apple was keeping on. And damn it, her love *was* powerful. It was the mother f-ing bomb.

And it *could* change a person.

Just wait and see.

If there was a tiny little part of her that worried there was some truth to their words, she was bent on ignoring it. She was bent on ignoring the aching uncertainty they stirred up inside her. And she was most definitely bent on ignoring the sharp darting pain they created in her chest.

Why?

Because her heart couldn't handle it being any other way.

Chapter Sixteen

THE CONCERT HAD just ended and everybody was making their way through the dirt parking lot, but Jake lingered behind with Apple behind the rest of the bunch. Sean and Shannon were directly in front of them, his arm wrapped around her and hugging her close. Thinking that looked like a swell idea, Jake was just stretching out his arm when he thought he heard someone from behind call his name.

"Did you hear something?" he asked Apple, his brows drawing together. "I swear it sounded like my old man."

Apple's sexy little lips puckered as she tilted her head and listened, hands on her lush hip. Damn she was cute. "I don't think so, sorry."

Jake ran a hand through his hair and blew out a breath. *Okay.* Maybe he was starting to hear things. God, hopefully he wasn't starting to go crazy now too. "Never mind."

They'd just started walking again when someone behind them called, "Jake!"

Stopping, he spun around and came face-to-face with his father. When he saw his pop's expression, his shoulders relaxed and tension eased. He smiled, noting automatically that Verle's eyes looked clear. "Hey, Pop. What are you doing here?"

Verle shifted from one Chaco-covered foot to the other, gently wringing his hands together. "I-I came to watch my boy play music." His lean, tan face broke into a grin. "I'm so proud of you, Jake. You always had such talent."

Caught off guard by the unexpected emotions, Jake cleared his throat and glanced over his shoulder at Apple, who was standing quietly by his truck, her gaze averted to give them privacy. "Thanks, Pop. But I didn't think you remembered that I used to play with Elijah and the guys. That was so long ago." And yeah, it had bothered him some, but he'd gotten over it. There were worse things in the world than one's dad not being able to remember he'd almost been a rock star.

Verle's dark brown eyes filled with emotion, and his lips pressed together in a thin, tight line. He crossed his lean arms, hugging them close. "I-I'm sorry, Jake. I'm so, so sorry I took that away from you. I know I did."

Saddened and not really up for taking all of that heaviness on right then, Jake held out his hands to his father. Besides, it didn't matter anymore how he really felt anyway.

"It's okay. Really. Hey, Dad," he said when Verle started to blink rapidly, trying to snap him back before he was lost completely to wherever he went when he had his episodes. "You didn't take anything from me. Look at me, I'm fine," he ended, placing his hands on Verle's slender shoulders.

It shocked him a little to remember how robust and muscular they'd been in his youth. Had his father been slowly slipping away since then, or was this a more recent development? Shit, was Verle not even eating properly without Harvey to look after him?

Before he could explore that new and very real concern, Verle pulled him in for a fierce hug. And just like always, Jake was filled with love, acceptance, and—at the same time—a profound weariness. "You should have had that life, Jake," his father said quietly.

The thing was, he really shouldn't have. He knew that 100 percent. His father really didn't need to worry about that. It had worked out exactly as it had been meant to because bottom line, Fortune was his home. Straying over to Archer State to get his chemistry degree had been the farthest he'd ever roamed, and that had been plenty.

Besides, sticking around had just kept things simple.

"I'm happy, Dad, really. You don't have to worry about me. I've got the brewpub and the cabin. Friends. Look, I'm even seeing someone." He hooked his thumb toward Apple. "Remember Marty Woodman's girl?"

His father caught sight of Apple and abruptly pushed Jake away. "What is *she* doing here?" he demanded, his eyes going round and paranoid. Panting all of a sudden like he'd just ran five miles, he stood with his shoulders hunched protectively.

"She can't have it!" he yelled. His whole body began to shake terribly, his coloring going blotchy red. "She *knows*, Jake. She knows, and she's going to take it."

While Jake wracked his brain for a way to calm his father down, a part of him realized the scene his father was making. He hadn't missed the dirty looks. The furious whispers as concertgoers passed.

Ah well, fuck them.

They were the ones who didn't know a goddamn thing about real love.

"Pop, she's not going to take anything from you, really." He glanced over at Apple, who was busy chewing her bottom lip, her eyes huge and filled with worry. "Isn't that right, Apple?"

Hopefully affirmation from her would be enough to snap his dad out of it.

She gave his dad a friendly smile meant to be disarming. "That's right, Verle. I'm not interested in taking anything of yours. Promise." And she stepped toward him, raising her hand to her chest. "Cross my heart."

"Liar!" Verle launched himself at Apple.

"No, Dad!" Jake yelled. Moving quickly, he stepped between the two of them, to protect her.

Suddenly Verle's face registered shock as the color drained from it. Then he jerked to a stop and bent over in one single motion, clutching his hands to his chest.

He fell to the ground just as Jake reached him. "Pop!" Crouching down next to him, he placed a hand on his father's shoulder and yelled to Apple, who was already pulling her phone out of her purse, "Call 911!"

"Doing it now. Hold on, Verle!" she called, raising the cell to her ear.

Locking out the panic he felt slamming at him, Jake focused on the Red Cross emergency training he'd obtained a few years back and checked his father's breathing. A crowd gathered around them, and Sean, Shannon, and Aidan had pushed their way through.

"What can I do?" It was Aidan, his face set in concerned lines.

"I think he's having a heart attack."

That's exactly what was confirmed at the hospital by the emergency room doctor later, the whole hour or so in between a blur to Jake. But as he stood in the hospital waiting room listening to the doctor explain to him that his father had suffered a mild coronary and he would be okay, he didn't feel better. He didn't even feel relieved.

Because the doctor had pulled him aside and privately told him something else. Something that Jake had been suspecting for a while because of the increased erraticism of his father's behavior. The physician had given him that practiced sympathetic doctor face and dropped the bomb: "Your father is going to be fine from the heart attack, but his glioma has grown to a dangerous level. You know from the last time you came to me and we discussed his condition, it's inoperable because of its location." The silver-haired doctor had paused, cranked up the fake sympathy. "Jake, I'm sorry to say this, but your father has only a few months. Maybe less."

With a heavy heart, Jake had thanked the doctor and went back to the waiting room, glad that he was surrounded by the support of his friends.

Seeing them all there, for him and his dad, filled him with gratitude. He was a blessed man, surrounded by such support. Yet it didn't stop the pain, the hollow ache in his heart at the knowledge that he was losing his father. Deep down he'd known this day would come, and he'd thought he'd prepared emotionally.

But he hadn't.

His heart was weeping.

All the worrying. All the waiting in trepidation, *every single day.* Jesus, even all the internal bracing of mind and spirit he'd done, preparing for that one sad, heavy day. Turned out there was just no preparing for the death of a loved one.

It'd been a hell of a weight to bear.

Yet, he had to be honest and admit that he'd hated the waiting game of seeing what was going to get his old man first: the booze or his brain. Considering how much effort Verle had put into the first part, it was more than a little bit of a surprise that the tumor was going to be the thing that did him in.

Apple came over and hugged him. "I'm so sorry."

"We're here for you, brother." Aidan placed a hand on his shoulder. "Anything you need, you just say the word."

Jake nodded, grateful. "Thanks, man." Knowing there was nothing else to do, he looked down at Apple with his chest aching and knew he needed her tonight. With a depth and intensity like he'd never known. "I'm going to just go home."

It was like she understood what he wasn't saying. Her eyes never left his as she nodded. "I'll ride with you."

A little while later after saying their good-byes, Jake and Apple were at her place putting a kettle on for tea.

"I'm so sorry about your dad, Jake. How are you holding up?" she asked, her blue eyes filled with concern.

He took a look around her pink kitchen and blew out a breath, feeling fried. "I don't know, honestly."

She placed a small, soft hand on his arm. "That was tough, baby. It's okay to feel off."

Looking into her eyes, so full of worry and affection, he felt himself start to tremble. It started on the inside and worked outward. Pretty soon his whole body was shaking.

"Hey now," she said softly. "It's all right." Pulling him into her arms, she rubbed his back in calming motions. "You have to let it out."

Suddenly pressure exploded in his chest, and he gulped in air as emotions came over him: pain, grief, fear. The feelings had been buried for so long because there'd been no other choice but to just knuckle down and bore through life. He'd had to ignore them to the best of his ability. Now they rose up like a tide and came out all at once. "Apple," his voice broke on a sob.

"Shhh, I'm here, Jake." Arms so tender and yet so capable hugged him tight, like he was something special that she wasn't ever letting go. "Let me love you better, baby."

Spilling over with emotion for his father, for her—for *him*—Jake took her mouth in an almost desperate kiss. Everything seemed to be unraveling, crashing over him, and he didn't know what to do, how to think. The only thing he knew was the feel of Apple in his arms and an emotion so strong, so pure that it overwhelmed him.

He needed his anchor.

Jake wrapped her in his arms and headed directly to her bedroom, letting his heart lead the way.

Chapter Seventeen

THE NEXT MORNING Jake woke early and slipped from the bed while Apple was still asleep. Heaviness and heartache weighed him down. But it wasn't all for his dad.

It was for her too.

Because somewhere along the way, like an asshole he'd gone and fallen in love with Apple. Against his intentions, against his plans—hell, against his *will*. Still, last night when they'd been together, he'd felt it. Maybe more accurately, he'd been unable to deny it. It had revealed itself so clearly.

He'd been in love with Apple his whole life.

And he sure as shit didn't deserve her.

His stomach went achy. There was so much that he'd hidden from her, so much to come clean about. Because the guilt was eating him alive and he couldn't stand it anymore, regardless of the promise he'd made his father. How would Apple feel once she found out that he'd been withholding more from her this whole time? Keeping his ancestors' story from her was bad enough. Now that things had turned serious between them, there was another issue to address as well: his unwillingness to have children. Before things went any further, any deeper, he had to tell her so she could make up her own mind. Before she could get hurt. She deserved better than that.

And he was going to give it to her.

He'd realized last night after she'd fallen asleep on his shoulder and he'd lain there awake thinking about his pop, life, and choices, that he wanted a real relationship with Apple. Like the most natural decision in the world, it had come to him and settled over him like his favorite sweatshirt. He wanted the whole damn thing with her: the dogs, the house, the picket fence. He wanted whatever she wanted. Whatever made her happy and smile like she did. No matter what it was, he was all in. One hundred and fifty percent.

Except for one thing.

And it was a big one.

He had to come clean with her, and it could very possibly drive her away, if the fact that he'd lied to her about his ancestors wasn't enough.

"Christ, I've made a mess," he said to Waffles as she lay curled up on her girly dog bed, looking at him in interest with her head cocked sideways. "You know she's going to dump my sorry ass when she finds out I won't have kids, right?"

"What do you mean you won't have kids?"

Jake's heart seized. Turning slowly, he flinched when he saw the confused, shocked look on Apple's sweet sleep-flushed face. "Good morning," he evaded. "How did you sleep?"

He watched as she eyed him warily, hoping beyond hope that she'd drop it until he had a better way to break it to her. This was the last thing he wanted. Christ, he'd hoped to ease into the conversation.

Instead of answering, she moved away from the doublewide archway, the wide legs of her pajamas swishing with the movement. Reaching the cupboard, she opened it and pulled out the bag of coffee stored on the bottom shelf. In mounting silence, Jake waited while she performed her morning routine of making coffee. Once she hit the brew button, she dusted her hands together and finally looked at him.

"I slept well, thank you. You?" The words were warm, but the tone was a little chilly.

Anxiety crept up Jake's neck. When it came to Apple, he knew what that tone meant. "I was good. I had you with me."

Her eyes softened. "That's a lovely thing to say to me."

"It's the truth. Best sleep of my life is when I'm with you." Every morning he woke up rested and full of energy. It was kind of amazing.

She walked over to him then and kissed him so sweetly, so tenderly, that it nearly brought tears to his eyes.

Her eyes were a little dazed when the kiss ended. "You're an incredibly sweet man underneath all the gruff, you know that?"

Guilt slammed into him with a granite fist. "Apple," he started. "I—"

"Know exactly the right things to say to avoid getting yourself into trouble." But she didn't sound mad. She didn't sound *happy* either. Looking into her eyes, Jake searched their blue depths, and he didn't see anger there. Thank God.

"I'm sorry." It's all he could say. He was just plain sorry he hadn't told her before now.

The coffeemaker beeped, jarring them both. Stepping away from him, Apple went to the counter and retrieved her favorite mug from the wall rack. "Why don't you tell me what you meant when I walked in a few minutes ago while I make my coffee, okay? Because it sounded an awful lot like you said you won't have kids. But that can't be right, can it?"

There it was. The one conversation he'd been dreading for weeks. The same one that he knew he absolutely had to have with her if they were going to have a real future together.

It killed him, knowing how much it was going to hurt her. "I didn't want you to hear it this way, Apple. I'm sorry."

"Tell me everything, now, please. I'd like to clearly understand what's going on."

Jake took a deep, fortifying breath. "I'm not having children."

She set the mug very carefully back onto the counter before slowly rounding on him. "Why ever not, pray tell?"

Shit, she'd gone Jane Austen. That was not a good sign. He held out his hands, leaning his butt against the counter. "Apple."

"Don't you 'Apple' me," she snapped, her eyes cloudy with hurt and uncertainty. "I've only been up ten minutes, for chrissake, and I haven't had any coffee. Do you have any idea how hard it is for me to have a serious conversation before I've even had a chance to fortify myself?"

He didn't know what to say. She looked so confused and defensive and soft. All he wanted to do was walk over to her and wrap her into his arms. To beg for her forgiveness. To tell her he was sorry.

But he didn't dare.

Not when she had eyes like that.

Instead he simply tried again, "Apple, please."

"What do you mean you're not having kids?" She tipped her head to the side to study him, her long loose hair cascading over her shoulder. "Is this a 'single guy, bachelor sort of thing,' or are you really truly serious?"

Nerves gripped him, made his stomach jittery. But she needed the truth. "I'm serious. I'm sorry, Apple, but I really am."

Now she crossed her arms and frowned at him. "What's wrong with kids?"

"Nothing," he instantly replied, meaning it.

"Then what's the problem?" she asked, giving him a look that obviously said, *WTF, idiot?*

She wasn't wrong. He felt like an idiot for not telling her the truth way back at the beginning. "There's nothing wrong with them, Apple. It's what's wrong with me."

"There's something wrong with you? What?"

He tossed her a small crooked smile. "Isn't it obvious?"

"Actually, no," she countered with a tense voice, her agitation clearly growing. "What's going on, Jake?"

He could see that she was on the verge of tears, and it made him feel about two inches tall. God, he'd thought the vasectomy was the responsible thing to do!

Now he was pretty sure it was going to be his ruin, regardless of responsible or not. *Fuck.*

"I really just wanted to do the right thing. I swear," he muttered, mostly to himself, feeling at a loss.

But she heard him. She scooped up Waffles and hugged her close, Apple's hair tumbling down her back in a shimmering blonde mass. "I don't want any excuses, Jake. Not anymore. I want to know everything that you've been hiding from me. What is this thing you did that you thought was so responsible? And what does it have to do with not wanting children?"

Seeing that it was pointless to hedge, he scrubbed his hands over his face and said the truth with a sinking heart. "My family has a genetic disorder that has affected almost every single male in my family for as long back as anyone can remember. It's called familial glioma, and it's a fairly rare genetic condition that causes brain tumors and cancer in the males of my family. It's an awful, horrific sex-linked gene mutation, Apple."

Her eyes went wide. "It causes brain tumors and cancer?"

Jake nodded, hating what he was going to say next. "Yes. Harvey was one of the very few in my family who didn't have it, Apple." He sucked in a breath, gathered courage. "My father has it though."

"Oh my God," she said, her hand flying to her breast. "Was that what you were talking to the doctor about when you disappeared with him?"

"Yes." His hands ached to reach for her. He rubbed his palms against the edge of the counter instead.

"Jake, I'm so sorry. Did you already know? Was last night when you found out?" She gave him a sympathetic look. "Are you still processing?"

He shook his head. "I've known for a long time. Probably since I was about twelve."

"Wow, what a heavy load for a kid to bear."

He nodded, still wanting nothing more than to go to her, but knowing that as soon as he confessed it all she'd probably rather kick him than hug him. And she sure wouldn't be sympathetic. Swallowing, he raised a hand out toward her, needing to feel her touch, but dropped it back to his side. "My dad's crazy, Apple, but it's not from the alcohol. It's from a large tumor pressing on his amygdala—the emotion center of the brain. It drives his behavior. The drinking is just how he's learned to cope."

Her lips pressed into a tight line, and her eyes went wet. Turning, she set Waffles back down. "Oh my God, why haven't you told me before?" She stopped dead like she had a thought. "Wait. Have you told *anyone*?"

He gave a grim shake of his head and shrugged. "Why? What good would it do? This whole damn town's made up their minds about my old man. Besides, he's still a drunk, Apple. People might like me because I'm a Bachelor and have a shit ton of money; and they might feel sorry for my dad knowing he's sick, but they'll never forget he's a drunk, first and foremost. Or all that he's done. People are small that way."

She was silent for a moment, looking out her big kitchen window at the sun rising outside. "Not all of us," she muttered, then asked, "Why won't you have kids? Do you have the gene too?"

The one question he truly dreaded.

Instead of answering, he looked her straight in her blue eyes and hoped for a miracle. "Is having kids a big deal for you?"

She crossed her arms, stating flatly, "You know it is."

He did. She'd been vocal about her desire for a big family for as long as he could remember. Jake sighed, giving it up. Maybe it was best this way. Apple could do so much better than the likes of him anyway. She deserved better.

"I don't know if I carry the mutated gene, Apple. But I've been keeping tabs over the years on a test that's being developed that screens for the gene sequence, but it's still in the pre-publicly-available stage—and it might be for a really long time still. It's already been in this stage for years." He shook his head, his gut feeling hollow. "That's not the only thing though. I, um, saw a doctor when I was twenty-one about my family's inheritable gliomas and mental illness. After reviewing my history, she agreed that there was significant risk of transmission. I asked her to perform a vasectomy so that I could never pass my genes on. Without a test to confirm my health clearance, the vasectomy was my only option, Apple. It was the right and responsible thing to do."

"You keep saying that." Tears welled in her eyes, and her chin trembled, killing him. "So you're never having babies, is that what you're really getting at? No two ways about it—just no babies. None?"

Keeping his eyes steady on hers, he shook his head, dying a little inside. "No, I'm not. You know my father, the way he is. I refuse to subject a child to that. It was really hard growing up under that weight, and I just won't do it to someone else. If I'm going to start exhibiting traits of this damned disease too, I'd rather do it alone, without risking putting someone else through hellish agony."

"And what do you mean 'exhibit traits'?"

"I'm healthy now, but I might not always be, Apple. I'm not in the clear. The really crappy thing about this fucking disease is that it doesn't tend to affect males until their mid- to late thirties. Right about now for me, actually. I've had MRIs, and everything is normal so far, but that can change drastically almost overnight. Tomorrow might be the day I begin to unravel. I just don't know. Every single damn day I wake up wondering if today is the day I'm going to lose my mind. It's kind of a shitty way to start your day."

Apple raised a hand and closed her eyes briefly like she was having a hard time taking it all in.

"Don't you remember my dad when we were kids, Apple? He wasn't always the way he is now."

"I remember." She crouched and picked up Waffles again. It was almost like she needed something to do with her hands. "He used to coach your Little League team, didn't he?"

"Yeah," Jake said with a crooked smile, feeling warmth spread across his chest with the memory. "Me and Aidan's. He loved it so much. At the end of every season he'd take the team out for ice cream down at the Lazy Cow Creamery, and afterward we'd all dump a bucket of water on his head." His smile faltered some as sadness crept in. "I can still recall the way he'd roar in surprise and then start laughing. Just laugh and laugh." He glanced at Apple. "It was the best."

"You miss him," she stated softly.

Coughing over a sudden lump in his throat, Jake cleared it and replied, "Yeah, I guess I do. He was a good dad. A good man. It saddens me to see it end this way for him, you know?"

She didn't answer. Didn't have to. The warmth and sympathy in her gaze told him enough. She understood. And it hit him then how much that meant.

He needed her understanding.

Always had.

"When did things start to change with him?"

"Around the time I was five. Or at least that's what my mother said before she left. But I don't remember that. I remember things with him like Little League and camping. So I think she really meant that he started drinking when I was about that old. I don't remember his behavior actually becoming erratic until I was about twelve or thirteen."

"And you're afraid that yours might follow in his footsteps."

The lump in his throat was back. Damn thing. "I am."

She was silent for a moment, watching him. "And you didn't think all this information was important to tell me?"

He told the truth. There was nothing else he wanted to give her. "I didn't think a relationship with us would grow to a point that it mattered, honestly."

"Sleeping with me wasn't a good enough indication for you?" she snapped, her sudden sharp tone slicing him like a knife.

Well, when she put it that way...but no, it never had before. "I've never been emotionally involved with someone I slept with, Apple. I know what that says about me, and it's the plain ugly truth. I'm a shallow asshole. My personal history has just never mattered to a woman I've dated before. It didn't enter my mind that it did with you. That it would." He gestured between them. "With us. I'm sorry, Apple, I really am."

Her eyes were dark and unreadable. "You know how much I want a family, Jake. You've heard me go on and on about it since we were kids. I can't believe you honestly didn't think it was information worth sharing with me, trusting me with."

"I didn't think our feelings would get involved. Didn't think it would matter."

She glared at him. "So when this whole thing started you never expected to have feelings for me? Wow, that hurts, Jake. A lot."

"No, it's not that! I just didn't think. Period."

"Damn straight you didn't think," she muttered.

He stepped toward her but froze when she gave him a look that promised something very bad would happen if he made another move. "That's not what I meant, you know that."

"No, I don't know that, Jake Stone," she said, loud enough this time that Waffles whimpered. "I'm sorry about your dad and your family disease. I really am. I'm sad and outraged for you." She waved her hand around the kitchen and at them. "But *this* is too much. You've been lying to me about a lot of stuff, and I'm really sincerely hurt. You should have trusted me. Out of all the people in your life, I'm one of the good ones, and you know that. So I'm really upset that you felt like you couldn't talk to me. Oh, and side note: when you're sleeping with me, there's going to be feelings involved, all right? It's how I'm made. I deserved the truth, and you know it." She threw up her hand, clearly overwhelmed. "Jeez, Jake, now I'm also wondering what else you've got that you've been holding out on. What else haven't you told me?" She planted a hand on her hip and cradled her dog in the other arm. "You'd better come clean *now*."

The world crashed in on Jake right then, and he just couldn't deal. His dad was in the hospital, his life was in upheaval, and the woman he'd loved most of his life was slipping through his fingers. It was too much.

Shoving away from the counter, he began pacing the big kitchen and decided to get it all out there, because Apple was two steps away from hating him anyway, and the secrets were like poison in his veins. He wanted it gone. "You know that I've known all along about what really happened to my ancestors. But I made a promise to my father not to tell you."

She froze, and her mouth dropped. For several long seconds she stared at him unblinking, her breathing shallow and rapid. Then, she slowly bent down and placed Waffles on the floor. "Cover your ears, honey," she said to the dog before straightening. "It's about to get ugly."

His stomach sank. This wasn't good. "I can explain."

Hands on her hips, she smiled tightly, clearly seething. "Please do."

He frowned, feeling like he was walking a very thin line and not knowing what was going to push him off. "Look, you know my dad. And I just explained about the family condition."

"Did you promise him from the beginning, or is it a more recent thing and you were just fucking with me there for a while? Or maybe the whole while? Exactly how fun has this been for you, Jake?"

Warning bells fired off all around him. And damned if he couldn't smell smoke.

One wrong word and this whole thing between them would be torched to the ground.

"What can I say that will make this better?" he asked, knowing it wasn't the most macho thing to say, and maybe a little bit of a copout. But he didn't give a shit about masculinity. Right now he just wanted to save what was left of him and Apple.

"The truth."

Smolder.

"Christ, Apple." He raked a hand through his hair, feeling the air around him grow stuffy and hot. "Please."

"*Truth.*"

Crackle.

Snap.

"Okay, Jesus, *fine*. At first it was for fun. But only at first, I swear. I made the promise to Pop a month or so ago. But I admit that yes, at first I was holding out on you because I liked seeing you get all riled up. You have no idea how pretty you are when you're pissed."

"That's about the dumbest thing I've ever heard."

"You're pretty?"

She waved a hand again. "*Pfft.* No, I knew that."

He was confused. "Then what?"

"That you felt you couldn't be honest with me and just tell me Verle was asking to be left alone. Like I don't know how to respect people's personal space, even if it means not getting everything I want. I would have left you alone, Jake. *Should* have, clearly."

"Wait, I don't understand. You've been so insistent on talking to me. How can you say you'd have backed off, when you've been at Two Moons for the past four months pushing at me? Your writing career is everything. You've said that to me more than once." This time, he was the exasperated one. Raking both hands through his hair, he added, "I'm so fucking confused right now."

"Then let me clarify. Yes, my writing career means the world to me. But *not* at the expense of others. If you or Verle had told me there were private matters you wanted to keep that way, I'd have struggled with that, but I'd also have respected his wishes. In fact, I'd have written my book without it and had it finished and submitted months ago. Damn it, Jake. You made this so much harder than it had to be."

"I wanted you around," he admitted quietly.

"Not good enough." She stared hard at him.

Jake sucked in a breath, feeling his chances to redeem himself slipping with every exhale. "I needed to be with you, Apple. I had to. I have feelings for you. I always have."

She ignored him. "Have you known for a long time about your ancestors?"

He nodded, his heart hammering heavy and dull in his chest. "Yes. Harvey told me once when I was a kid. I spoke to my dad a month or so back about telling you. I tried to convince him to talk, but he just flipped out every time I mentioned you." He frowned. "I still don't understand why he does that."

"So, what's the story? How'd they all die?" Her face was so impassive, he couldn't tell where she was at.

It was down to this. He loved his pop, he did. With all his heart. But if he was going to save what was left of him and Apple, then he had to tell her the full truth of it now. For a heartbeat he weighed his loyalties, but the answer was clear.

Sorry, Pop.

"My ancestor, Jesse Stone—the one who owned the Bible I gave you—had the family disease."

"Meaning?" she pushed when he paused for breath, her gaze shards of ice.

He couldn't handle it, couldn't handle seeing his warm, sweet, soft Apple go cold on him. "He killed them, Apple. That's what it means. It means that my goddamn ancestor went ballistic from this fucking familial disease that runs through our blood—*my* blood—and slaughtered and ate almost everyone in the encampment one horrible spring night. Including *his own wife*. And then he killed himself. Bodies were buried in a spring avalanche and never discovered. And that's how the goddamn awful story ends."

Jake leveled his gaze on her. "This is my truth, Apple. It's who and what I come from. Crazy people and murderers." His lips twisted in a hollow, self-deprecating snarl. "Still like me?"

Apple leveled a look at him, letting her emotions show now. Her face flushed and her eyes pooled with tears. "Get out."

He flinched. "Please, Apple," he pleaded softly.

"No! There's no 'please, Apple' anything. I need you to leave so I can think. Do you know how much anguish you've caused me? For months, Jake. Months! Why? What did you get out of it?"

He raked his hands through his hair, fisted there. *Her.* She was what he'd gotten out of it. And she was everything.

But he had fucked it up.

"I got you."

"Was it worth it?"

"It was." No truer words had he ever spoken.

"Good, remember it. God, those women were right about you. You haven't changed at all."

But he *had* changed. "I think I love you."

She sized him up from his head to his toes—then dismissed him, breaking his heart. "You don't know what love is, Jake Stone."

Maybe. But he knew what he was feeling, and it was real.

"Apple," he tried again, hoping to break through to her.

She wasn't in the mood to listen. "Enough talking, Jake. I want you to leave. I need to be alone right now."

Though it went against everything he wanted and needed, he didn't argue. Why would he when there was nothing to argue about? She'd made her decision.

With an aching heart, he gathered his things and left.

And wished like hell he could be different.

Chapter Eighteen

THREE WEEKS PASSED, and autumn swept over Glacier Valley. Jasper's Peak became a spectacular sight, all gold and rust and green with pine. The elk appeared to the delight of tourists and locals alike, making their annual pilgrimage down the mountains, rutting and occasionally rioting on their way to their winter grounds in the amber-hued meadows tucked between peaks.

During that time, Apple buried herself in her work—both at the library and with her book—and tried desperately to ignore her wounded heart. It was the hardest thing she'd ever done. Everything reminded her of him. Literally *everything*. Even Mrs. Walton's dog dumping in her yard made her think of how she'd had that fantasy of him being her Mr. Perfect, and it had her feeling sentimental over dog crap.

Dog. Crap.

She was pathetic.

Not even binge eating brownies and knitting Waffles more than a dozen sweaters had cured her or cheered her up. All it had done was succeed in giving her a monster blister on her finger and a little extra plump around the thighs. Although to be fair, Waffles did look adorable in her fuchsia Fair Isle–inspired turtleneck. So her time spent wallowing in depression hadn't been a total waste. Just mostly.

Still, she didn't feel any better. Couldn't. Not even finishing her book had helped.

Yes, she finished her book. Hooray. Wasn't she just ecstatic?

She wished she could be.

She *should* be.

Having a broken heart tended to take the shine off things.

After Jake had made his confessions and she'd asked him to leave, to avoid feeling her feelings for as long as she could, she'd buried her head in her work. It was surprisingly hard and uncomfortable sharing the truth of Fortune's first settlement and its gruesome end—like she was being somehow disloyal to Jake and Verle by highlighting that part of the town's history. Even knowing that she wasn't, and that it truly was for posterity's sake, hadn't made it settle on her shoulders any more comfortably.

So after dreaming of it her whole life, she'd sent her completed manuscript off to her publisher. Her real-life publisher. And it would have been great if she weren't so miserable.

Being without Jake sucked. With a side of blew.

Everything seemed duller. The sky, the trees—her spirit. But how could she ever be with him again when he'd lied and hid things from her—important things like him refusing to have kids? She asked her reflection in the mirror every morning before she went to work, "Can you live a life with no children of your own in it?" And she asked it again every time she walked by Two Moons and refused to look inside in case he was in there. Yet she hadn't come up with an answer. Not yet. It wasn't like him not being willing to have children wasn't a big deal to her. Because it was. It was a *very big deal*.

She'd been born knowing she was meant to be a mother.

Then she had to go and fall in love with the one man who couldn't give her what she needed most. So she'd kept busy. Ridiculously so. She'd written, knitted, hiked—comfort baked like a champ.

She'd done one hell of a good job avoiding Jake.

Until today.

Today was *the* big day where the Bachelors of Fortune were finally going to put on their puppet performance at the library. She hoped—*really* hoped—that it would work, because just yesterday the bag boy at the co-op had given her the up-and-down and said, "Day-um, girl. Stone sure knows how to pick 'em." Which alone was offensive enough. But after she'd grabbed up her bags and was stomping away in irritation, she still managed against her will to hear, "Mmm-hmm, like a juicy peach." And then to her utter outrage, *"Chomp."*

When nineteen-year-old boys had her feeling degraded and dirty, there was a problem. A real problem. A big, fat, stinky pile of a problem.

Furthermore, what made everyone just automatically assume that *he* had picked *her*?

It was time to set the record straight.

After Aidan had confirmed dates with her (she had refused to call Jake, for obvious reasons) she'd gone a little insane trying to get the word out about the Bachelors' play at the library. Apple had media blitzed the event all over town and the cybersphere as much as she possibly could.

Judging by the huge turnout, it had worked too.

Apple smiled at Mrs. Butler, who'd brought her three youngest in to watch. "I'm so glad you could make it," she said with a cheer she didn't feel and wondered if she'd ever feel again. "I know you've been looking forward to it."

The brunette leaned in close, hitching a toddler on her hip. "Kay's coming too. There's no way she'd miss this chance to see the Bachelors in action."

Speaking of the men, Apple scanned the crowd of women, children, and the occasional Mr. Moms looking for them. It had been weeks since she'd seen Jake, and even though she'd done her best to prepare (affirmations, avoidance of reality, lots of chocolate—the usual things), she just never knew how it was really going to go with him.

And that made her stomach drop. "Well, I'm sure it will be memorable for all in attendance. Now, if you'll excuse me, I need to see what's holding the Bachelors up."

Making her way through the rows of chairs, Apple approached the wooden stage, her body so tense over the impending meeting with Jake she could barely walk. She wanted to see him. She didn't want to see him. She wanted to forgive him. She never wanted to speak to him again. The emotional Ping-Pong was killing her.

So she focused on her cousin's gift for the library instead. It still amazed her that Aidan had whipped out this incredible work of art for her to use permanently at the old mill. He'd even stained it a glossy honey color. He had such a good heart; he really deserved someone who would treat him right, someone who would cherish that inherent kindness and generosity of his.

"Jesus, you scared me!" Apple jumped in surprise when Sean's head popped out from behind it, her hand flying to her breast.

The Irishman laughed, his green eyes bright with humor. "Sorry about that, lass. Aidan just texted me that he was running a few minutes behind and he wanted me to double-check some of the screws at the joints to make sure they hadn't come loose."

Ah, well. "Is Jake coming?" Just saying his name made her hurt. *Everywhere*. And here she thought love was supposed to be comforting.

Sean nodded as he tightened a screw. "He's already here."

Apple's head whipped up, and she darted a look around, not seeing him. But her body reacted to the information with a pang of longing so poignant it took her breath away. "Where?" she managed to whisper.

"In the toilet, I think. Don't worry, he'll be out in plenty of time for this."

Just then a small group of women came up and claimed her attention. "Excuse me, can you tell us about the pre-school story-time program we heard you're expanding on? We've got some ideas we'd like to share."

"Of course!" she replied behind a glass smile. "Let me take you to the reading tree, and we can chat." Apple led the way across the room and didn't see Jake come in. In fact, the women had so many questions and kept her so occupied that she didn't see him until it was time to introduce the Bachelors to the large audience.

A very, very large audience.

And it was all thanks to Apple. Well, and the guys. But mostly her. She'd done all the PR grunt work.

Barbara Keeley and her "she's overcompensating with advertising" could kiss her ass. Look at the turnout. It had totally been worth it.

And if she'd buried herself in the work as a coping mechanism against a broken heart, well, that was for her—and *only* her—to know.

Taking a deep breath, Apple walked up the middle row until she stood directly in front of the closed velvet mini-curtain. Jake, Aidan, and Sean were standing together off to the side, and she did her best not to look at him. She didn't even need to, really. She could feel him—his presence, his energy, his rugged masculinity. Just knowing he was there made it hard to breathe.

"Thank you so much for coming out to the library today, everyone," she said brightly, noting all the happy little faces in the crowd. It made her heart squeeze. *Hard.* God, she wanted kids. Innocent and precious, and so full of possibility. She yearned for the adventure of motherhood—of growing and becoming more than she was now. More than anything, Apple wanted her own family. And for a while there, she'd been thinking she wanted to make all those beautiful would-be babies with Jake.

It still hurt knowing he'd kept that from her.

Taking a breath when a pang in her heart caught her off guard, Apple continued, "I am excited to introduce our very special guests. They've put together a unique performance for you that I think you'll enjoy." Her voice broke slightly on the last word, and she pressed her lips together, feeling them tremble. So much for the longer speech she'd memorized. She couldn't do it. The more she talked, the more likely she was to break down. Damn him.

Time for the abridged version. Bringing her hands together, Apple beamed. "Without further ado, let's put our hands together for the Bachelors of Fortune!"

The audience broke into applause, and Apple quickly slipped off to the side, gratefully letting the guys take over. And she finally looked at Jake. She immediately wish she hadn't. He was staring at her, his eyes dark and unfathomable—and her heart flip-flopped against her will. "Why?" she muttered under her breath, having no idea who the question was for—or *what* it was for.

She needed air.

Looking a little desperately over her shoulder toward the corner storeroom with the tiny balcony off the back, where she could take in some fresh air and calm, Apple was about to slink off when Jake's unmistakable voice rang out and silenced the crowd.

"Thank you all for coming out today. We're so honored to be here and to have the opportunity to entertain you all. But before we do, there's an announcement I need to make."

Apple stopped dead in her tracks.

Announcement?

Slowly spinning around in her flats, her pulse racing, she shoved her glasses up her nose absentmindedly and waited with shallow breaths for him to keep speaking.

"Apple, would you come here, please?" Jake's dark gaze bore right into her.

Yes.

No.

Definitely no.

No, wait, yes. Shit. She didn't know. What could he possibly need her for?

With wide eyes she scanned the room and realized everyone was staring at her expectantly. And that was enough to make her feet move, all on their own. Feeling awkward and super uncomfortable under the sudden scrutiny and open curiosity of her fellow townsfolk, Apple was at Jake's side before she knew it. And she didn't want to admit to herself how good it felt to be there, right by his side.

"I'm here," she said under her breath for only him to hear. "What's going on?"

"I'm sorry—" he started quietly, his gaze out on the crowd.

"Is *that* your announcement?" The edge in her voice as she cut him off surprised even her. Wow. Resentment much?

He stared at her, hot and intense. "No."

The honesty in his voice surprised her and had her gaze darting up. She looked him in the eye and instantly began to fall into their dark, unreadable depths. It hurt and it was heaven all at once.

"As you all know," he began to address the crowd, "every year Two Moons Brewery and Pub holds Theme Night. And each year I pick a charity all the proceeds from Theme Night go toward. Last year was the elementary school, and the year before that it went toward helping the revitalization of the Senior Center. Remember how thrilled Pete McGuckin was to have that ramp rebuilt on the south-side entrance? He couldn't get up it fast enough. Remember how in all his excitement he left a wheelie mark with his scooter on his way in to ask Alice Ford to dance?"

The crowd chuckled at the collective memory. Even Apple felt her shoulders tremble with unshed laughter.

"Now, since I recognize most of your faces from this year's fundraiser at the pub, you saw the sign stating that 'computer literacy' was this year's charity of choice. And I've been talking in depth these past few weeks with our lovely town librarian, Ms. Woodman here"—Jake gestured to her and winked when she gave him the crazy eye—"about the library's unfortunate lack of modern equipment, as well as the new computer classes starting next month for all senior members of our community.

And I thought to myself, 'Boy, ol' Pete sure did fancy that ramp. I bet he'd be outright thrilled to learn Microsoft Word on a brand-new computer.' " Jake turned to Aidan and Sean and motioned with his hands, adding, "So, without further ado…" Taking something from them, he straightened and continued in his deep, confident voice, "On behalf of Two Moons Brewery and Pub, I'd like to present Ms. Woodman with the proceeds from Theme Night—all twelve thousand and fifty-nine of them—in the form of this awesome oversize check."

Apple's mouth dropped.

The crowd cheered and hollered like true Fortunites. They might have even whistled some, but Apple was too in shock from what Jake had done to really know. All she could do was gape at him and the enormous check he was holding out to her. So much had just happened, and her brain was saturated. She could barely register what it all meant. In less than five minutes Jake had killed the gossip running around about them. He'd also done another great thing for the town. It was so much to process.

Taking mercy on her, Jake placed the check in her hands and leaned down to whisper in her ear, "All of this is for you."

Blinking hard against the sudden wave of tears, Apple swallowed and nodded, unable to talk.

"Thank you," she finally managed, completely overwhelmed. "I'll just go put this somewhere safe." With that she made her exit, glancing at the gossip queen's surprised expression as she went. And it hit her: Jake had singlehandedly saved her reputation and her job. With this one act, he'd restored her credibility with the town busybodies and everyone else, up to and including her boss. Because of what he'd just done, she didn't need to worry about her job security anymore. Surely he hadn't done it because he cared what they thought of him.

He'd done it because he knew that *she* cared what they thought of her.

Aidan started talking then to the crowd, and she scooted farther away, looking for a nice out-of-the-way nook to cozy up in and watch and process. Before long, a G-rated puppet version of Robin Hood was in full swing, much to the delight of the crowd. Even Apple had to laugh at Jake's high-pitched voice as he played Lady Marianne.

For thirty minutes the Bachelors entertained Fortune's youth. When it was over they received a standing ovation and definitely more than a few whistles. As soon as the show was over, the crowd dispersed and began browsing books. Apple and her assistant became busy answering questions and searching for titles for what felt like hours. In reality it was only about thirty minutes of hectic activity.

She'd just returned from the back room when she saw Jake waiting at the children's help desk, and her heart squeezed. "Apple," he said, his eyes intense and a little sad. "How are you?"

Being in close proximity to him was so freaking hard. She didn't know whether to kiss him or kick him in the shins for being such a thoughtless, selfish jerk and letting her fall in love with him when he knew he was all wrong for her. In the end she decided to do neither. "Thank you for the donation. It's extremely generous and will be put to good use. And I'm well," she managed, feeling like a robot. How weird it was to talk to him now. "Finished my book."

"I'm glad." His voice was barely more than a whisper. "I miss you, Apple."

Tears welled in her eyes instantly, and Apple crossed her arms, blinked them back. "I can't," was all she said. She needed more time to sort things out. Seeing him today was confusing. She wanted him, but how could she ever really fully trust him again? And honestly, she just didn't know if she would be happy in the long run being with him but not ever having babies. Was he even open to adoption?

His dark eyes pleaded with her. "Can we go grab coffee and sit and talk or something?"

As much as she hated it, a big part of her was seriously tempted. But she resisted and repeated, "I can't." Before he could say anything else, Apple picked up her tattered emotions and left him standing there staring after her.

One thing she did know: this heartbreak from Jake was enough to last her a lifetime.

Chapter Nineteen

APPLE NEEDED HER mom.

After closing up the library, she walked the few blocks to Cedar Street and her parents' Craftsman. Her pace was brisk because of the chill that was quickly falling as the sun set low on the horizon. Still, she took the time to ogle the gorgeous display of fall color from the russet-leaved oak trees to the potted mums. It activated the melancholy inside her, sent it on a slow, meandering roll through her spirit. Most of her life she'd envisioned raising her own family here.

But maybe it wasn't meant to be.

Pulling her cardigan closed around her as a gust of wind kicked up a few fallen leaves and sent a chill up her skirt, Apple glanced up at the darkening sky, noting the gathering clouds. It somehow seemed fitting with her mood.

Reaching her childhood home, she didn't even bother knocking, she just burst in and declared, "I need advice, Mom!"

Sedona looked up with a startled expression from the overstuffed couch where she'd been reading. Sitting up, she swung her bare feet to the floor, all instant concern. "What's wrong, honey?"

"Jake." That's all she said. And by the instant sympathetic look in her mom's eyes, it was all she'd needed to say.

Patting the green chenille cushion next to her, Sedona let out a sound of sympathy. "Oh, darling, he got to you, didn't he?"

Apple flopped down and laid her head against the back of the couch, closing her eyes. "*So bad.*" Tears stung the backs of her eyes. "You've been in Berlin at your shows, so I didn't call to talk about it. I didn't want you to worry."

"The complicated ones usually do." Her mom sighed, a little wistfully. "And you know you can call me anytime, honey. I was never too busy for you."

"I know, Mom, thanks." Apple popped one eye open, intrigued despite her heartache. "Wait a minute, who in the world are you talking about?"

"Your dad, of course." Sedona arched a blonde brow at her, like that was the most obvious question in the world.

"That's funny." Apple laughed. Just flat laughed at that.

"What's so humorous about it?"

Apple gave her mom a look. "Come on, Dad? He's Mr. Mellow."

"Oh, honey, no." This time Sedona laughed, her long blonde hair billowing down her back.

"Nuh-uh." Apple raised her head, disbelieving. No way was her dad anything *close* to being like Jake. It was hilarious that her mother would even compare the two. Marty Woodman had more patience in his pinkie than Jake did in his entire body.

"Yes-huh," her mom retorted. "Your father was not the man he is today. It has taken time, patience, and acceptance to get him where he is. When we first met, Apple, he wanted to work on Wall Street. *Wall Street*, honey."

For a person like Sedona, that was one of the gravest of offenses.

"So what did you see in him, then? Why did you give him the time of day?"

"I saw beneath the surface, Apple. I looked where most people didn't. They saw a hotshot Harvard-educated financier. But I took the time to see the poet beneath the gloss."

"Why?" Apple brushed a stray hair back and looked at her mom. "Why did you take the time if who he was wasn't what you wanted?"

Sedona raised a brow, clearly surprised. "Who was I to know what I really wanted, much less needed?" She shook her head and reached for a plate on the coffee table. "Brownie?" she said before taking one for herself.

"*Yes.*" Apple grabbed two.

Talking around a bite, Sedona continued, settling back into her comfy spot on the couch. "Life has a way of bringing the people we need most into our lives, but they don't always look like we want or imagine them to. When I met your dad, I was an art student at Berkeley and he had just taken a job in the stock market. He worked for everything I stood against."

Apple took a bite and almost groaned in pleasure. God, she loved chocolate. "But you dated him anyway."

"I did. He was so persistent that I finally caved."

Apple took another huge bite, already eyeing the plate for a third. "And you're happy."

"I am, yes. But back then I had a whole different life planned for myself. One I thought was the *only* path for me to find happiness. I wanted to live in Paris with my artist husband. He was supposed to be sweet and deep and profound. He was *not* supposed to be an ambitious stockbroker. And I was so narrowly focused on that idealized life that I almost missed the greatest gift."

Apple sighed, resisting the chocolate temptation and already regretting it. "This is different, Mom. Jake won't have children, and he didn't tell me about it until I'd already fallen for him. I feel duped."

Her mom's hand covered hers and squeezed reassuringly. "Yeah, love's a bitch that way."

Apple's gaze whipped to her mom's. "Excuse me?"

"I wanted to marry a liberal. That didn't happen. Life's not fair. So what?" She shrugged.

"But—" Apple broke off. "Damn it, give me another brownie." She grabbed the last one off the plate rather defiantly. Screw the extra five pounds. It was worth it. "He's made a lot of mistakes, Mom. Like, *a lot*."

"Your dad voted for Reagan." Sedona held up two fingers and gave her a pointed look. "*Twice.*"

Apple flinched and felt a grin start to form. See, this was why her mom gave the best advice. She made her think—and she also made her laugh when she didn't think it was possible. "And yet he survived for you to tell the tale."

"*Hmph,*" Sedona just said. "Don't get me started."

"I'm not sure I can trust him," she blurted out, staring down at her brownie, needing to finally get that fear out in the open. "He knew how much it meant to me to have a family of my own and to write my book, and he was dishonest with me about both."

"Stop for a second. Why won't he have kids?"

Apple sighed, still sad for him about it. "It's awful, Mom. His family has this horrible genetic disease that causes brain tumors in the men and makes them go insane. It's what's really wrong with Verle—"

"Ah, that makes sense."

"I know, right? Poor Verle! It must be so terrible to live with. Anyway, Jake finally confessed to me that it's what happened to the first settlers, and it's the stuff horror movies are made of. Seriously. His great-great-great-whatever ancestor Jesse Stone had the familial glioma disease. He went crazy one night and killed almost everyone—including his *wife,* can you believe it?—before he turned the gun around and shot himself. It's terrible, awful stuff, really."

Sedona nodded. "Sounds like. Eesh. Poor guys."

Apple agreed. "Yeah. So anyway, when Jake turned twenty-one he got a vasectomy done so he wouldn't pass the genes on by accident."

"And that's why he can't have kids? Does he have the gene?"

"Yes, and he doesn't know. There was no test for it when he had the vasectomy done."

"Let me get this straight," Sedona said, her blue eyes thoughtful. "Jake's family has a hereditary disease that does tragic things to those with it, and so Jake took measures to make sure no one else would suffer from it—at least not through him. Is that correct?"

"I suppose so," Apple hedged, not sure where her mom was going with things.

"So you're upset at him for being a responsible young man?"

"No, I'm mad at him for not telling me from the beginning. About any of it. I wouldn't have gotten involved with him and had my feelings crushed if he'd have come clean about it all."

"Not true." Sedona patted her knee and stood. "You're you, Apple. You still would have jumped in with your arms wide open. You wouldn't have turned from the chance at love. The real question is what you want from here: an imperfect life with Jake or an imperfect one with someone else. Because, honey, there's just no such thing as 'a perfect life.' Just imperfect people who are perfectly meant for each other. It's up to you to decide if he's that one for you."

She pictured Jake. And the minute she did, her heart began hurting again. "I don't know, Mom. I would need him to change a lot of things, and people just don't change that much."

"No, that's true. But they can love enough to grow."

Apple sighed. "He said he loved me, but it can't be true."

Sedona leaned her elbows on the back of the couch. "Why not?"

"Because that's not how love goes!" Apple burst out.

"So how does it go, then?" Her mother gave her a skeptical look.

Suddenly filled with confusion and uncertainty, Apple pushed off the couch and began to pace. "Not like this. God, he's not who I imagined I'd fall in love with, Mom. For chrissake, it's *Jake*."

Sedona leaned across the couch toward her then, her expression uncharacteristically serious, and pegged Apple with a stare. "Let me tell you something about love, Apple. And it's a big, important bit of life wisdom I'm about to impart, so listen. Love is many things, but perfect isn't one of them. It's flawed as hell. Still, if you're lucky enough to find it, honey, it's a real blessing. So don't be so hasty as to toss it aside, even if it is *Jake*."

"But it's not how I pictured it would be. He's not who I pictured. He's certainly no white knight."

She just raised a brow again. "So what? They're for little girls anyway. Apple, I've seen Jake with his dad. You think that boy doesn't know a thing or two about love and loyalty? Look at what he's dealt with day in and day out for his entire life. And never once has that boy uttered a bad word about his father, even when there had been good cause for it a time or two. Just the opposite, actually. I've seen him stand by and support that man when everyone else had turned their backs."

In midstride, Apple stopped and slowly turned toward her mom. "Oh. My. God." Sedona was right. It had been in front of her all along. The way that Jake loved and accepted Verle clearly showed that he knew a whole damn lot about love and commitment. He had staying power—the unwavering kind that was rare and precious. And anyone who could love that fully deserved to be forgiven. To be given a second chance. Filled suddenly with a ton of energy, she rushed forward and hugged her mom. "I have to go."

She was out the door before her mom could even finish saying good-bye. She was on her way to Jake. God, she'd made a mistake turning him down at the library today.

The sky opened up and starting pouring.

Apple refused to take that as an omen.

Please, don't let it be too late.

JAKE FROWNED AS he lit another candle. The storm had finally broken loose, and he'd lost power about half an hour ago. Which suited him just fine. Sitting in the dark while rain pounded the windows outside sounded right up his alley. With Apple gone, everything felt wrong. No, it didn't just feel wrong—it felt empty. Like a black hole devoid of any light or warmth of any kind, whatsoever.

Apple brought the sun into his life.

It had been too long since he'd seen her smile. Far too long since he'd heard her laugh. And way, way too long since he'd held her in his arms. God, he wanted that in the worst way—just to hold Apple again. The need overrode everything else in his life. All his fears, all his misgivings and beliefs. They melted like snow in spring when he thought of having her in his life again—for the rest of his life. Being his partner, his lover, his friend. Challenging him and helping him grow.

And one day being the mother of his children.

It had taken a lot of painfully honest soul-searching, but he'd come to realize that he wanted that. More than he'd ever wanted anything. He wanted a family with Apple no matter what health risk there might be. He'd finally realized over the past few weeks that if he were blessed enough to make a child with her, then he'd love it no matter what. No matter *what*. He'd just love it with everything he had inside him, because it was theirs.

A car door suddenly slammed outside, and Dregs barked. Jake's head whipped up, and his eyes narrowed on the front door. He wasn't expecting anyone. Who the hell was showing up at his place now? It was storming like shit out.

Jake placed a reassuring hand on the old bulldog's head. "It's okay, boy," he said and began crossing the open living room, tension settling between his shoulders. After Sean's run-in last year with the mob unexpected visitors made him wary. "Who's there?" he hollered.

He had just stepped in front of the huge woodstove when the front door swung open. A gust of wind and rain and Apple came blowing in.

"I'm so sorry!" she hollered over the storm, pushing the door closed with her shoulder and floundering with it for several seconds. Once it was finally shut, she brushed her hands down her soaked and clinging dress and gave him a shy smile. Her bun was drenched and sagging steeply off to the side. "Hi."

His gut clenched like a vise at the way her wet dress clung to her curvy, beautiful body in the candlelight, even as his heart throbbed painfully. Christ, he'd missed her. Just plain missed the sight of her. Thunder boomed and lightning struck, flashing blinding white through the windows behind her.

"What are you doing here, Apple?" he managed, his throat starting to tighten with emotion. All it took was one look at her sweet face, and his chest squeezed so hard he thought it might break him in half. He would do anything to have her back. Anything in the world.

It had stung that he'd tried to reach out to her today at the library and she'd slapped him down, but now he didn't care. Not even remotely. Just the fact that she was there in his living room had him happy enough to weep.

Kicking off her flats, Apple pushed her glasses back up her nose and took a step toward him. "I came to ask you my three free questions."

Jake frowned, not understanding, his pulse thickening at her nearness. God, the woman undid him. "But I thought you finished your book and turned it in."

She nodded and took another step closer, her navy blue dress clinging to her every luscious curve. "I did. But we had an agreement, remember? The one for three nudity-free questions? I've been doing a lot of thinking, and there're some things we need to air out between us. So I'm here to ask my questions."

"I thought you were done with me." It hurt to even say the words. It had been killing him, accepting a life without her.

Thunder exploded then, lightning coming almost instantly on top of it. Dregs barked and came running as fast as he could on his stubby bowlegs, cowering beneath Jake. But he barely noticed because Apple was taking another step toward him, and the play of candlelight on her skin was mesmerizing.

Exquisite Apple.

"I'm not done." She smiled shyly.

Thank you, God.

Breath exploded in his chest, and he sucked in air. Maybe he still had a chance.

"Ask me a question," he said firmly. Definitively. Anything she wanted to know he wanted to tell her. No secrets. "I won't lie. I'll never lie or hide anything from you again. I promise."

She chewed her bottom lip and eyed him, like she was considering the authenticity of his words. He crossed his arms to keep them from reaching for her. "Whatever it takes, I'll make things up to you, Apple. Just give me a chance."

"Not quite yet," she said, smiling more fully now. "This first one's a biggie." Inhaling deep, she looked at him through her lashes and asked, "Do you still love me?"

Jake went very still. Then his heart thumped hard. Once. Twice. It began to pound hard in his chest. There was no lying. Only truth.

"I do."

"You do?" she replied, her hands moving slowly up her body and over her hips, distracting him, making him yearn.

He nodded and swallowed hard. That stupid lump was back and bigger than ever. "I do."

"Say it, Jake." Her hands smoothed up her waist, around to the front row of buttons, and she began to play with them. "Talk dirty to me."

His gaze zeroed in on her fingers between her breasts. "Are you doing what I think you're doing?"

"Do you think I'm about to take off my clothes?"

"Yes." He nearly groaned, his hands clenching hard. She was killing him.

"Then say it," she urged, her nimble fingers undoing a button.

"I love you, Apple." The words fell from his lips, naturally and easily, like they'd just been waiting there his whole life to be said.

And he knew they had. Always, just for Apple.

"I'm so sorry for keeping my vasectomy and family's history from you," he added, wanting it all out there and behind them.

"I know, and I forgive you." She popped another button. "Just don't ever do it again."

"Never," he promised. And meant it. He absolutely meant it.

Her smile became brilliant, and she took another step toward him, dropping her dress. She was almost within arm's reach now—every inch of her gorgeous, luscious skin. "How much do you love me?"

He didn't even have to think about it because he already knew, although it was going to hurt like hell. But he didn't give two shits about the pain. "Enough to get my vasectomy reversed, Apple."

Her eyes went huge. "You must love me a lot."

She dropped her bra.

He growled, and lust pooled heavy in his groin at the vision of her. Love and desire mixed a heady concoction inside him. Christ, he loved her. Always had.

And that was the damn truth. But there were some things they had to get straight before he scooped her up in his arms and took her to bed to give her a personal demonstration of his love and devotion. "I'm not a perfect guy, Apple."

"I don't want perfect. I want to be loved."

He nodded, reaching for her and pulling her into his arms. "I can do that, better than anyone else."

"And I still want babies, Jake. I know the reversal will hurt, but I want them."

"I can do that too." He kissed the top of her head, relief and gratitude and appreciation for the woman in his arms flooding him. What had he done to get so lucky?

She cozied up to him, and he didn't give a flying shit that she was cold and clammy from the rain. She was in his arms. And she was his. "I get one more question," she said against his chest. "But this one's for me. Ask me if I know what love is."

Jake felt himself melting inside at the warm, sweet look of love in her beautiful eyes. The very look he'd dreamed of but never actually hoped to see. He'd always thought of her beyond him. But she wasn't. She was right there in his arms, right within reach. And he wasn't letting her go.

He lowered his forehead to hers. "What's love?" he whispered.

She slid her arms around his neck and held close. "It's acceptance. That's what love is, Jake. It's acceptance. And there's no one who understands that more than you. The way you just accept your dad for the way he is amazes me. Humbles me. You have more loyalty in your pinky finger than most people have in their entire bodies."

"But what about my family medical condition?"

Apple shushed him with a finger. "I don't care about that. All I care about is being with you, for as long as we can have."

Jake smiled as his heart filled with joy and love for this woman. "Then you're in luck, because that's what I want too. Every day for the rest of my life, honey. I want you driving me crazy."

Apple smirked. "Oh, I can do *that*."

"Nuh-uh." Jake slid his hands around her hips, cupping them and pulling her close. His breath fluttered across her curls, and she went beautifully, achingly soft against him. "I have a better idea."

Her head dropped back, and she sighed breathlessly. He was so in love, so filled with lust, and so incredibly, amazingly happy at life's unexpected gifts. It was a beautiful thing.

Apple laughed joyously and leaned into him, eager to experience his one-of-a-kind magic—for the rest of *their* life. Together.

"Oh yes," she whispered. "That can definitely work too."

Epilogue

APPLE SIPPED AT her lemon and honey tea and flipped through the old Bible Jake had given her months ago. It was the end of October, just days before Halloween. Verle had died almost three weeks back from a second heart attack placing too much stress on his heart, and they all felt the grief and sadness. Jake the most. After the funeral, he'd spent a lot of time going through the books in the old miner's shack. She figured it was how he needed to grieve.

But today, the two of them were enjoying a lazy morning fueled by the season's first snow. Jake was in the living room going through some old photos.

"What is this symbol?" she called out to Jake, referring to the crossed axes in the top corner of the old scripture. "I swear I've seen it before. I just can't place it."

Going back to puzzling, she absently heard Jake's cell phone go off and him answer. She stared at the symbol and continued to ponder it while his voice sounded in the background. The nugget and crossed pickaxes looked so familiar. She just couldn't figure out from where.

Jake appeared in the doorway then, a funny look on his face. "That was the doctor's office."

Apple tensed. Last week he'd gone in for the genetic test that had *finally* been approved by the Food and Drug Administration and made available to the public. It had the ability to code for the mutated gene linked to his family's disease. "What did they say?" She couldn't tell if the news was good or bad by the expression on his face.

A smile started slowly across his lips then, spreading until it was in full bloom. "We're in luck, juicy fruit. I don't have the gene. Somehow, some way that I don't understand, it's not in me." He looked at her, his eyes huge. "Holy fuck, Apple, I don't have it. I'm clean."

Relief flooded Apple, and she squealed, leaping out of her seat, knocking over her tea as she went. "I'm so glad for you!" she said and kissed him. Then she pulled back. "Wait, I don't have the gene, and now you don't have the gene either…" Joy flooded her when it sunk in. "Oh my gosh, we get to make babies!"

Jake wiggled his eyebrows in jest, but Apple could see the emotions beneath the amusement in his eyes. It must be life altering, knowing he was free. "We can start now if you'd like," he offered with a naughty grin. "I could use the practice."

Apple swatted his arm playfully and pulled away. Glancing down at her spilled tea, she let out a cry and pushed away from Jake. In her excitement she'd drenched the open Bible.

Wait a minute. Apple snatched it up as tea dripped from the last page. She stared at words that hadn't been there a few seconds ago. Words that her tea had brought to the surface like exposed secret ink. They were written in a flourishing scrawl. Jesse Stone's scrawl, to be exact. They said: *Below the miner's shack.—Jesse*

Excitement bubbled under her skin. "Do you see that?"

Jake was looking over her shoulder. "I do, yeah. Do you think he was referring to my miner's shack?"

She was already nodding. "Harvey's shack, yes. Yes, I do." She was about to pick up the book and had already bent over when she had a vision. And in it was a black-and-white photo of a young Harvey Stone. The same photo from the Mother Lode. The one with all of the prospectors standing together in front of that post. The post that had the same pickax symbol etched into it. "Holy shit." She breathed heavily, her eyes huge when she looked up at Jake. "I know what the symbol is."

"What is it?" Deep brown eyes looked into hers, excitement sparking in their depths.

"It means 'the mother lode.' Jake, I've seen the design at the coffee shop. It was in a picture that also had your grandfather in it. The photo was taken during that brief strike in the fifties. I bet your ancestor passed the symbol down the family tree."

She could see how it would have worked. "I think we should to go to Harvey's shack."

Jake was already heading for the door.

Twenty minutes later they were standing in the middle of the old miner's shack. A turn around the outside had yielded no door or hole to below ground, so they'd come inside to inspect. If there had been a gold strike below the shack, there'd be access to it somewhere.

She saw Jake look down at the wood floor. "Look to see if there's a door on the ground or something."

Apple was already on it. She'd spotted the only rug in the room under the kitchen table and was in the process of moving it so that she could roll the wool rug back and see if there was anything underneath. "I think I might have something."

Jake came over and helped her finish with the table, then grabbed the edge of the frayed Oriental rug. "Here goes," he said. With a flick of his wrist he pulled it back.

And revealed a trapdoor in the floor.

"Nice!" Apple laughed, excited by the adventure.

Jake grinned like the devil.

Then he pulled the door up by its leather strap and slid on a headlamp that he'd shoved in his back pocket earlier. He looked into the dark hole. "I'm going down."

Nervous, but not willing to be left out, Apple ran out to his truck and quickly grabbed the extra headlamp he kept there and followed him down the hole. Jake's hands guided her down from below, and when she landed on solid footing she saw that they were in an old mineshaft.

"Should we be doing this?" she said, suddenly unsure. But she couldn't turn back when Jake grabbed her hand and tugged her along. Focusing her lamp on the ground to keep from tripping, she gasped when she noticed that there were footprints in the dust. "Jake, people have been here."

"Pretty recently too, Apple. Look, that tread is clearly a running shoe."

Weird. A little creepy.

And *way* exhilarating.

They'd followed the footprints for only about twenty feet when they rounded a bend and stopped in total shock.

"Holy shit," Jake said.

There before them was a wall of shimmering gold.

"The mother lode!" Apple exclaimed. "I knew it! That *is* what the symbol was! Your ancestors found the mother lode!"

Jake picked up a small modern pickax lying on the dirt floor by his feet. "They weren't the only ones." Then he looked at a folding chair leaned up against the wall of gold, a look of surprise on his face. "I think this is what my dad was talking about, Apple. This is what he kept freaking out over when I talked to him about sharing the story with you. He thought you knew about all of this and were coming to take it from him." He shook his head. "I'll be damned. Him and Harvey, this whole time."

"Maybe they weren't so crazy after all." His eyes went dark with emotion.

Apple hugged him tight. "Let's do something with it that would have made them happy."

Jake kissed the top of her head and seemed to perk up. "Yeah?"

She nodded. "Absolutely."

He wrapped her in his arms. "I love you, juicy fruit."

God, she was never going to get tired of hearing those words. Not from him. Because it turned out that Jake was her knight after all—in all his beautifully tarnished armor. And every day with him was a gift, an adventure of epic proportions. One for the record books.

And that was *way* better than any fantasy.

Keep reading for an excerpt from

GETTING LUCKY

The first book in Jennifer Season's Fortune,
Colorado series!

Born into the infamous Charlemagne equestrian empire,
Shannon has been raised to do whatever it takes for the
family business. Even if it means going undercover and
digging up dirt on a competitor. It's easy enough when
she believes he's a bad guy whose success seems too good
to be true. In fact, Shannon's excited to put the aggra-
vatingly sexy Irishman in his place and get back in her
father's good graces. All she needs is to stay focused on
the goal...and out of Sean Muldoon's arms.

From stealing a thoroughbred racehorse from the Irish
mob to striking gold in the mountains of Colorado, there's
little Sean hasn't experienced. But when it comes to resisting his hot new stable manager, Sean's out of luck. With
the Irish mob hot on his heels, keeping Shannon off their
radar is all but impossible, and he's not about to put her
in danger too. Sean wants Shannon, but how can he offer
her a future...when he can't even guarantee tomorrow?

Available now from Avon Impulse!

Keep reading for an excerpt from

GETTING LUCKY

The first book in Jennifer Seasons's Fortune,
Colorado series

Bonafide the infamous Charlemagne-squad day, born the
charmed life, been raised to do whatever it takes for the
family business. Even if it meant going undercover and
dressing up dirt on a competitor. It's easy enough when
she believed she'd had guy who'd sworn was seems too good
to be true. In fact, Shannon's excited to put the aging
vultures were frantic to the place and get back in her
father's good graces. All she needs is to stay focused—if
the rest . . . and out of sean Muldoon's arms.

From stealing a thoroughbred racehorse from the Irish
mob to writing a bride industry of Colorado, there's
little Sean has ever experienced. But when it comes to resisting his hot new bunk manager, Sean's out of luck. With
the Irish mob hot on his heels keeping Shannon off their
radar is all but impossible, and he's not about to put her
in danger too. Sean wants Shannon, but how can he offer
her a future . . . when he can't even guarantee tomorrow?

Chapter One

"BE PREPARED TO use the ladies." Her sister pointed at her chest.

Shannon Charlemagne released a groan and bit her tongue, her patience already on the verge of deserting her. Her sister's rather unhelpful suggestion about her breasts at this particular moment had that patience packing its bags and furiously scribbling a Dear John letter on a sticky note.

The crap her family put her through.

Pushing away from the hood of the rental car she'd been sitting on, Shannon glanced at the entrance to a horse ranch in the mountains outside Fortune, Colorado, and sighed heavily. Where would she be without her patience? It was her armor, her protection. Losing it would be worse than being thrown to a bunch of wild jackals with bacon-wrapped sausages strung around her head like a Christmas wreath. And with the insanity she was about to fling herself into, she needed it more than ever. Not for the first time, she wondered how she'd been roped into such a stupid situation.

Oh, that's right, because she could never really put her foot down and say no when it mattered.

If she had a dime for every time her family obligated her to something against her will, she'd be richer than Oprah and living it up on Martinique with a French cabana boy named Pierre.

Sometimes she really wished she were part of a nice, average, *normal* family. One where there weren't so many expectations to live up to the legacy that was her family birthright. So much pressure to conform. She was a Charlemagne—the oldest and most prestigious family in all of American horseracing. The most renowned and well-respected family in the industry.

Yeah, it was like that. She was one of *those* Charlemagnes.

Which ultimately meant that, as much as she balked (which wasn't as much as she'd prefer, granted), deep down she was a good girl who was loyal to a fault and never went against her father. No matter how overbearing and authoritative he might be. She understood her duties and responsibilities to the Charlemagne name.

Didn't mean she had to like it, though.

Sighing again, Shannon pushed back a clump of her light auburn hair that had fallen loose from the braid she'd hastily made that morning and resigned herself to her ill-conceived fate. Her father had asked her to do this. Good idea or bad, it didn't matter. He'd said it was important for the family—crucial even.

And that's why, even though she disagreed with pretty much every aspect of his request, she was currently standing on a gravel road in the Colorado mountains about to do something not entirely on the up-and-up. She and her sister were squinting against the brilliant afternoon sun as they gave the plan one last run-through before she set off alone into the great unknown.

Still, there *were* limits to what she was willing to do, family or not.

"Why does everything always have to be about sex with you?" Shannon asked. She pointed a finger at her breasts, giving her sister a slight frown. "You know these ladies only come out for very special occasions. They're highly selective. And this, shall we say, *undercover* job I'm about to partake in, certainly doesn't qualify."

"Does too," Colleen scoffed. "Your boobs come out far too infrequently, if you ask my opinion," her sister added, somehow managing simultaneously to sound both affronted and amused. Colleen didn't usually wait for anyone to ask her thoughts. She just spoke her mind. Whether or not her opinion was wanted was, often, a toss-up.

"And why would I do that?"

"Because I'm practically a doctor? As an upcoming graduate of Harvard Medical School, it's my almost-professional opinion that you don't have nearly enough sex."

Shannon laughed outright at that. There her little sister went saying crazy things again. "Thank you so much for caring about my love life and well-being, but I think I'll be fine."

Humor shimmered in her sister's hazel eyes as she tipped her head toward the huge Pine Creek Ranch sign that hung suspended from wooden beams arching over the entrance. Her blonde hair brushed across her freckled cheeks as she said, "I wouldn't be so hasty in keeping those girls on the shelf if I were you…I saw Sean Muldoon in person."

"When?"

"During the races in Kentucky this past May with his Triple Crown winner, Something Unexpected. This guy that Dad is sending you to spy on is full-on Irish—with the accent to prove it—and downright sexy. He's like an Irish Dove bar—you know just by looking at him that he's dark, smooth, and addictive. He moves with this loose, long-limbed gate and has an easy smile, but there's something almost dangerous about him just bubbling under the surface. It's seriously potent." Colleen fanned herself and grinned. "It's too bad I'm such a blabbermouth, because I'd dig up the goods on him, all right."

Shannon remained silent and waited for it. It had to be coming.

"Of course, I'd see if Muldoon was as fast to the finish line as his racehorses are while I was at it, if you know what I mean." Her sister finished with an overly dramatic eyebrow wiggle and wink.

And there it was. Right on schedule. That's one of the things she loved most about her only sibling—she was reliable. If there was ever an opening for a crude comment to be slipped in, you could bet she was all over it.

That's what she said, Shannon thought.

Crap! Damn it, now Colleen had her doing it too. Figured.

"Let's go through this one last time," Shannon said briskly. "I'm supposed to find this Sean Muldoon and tell him I'm responding to his ad for the stable manager position and convince him to hire me." She stared down the long gravel lane beyond the ranch's entrance as it lazily rounded a bend and disappeared into a sea of aspen, spruce, and pine in the distance.

Into Sean Muldoon's ranch.

She'd learned from her father that Pine Creek sat on about one hundred acres, though it was hard to tell at the moment from the thick grove of trees that flanked each side of the single-lane road. It looked more like the entrance to a state forest, not a sprawling horse ranch.

But, as Shannon knew better than most, looks were most often deceiving. Nervously swiping her hands down the thighs of her worn denim jeans, she continued reviewing the plan that their father had designed, hoping that repeating everything would help her focus.

Colleen opened her mouth and started to say, "That's why you should—"

Shannon held her hand up like a crossing guard. "I know, use the ladies. I get it." She probably could if she wanted to, honestly. They weren't bad. A quick glance downward confirmed that claim. Not bad at all. A little on the small side, but so what? What she lacked up top she made up for on the bottom with an ample and curvy derriere.

Depending on the day, that was either a blessing or a curse.

However, given that she was a professional equestrian and spent half her life bouncing around on a horse (with skill and grace, of course), having the extra padding was more often a bonus than not. Her butt was like a car's suspension system—it absorbed the shock and made the impact of jumping her horse feel like the smooth ride of a Rolls Royce. Not that she was going to upstage big-butted celebrities or anything, but it wouldn't be a runaway victory if they *did* compare backsides. Only she had earned hers the cheap and easy way: genetic inheritance.

Colleen cleared her throat. "Dad's gut is saying that either Muldoon or one of his trainers is doping the Thoroughbreds with steroids before the races." Her sister's eyes flickered and unfocused briefly, like she was recalling a memory. "I've seen them run. They've got rockets for hooves, Shan."

No wonder all of the company's clients had bailed on their breeding program over the past few years. Shannon knew they were down to a teeny-tiny trickle, and if she didn't find a way to reverse that fast, then they were going to go bankrupt and lose the farm. And it was the only thing of material value they had left. Over the years her father had sold off everything else. All the jewels, cars— everything. It hadn't escaped her notice that the walls of her childhood home were now mostly bare, when priceless Monet originals and the like had once hung there.

Not for the first time, she wondered what had happened to all the family's money. Where were all their millions disappearing to? It didn't make sense. Not in the least. But pondering that made Shannon's stomach go tight and queasy, so she stopped. With effort she grappled with her thoughts and redirected them to the immediate problem at hand.

Shannon glanced at a stand of early June aspens swaying in the gentle breeze and smiled softly. The leaves were such a tender shade of green against the white of the bark; there wasn't anything like them back home in Saratoga Springs, New York, which was too bad because they were beautiful. The leaves danced on the wind like gypsies around a campfire.

"It's beautiful here." She couldn't help admitting it. Even the sunshine on her face felt amazing. "It's such a gorgeous day, isn't it? If this guy doesn't hire me, I'll hike back down to the entrance here and meet you. I'll text you once I know if I got the job."

Colleen shifted and crossed her arms, her voice oddly neutral when she replied, "Of course. I was planning to wait."

Shannon narrowed her eyes, suddenly suspicious of her sister's tone. "Did Dad tell you to leave me here anyway?" It would be so like him to force his will on her even from two thousand miles away. No way did she want to be stranded out in the wilds of the Colorado Rockies with no transportation. It was something like seven miles back into town. Not exactly a leisurely afternoon stroll in the park.

"I'm sorry, Shan, but I have to. You know how Dad is. In his mind, you'll work harder to secure the job if you don't have any backup waiting for you. He called it 'added incentive.' " Sympathy and understanding shone in her eyes. They both knew all too well what that meant. "I wish I could stay here to make sure it all goes well, but I can't. My orders are to head straight back to the hotel and call Dad to receive instructions. Before you ask, I have no idea what he has planned for me."

Instinctively Shannon's back went up. Callum Charlemagne was so very fond of his orders. How else best to rule the kingdom, right?

Feeling that old tension settle between her shoulder blades, Shannon began to pace. Some things just never changed, no matter how old she was. His penchant for bullying made her as angry today as it had when she was a teenager.

Colleen placed a hand on her arm, gently stopping her midstride. "He loves us, Shannon. In his way, the best he can. And he legitimately needs your help." Her fingers gripped tightly for a brief moment and then released, her expression suddenly pensive. "This time we all do."

That simple truth took the fire out of Shannon. They all needed her to step up. Her family was the majority shareholder in the company, but for how much longer, no one knew. They'd had to borrow against the stock, and there was no money to repay the loan since they had so few clients generating cash flow.

No income, no majority control of the company—no farm.

Why? Because her *family* farm was owned by the company. And without the security of owning 51 percent of the stock, they could be booted off the place without a moment's notice. In every way, they and the business—their very *future*—would be at the whim of the company.

It still grated, knowing that truth. Not only had the business been in the Charlemagne line for generations, the farm was home. It held all their best memories—like how every Christmas her mother made homemade cinnamon rolls with cream cheese frosting for breakfast and everyone sat in front of the fireplace with their newly opened gifts and chowed down. They all got to eat with their fingers. It was *heaven*.

And in all actuality, it was the one time of year that her parents really and truly relaxed. They laughed and smiled, and seemed to leave the bad stuff behind—or at least alone. The rest of the year the stress of simply being a Charlemagne and managing everything that entailed wore them down. Christmas was their time to breathe.

It had been tough growing up with parents who were too busy maintaining the family name to spend any quality time with their children, but she'd had Colleen. As much as her sister made her sometimes want to wash her mouth out with soap and sit her down with a wholesome Hallmark made-for-TV movie to cleanse her corrupted brain, she was thankful every single day for her.

It helped telling herself that dissecting cadavers during medical school had warped her lovely sister's mind, so having it permanently in the gutter wasn't her fault.

She was joking.

Mostly.

Taking a big breath to help soothe her quivering stomach, she gave her sister's hand a quick squeeze. "You're right. I know you are. I just get so frustrated with him sometimes, you know?"

Colleen pulled her in for a swift all-business hug, the time for emotion clearly behind them. "I know. But hey, think of this adventure as fodder you can use later to write that Great American Novel you've always dreamed about."

A snort escaped Shannon. "Clearly you're delusional if you think I want to write a novel, much less have the capability," she couldn't help teasing.

Colleen rolled her eyes and gave Shannon's arm a playful shove. "See what I get for being sympathetic? Sarcasm. I get sarcasm and derision from my only and most beloved sibling." Her expression remained serious for a moment, but Shannon knew it was about to crack. Seconds later a grin split her deceptively wholesome face and she laughed. "Thank God I'm rarely sympathetic, or else that might hurt."

Shannon laughed at that. Sensitivity wasn't the youngest Charlemagne's strong suit. Not by a long shot. It was one of the things that made her so incredibly strong. And it was one of the main reasons she was at the top of her class at Harvard. She was the most goal-oriented person Shannon had ever known. Colleen didn't let pesky things like emotions get in the way of her achieving her dreams.

If only she could say the same for herself.

At that moment a very large semitruck rounded the bend in the highway behind them and lumbered past, its trailer swaying from the constant turns along the tight mountain roads. When the flannel-clad driver spotted the two of them on the side of the road, he blared his horn and made a highly inappropriate hand gesture out the window toward them. It seemed that she and her sister were being invited to take a little lap nap with him.

"In your dreams, jerk!" Colleen yelled to the retreating semitruck, making a hand gesture of her own, and then gave Shannon an incredulous look. "Can you believe that guy?" Shannon shrugged and started to talk, but Colleen cut her off by exclaiming, "Like I'd ever do that with a guy who wore *flannel*!"

Her sister sounded so offended that Shannon couldn't stop the burst of laughter that let loose. "Heaven forbid!"

Colleen leveled her with a stare and said flatly, "It was plaid, Shannon. *Plaid.*"

Trying to wrangle her laughter but finding the effort futile, she gave into the giggle fit and braced herself against the rental car for support. It occurred to her the laughter might be misplaced nerves and that she was really just an anxiety-ridden mess over the duplicitous mission she was about embark upon.

But then again, maybe not. The look of horror on her sister's face at the thought of sleeping with a guy who wore plaid flannel was outright hilarious. And priceless. Turns out, there actually *was* one thing in this world that could make the unflappable Colleen Charlemagne flappable.

"What about this Sean Muldoon?" Shannon asked her sister after the giggles had subsided and she could speak again. "You said he's pretty hot. Would you do him if he wore plaid flannel?"

Colleen appeared to contemplate the question, but only made a little hum in her throat. "Dad's waiting, Shan. Why don't you get this show on the road and find out for yourself?"

Sighing at the twinge of guilt that told her she was indeed procrastinating and they both knew it, Shannon took one more calming breath and then grabbed her small duffle bag from the backseat. Everything she needed was in there. Much as she didn't like the truth, it was time to do this thing.

Suddenly swamped with anxiety, she spun to her sister. "I can do this, right?"

Receiving a fierce hug in response, Shannon squared her shoulders and settled the duffle bag strap more comfortably across her body. She glanced down the long lane again and felt her insides shiver. She could do this. No big thing.

All that was at stake was *everything*.

About the Author

JENNIFER SEASONS is a New England transplant. She lives with her husband and four children in the rural mountains of the Northeast, where she enjoys gorgeous views every day. A dog and several cats keep them company. When she's not writing, she can be found in her studio playing with vivid color, be it pastels for painting or acrylics on canvas, or even funky, chunky yarn for knitting and glazes for her hand-thrown pottery. For Jennifer, it's all about self-expression through colorful creations. She also loves spending time with her family outdoors exploring her beautiful adopted home state, practicing yoga, running, gardening, and lounging in her hammock under the trees with a good book and a home-made chocolate chip cookie—or three.

You can find her online at:
www.jenniferseasonsbooks.com

www.facebook.com/jennifer.seasons.3
http://twitter.com/JenniferSeasons
www.instagram.com/jenniferseasons

Discover great authors, exclusive offers, and more at hc.com.